AIRSHIP 27 PRODUCTIONS

AN AIRSHIP 27 PRODUCTION

Tales from the Hanging Monkey–Volume 2

"Black Diamond, Black Death" ©2017 Bill Craig
"Prophecy of the Firelord" ©2017 J. Walt Layne
"The Star of the Sea" ©2017 Don Gates
"The Merciless Mermaid" ©2017 Lee Houston Jr. & Nancy A. Hansen

Published by Airship 27 Productions
www.airship27.com
www.airship27hangar.com

Interior illustrations ©2017 Michael Harris
Cover illustration ©2017 Rob Davis

Editor: Ron Fortier
Associate Editor: Jonathan Sweet
Promotions and marketing manager: Michael Vance
Production and design by Rob Davis

ISBN-10: 1-946183-21-0
ISBN-13: 978-1-946183-21-7

Printed in the United States of America

10 9 8 7 6 5 4 3 2 1

Tales from
THE HANGING
MONKEY
VOLUME TWO
Table of Contents

BLACK DIAMOND, BLACK DEATH

By
Bill Craig

Motugra, South Seas 1935

The S.S. Southern Light was being tossed about in the squall despite being fully loaded with cargo. Captain Hans Vorlund mopped the sweat from his forehead as he strained to see out the front window of the bridge. He glanced over at the navigator. "Where is the nearest port? If we stay out here we'll be swamped."

"We're near the Motugra chain. Motugra Island has a deep water port where we might be able to ride out the storm," the navigator replied.

"Give the coordinates to the helmsman and get us there. Neptune alone knows when this storm will blow itself out," Vorlund shook his head.

"Aye, Captain," Dougal MacTavish, the navigator relied.

"Grover, follow the course he gives you. Mitchell, you have the bridge. I'm for some hot coffee if I can keep it in the cup," the Norse captain ordered, heading for a hatch that led deeper into the ship. The storm had hit not long after they had left Borneo, and he knew that some of the crew blamed it on the passenger they had picked up there.

Kit Murdock kept to himself, but some of the crew thought the young man cursed as bad things tended to happen when he was around. For some reason, no thought was given to any of the other passengers, only Murdock. That in itself was reason to investigate, Vorlund told himself as he headed for the galley. Hopefully the cook had steaming coffee on for the night watch was going to be a long one in this damnable storm.

Vorlund had spoken to Murdock when he had first boarded the Southern Light. The young man seemed haunted by things he had seen inland hunting for diamonds. Murdock refused to speak of it, but he seemed incredibly relieved once they had sailed from the port in Borneo.

Then other things started to happen. Shadows seen darting in the corridors near his stateroom; a break-in. Murdock had blockaded himself in his stateroom and become a recluse after that. Sailors being the superstitious lot that they are began to talk and pointed out the young man's strange behavior. Soon, they began to say either he was cursed or had brought some cursed cargo aboard.

Vorlund had visited the young man's cabin after that to make sure the man had a revolver at least to protect himself. Murdock had accepted the gun stoically and assured him that he would remain sequestered in his cabin if the Captain would at least provide him with food and drink. In the young man himself, Vorlund could sense no evil, but something in the man's cabin made him uneasy. Vorlund shook the thought off as he reached the galley and entered, greeted by the scent of freshly brewed coffee.

•••

Kit Murdock opened his eyes. The motion of the ship being battered by the waves had not changed, yet some small noise had awakened him from his slumber. He reached beneath the pillow on his bunk and drew forth the Smith & Wesson police positive .38 Special that Captain Vorlund had presented him with shortly after they had left port in Borneo.

Murdock rolled to his feet, the pistol held loosely in his right hand. It was that damned black diamond that he had stolen from the temple deep in the heart of Borneo. Someone knew about it, knew that he had it. Whoever it was wanted it badly enough to kill for.

He could hear strange noises from the dark corridor outside his room but he made no move to turn on the lights. He clutched the revolver tightly, feeling the checkering in the wooden grips bite into the flesh of his palm. Murdock wondered if he had been followed out of the jungle, though he didn't see how that was possible.

He had been washed downstream faster than anyone could have made their way through the jungle and he had booked passage within hours of reaching civilization. No, there was no possible way that it could have been natives from that tribe. It had to be someone else, someone who had a good idea of what he had found during his dangerous trek to the interior to hunt diamonds. For the life of him he had no idea who that could be. He heard a soft scuffing noise again and the doorknob started to turn.

Murdock threw himself against the dresser he had shoved across the doorway, slamming it into the door and keeping it closed. He heard a muffled voice snarling what sounded like a curse, then a shout and the sound of running steps. Murdock gripped the Smith & Wesson revolver tighter, sweat beading on his forehead as he waited.

•••

Sean O'Malley was heading down the corridor towards his own quarters when he heard the slam of a door ahead. He looked up and saw a shadowy form stagger back from the door of the strange passenger. "Stop you!" O'Malley yelled, charging towards the shadowy figure. The shadow spun and leapt away from the door, racing down the corridor with O'Malley in hot pursuit.

The Irish sailor was not one of the group who feared the mysterious passenger; instead he appreciated that the man wanted his privacy. If the mysterious figure was a shipmate, he intended to haul him before Captain Vorlund so the man could account for his actions.

The light in the corridor was dim at best and O'Malley quickly realized that it was not one of his crewmates that he was chasing. His eyes narrowed with rage at the thought of a stowaway and he sprinted faster, keeping the figure in sight until he darted into a cross-companionway. O'Malley swung around the corner and something struck him in the gut, taking the wind out of him. As he doubled over he had a glimpse of oiled dark skin and a strange cloth sarong. O'Malley swung a fist and knocked the figure away, but before he had recovered enough to stand the man was on him again, knocking the Irishman into the bulkhead hard enough to stun him.

Muscular hands tightened around his throat but O'Malley wasn't done yet. The Irishman drove his knee between the other man's legs and heard a gasp of pain, then his own hands grasped the wrists of his attacker and he began to force the hands away from his throat. O'Malley was a scrapper from the time he was six years old, and he had learned many forms of fighting in every port he had ever visited. He sucked in air as the hands came loose and threw himself forward, head-butting his assailant and heard the crack of bone as the man's nose broke.

O'Malley smiled grimly as he turned slightly and drove his shoulder into the man, driving him back. Nails raked his face, drawing thin lines of blood. O'Malley roared in anger as his fists began to piston, slamming into his attacker with punishing blows, aimed at stomach and ribs, pinning the man to the bulkhead. A red rage filled him and a red cloud covered his vision. Then there was a tearing pain in his neck and a heavy weight drove him to the deck.

O'Malley reached up and grabbed a handful of hair, trying to tear the head away from his neck. He felt the hot spurt of blood and felt himself growing rapidly weaker. Sean O'Malley collapsed on the deck in a spreading pool of blood. His killer stood and helped the other dark skinned man up. Together they slipped away into darkness knowing they could do no more this night.

Sean O'Malley's shouts and yells had not gone unnoticed and soon other sailors were filling the companionways and corridors, searching for their shipmate who had sounded an alarm. Word quickly reached Captain Vorlund in the galley and he joined the search as power was sent to the lights and the corridors brightened. Cries of horror summoned the Captain to the companionway where the Irish sailor had been brutally murdered.

"All right, what happened here?" Vorlund demanded after fighting his way through the throng of angry sailors.

"Heard O'Malley shouting, Captain. By the time I got here, he was bleeding out on the deck. Nobody around that I could see," Nils Holgren announced.

"You were the first to arrive?" Vorlund glared at the man.

"I was," Holgren replied in a very challenging manner.

"How long 'til the next man arrived?" Vorlund asked, never taking his eyes from the Dutch sailor.

"Less than a minute," Viktor Andropolus replied. "I got here right behind him."

"What killed him?" Vorlund asked.

"Doc Mason hasn't got here yet," Jason Franklin replied. Franklin was Vorlund's first officer.

"Has anyone awakened him?" Vorlund asked.

"I sent a man to fetch him," Franklin nodded.

"Looks like his bloody throat was ripped out," Kevin Smythe, another sailor offered.

"Belay that talk and secure the area for Doc Mason. Then I want the first five men on the scene to come to the bridge," Vorlund turned and walked away. He knew what most of the men were thinking and he wanted to check on Murdock before any of them did.

Vorlund knocked on Murdock's stateroom door. "Who is it?" Murdock called out from behind the door.

"Captain Vorlund, Murdock. I need to speak to you," Vorlund replied. He heard the sound of something heavy being slid away from the door and then it opened just a crack and Murdock peered out at him. "Let me inside, Murdock." Murdock opened the door and ushered him inside shutting and locking the door behind him.

"What has happened?" Murdock asked; a deep sadness evident in his eyes.

"One of my men has been murdered," Vorlund met his gaze. Murdock never flinched.

"Someone tried to break in again, I slammed the dresser against the door and I heard a shout and the sound of running feet. I fear I am responsible for the crewman's death," Murdock sighed, hanging his head.

"If you were indeed here in your compartment, it was no fault of yours. Sean O'Malley was both a brave and fair man, not one of those who gossiped about folk he had never met. He met his death both bravely and with honor if he had spotted what was going on," Vorlund said softly.

"Forgive me if that brings little consolation," Murdock's shoulders sagged in defeat.

"Who pursues you?" Vorlund asked, finally speaking his unasked question, one that had haunted him since Murdock had come aboard his ship.

"I know not, perhaps the very Devil himself," Murdock looked up at him and Vorlund was stunned to see that the man believed his own words.

"Keep your door barricaded. We shall dock on Motugra Island in the morning. Perhaps it would be a good thing if you went ashore there," Vorlund suggested.

"Perhaps it would, Captain. Perhaps it would," Murdock nodded. Vorlund let himself out and he heard the dresser being slid once more in front of the door after it had closed. Jinx or not, Vorlund would welcome the moment when the young man was off his ship!

"Motugra," Kit Murdock rolled the name of the island around on his tongue, speaking it aloud several times. Would he find a buyer for the Black Diamond there? Or would he have to travel farther to rid himself of the damnable stone? One thing was for sure, he would be off the ship at the first opportunity. He owed that to the Captain and the crew.

•••

Nick Fortune took another sip of his beer as he watched his good friend Corky O'Brian move through the Hanging Monkey, greeting most of the patrons by name before dropping into the chair across from him. "That's a helluva storm blowing out there," Nick said.

"That it 'tis me lad," Corky agreed taking a sip from his beer.

"I've never seen the like in all my years at sea," Fortune admitted.

"It has been a monster of a storm. Few have had the courage to buck it," Corky admitted.

"I don't think Jimmy will be making it back anytime soon," Nick referred to Jimmy Dolan a good friend and competitor who ferried cargo between the islands on his Grumman Goose.

"I suspect not in this storm," Corky nodded sagely. Nick was in rare form this night, really in his cups, not something that happened often. Corky suspected it had as much with Grace Thomas being off the island as anything else.

O'Brian knew that Nick had a soft spot for the American journalist and that she did indeed feel the same way about him. "So where is Grace off to this time?" Corky inquired.

"Who said this was about her?" Nick looked at him through bleary eyes.

"You did, Old Friend, though in not so many words," Corky grinned.

"You know me too well, Old Friend," Nick sighed.

"I do. Khuna will help you home, Nick. Get some sleep, tomorrow will be another day," Corky smiled. He motioned for the native bouncer to come over and help Nick back to the bungalow that he called home.

•••

It was nearing dawn when the Southern Light sailed into the port of Motugra. Captain Vorlund sighed with relief when they sailed out of the heavy seas into the relatively calm waters of Motugra Bay. The old ship seemed to almost groan with relief. Unwilling to take chances, he headed for Murdock's stateroom, planning to escort him off the boat personally after hearing some rather violent threats being made by the crew. For some reason they wanted to blame Murdock for what happened to O'Malley even when it was evident that the young American had never left his cabin.

"I was waiting for you," Murdock said as he ushered Vorlund into the cabin.

"I thought you might be," Vorlund nodded.

"You fear for my safety from your crew, but I fear something far worse," Murdock shook his head sadly.

"Exactly what is that, Murdock? What is it you fear?" Vorlund inquired.

"Demons, Captain, demons from the darkest pits of hell," Murdock sighed.

"Surely you joke," Vorlund looked at him.

"Was it a joke that killed your sailor last night?" Murdock looked up with eyes filled with pain.

"No, it most definitely was not a joke," Vorlund replied stiffly.

"I know, Captain, but I had to make my point," Murdock said softly.

"Point taken," Vorlund replied.

"Are we docked yet?" Murdock asked.

"We are," Vorlund nodded.

"Then I want off this boat as soon as possible," Murdock said.

"I think that would be a really good idea," Vorlund responded.

Kit Murdock wasn't the only passenger leaving the ship. Two others were leaving as well. Two brown-skinned men slipped down the anchor chain and lowered themselves into the warm waters of the Bay. They swam unobserved to shore and moved quickly and quietly into the jungle where they were more at home.

•••

The sun was up when Nick Fortune opened his eyes. His head throbbed dully from his over-indulging the night before. Nick took his time getting out of bed, trying to spare his aching head. Coffee. That was the first order of the day!

He found a bottle of aspirin and screwed off the lid, popping two of them into his mouth and dry swallowing them. He then went to the kitchen and prepared the coffee pot before setting it on the stove to perk. At least with the sunshine he didn't need to light one of the coal oil lanterns. Looking out the window, the clouds were moving off and the blue sky was a welcome sight. Everything looked bright and clean after the storm. He hoped it was something that would last. With the storm he hadn't been able to run any cargo for the past week. His wallet was getting a little on the thin side.

Of course, spending as much as he had at The Hanging Monkey hadn't helped his cash flow. He needed to get back on the sea hauling cargo between the islands. It would take his mind off Grace and her absence from the island. She was off chasing down a story near the part of the island chain controlled by the Japanese. He was both angry and fearful for her. She should never have gone without him. Grace was far too headstrong for her own good.

Nick headed to the bathroom and lathered up his face to shave. By the time he had shaved and showered the coffee was done and he poured himself a cup. The aspirin had finally kicked in and was starting to take the edge off his headache as he sipped at his first cup of coffee for the day.

•••

Corky O'Brian opened the door to the Hanging Monkey. The chimp was on its branch watching and grinned at him, showing his teeth. "Top of the morning to ya," Corky grinned back at the chimp, saluting it with his cup of coffee. The chimp chattered back as Corky started laughing.

The monkey had been a great source of both consternation and amusement over the years. It had also been an inspiration as he had named the pub after it. Corky shook his head as he walked back inside. A few hearty souls would make their way in for breakfast and some early drinks. In all likelihood Nick would make his way back for breakfast.

Corky wished that he had some word on Grace Thomas but so far he had heard little to nothing about the American news correspondent. They were still awaiting the arrival of the Federal Bureau of Investigation agent that was coming to question Nick about his involvement in the deaths of Jane Mulgrew and Dane Carter. Corky had sent word that he was to be notified of anyone expressing interest in Nick that was headed for the island.

•••

Jacques Henrique watched as the captain escorted Kit Murdock off of the Southern Light. He frowned and nodded to one of his men who would also depart the ship and follow the young American. Jacques had spoke with one of the natives who had nursed Murdock back to health after he emerged from the jungle of Borneo burning up with fever. The man had told him of the black diamond that the young man carried out of the jungle.

Once the man had learned of the black diamond he had sent the American on his way as soon as he was healthy enough to walk. The native had feared the stone, said it was cursed. Given the murder of the crewman the night before, Jacques was almost inclined to believe it. However the value of such a stone, a black diamond the size of a man's fist, was almost incalculable. If he could acquire the stone and take it back to Europe, he would be a very wealthy man.

Murdock had proved very resourceful so far. Much more so than he had expected. It was something to consider as to the best way to deal with the young American and acquire the stone. Henrique's man moved down the gangplank and followed at a discreet distance as the ship's Captain steered the young American towards a specific destination.

Jacques returned to his cabin to pack his things. He wanted that diamond in the worst possible way. His mind turned to the shipboard murder the night before. It had been a horrible thing, the dead sailor looking like he had been set upon by wild animals.

It was a puzzling mystery to say the least. The natives back in Borneo had told him of a deadly curse on the great black diamond. Suddenly he found himself wondering if they might indeed be true…

•••

Corky O'Brian looked up as the bat-winged doors swung open. Two men entered, only one that he recognized. Captain Hans Vorlund of the Southern Light steered a young stranger inside. Vorlund nodded at Corky and the owner of the Hanging Monkey walked over with two cups of coffee. He sat them down in front of the two men. "Hans," he acknowledged.

"Corky. This is Kit Murdock, he needs a safe place to stay. Can you set him up?" Vorlund asked.

"If he can pay, I can," Corky replied honestly.

"I can pay," Murdock affirmed. Corky looked over at Khuna, the native Motugran who served as troubleshooter and bouncer for the Hanging Monkey.

"Khuna will show you to your room," Corky told him.

"Lord he's a big one," Vorlund whistled.

"He is. Khuna's a semi-reformed head-hunter, but he keeps the peace," Corky shrugged.

"I would imagine so," Vorlund shook his head. Then he looked sharply at O'Brian. "Semi-reformed head-hunter?"

"Well, I haven't been able to break him of the practice completely," the Irish ex-patriot shrugged.

"I think I would sleep better not having learned that," Vorlund shuddered.

"Think how I feel," Corky grinned.

"I'd rather not, I think," Vorlund replied gulping down his coffee.

"I gather the young lad had trouble on his tail?" Corky asked.

"More than his share, but I feel I should leave it to him to tell you what it is," Vorlund said soberly.

"Your crew coming in?" Corky changed the subject.

"They are, but they have no love for young Murdock. Keep him away from them if you would. That young man has more than his share of trouble as it is," Vorlund replied.

"I'll do for him as best as I can," Corky shook his old friend's hand and Vorlund took his leave. Corky pulled out a crumpled pack of Player's cigarettes and shook one free. He removed a battered lighter from another pocket and fired it up. Corky didn't smoke often, but when he did it was usually while in deep contemplation of a problem.

•••

Kit Murdock looked around the room. It was nice enough and he took note of the firm lock on the door and the latches of the windows. Murdock nodded in satisfaction. He put his bag in the closet and carried the revolver that Captain Vorlund had given him to the bed. He sat the gun on the nightstand where it would be close at hand. Fully dressed he lay back on the bed and closed his eyes, drifting off to a troubled sleep.

•••

Nick Fortune stepped through the bat-winged doors of the Hanging Monkey, taking a moment to let his eyes adjust to the lower light inside the building. Corky was sitting at a table smoking and sipping his cup of coffee. Nick walked over and dropped into the chair across from him.

"Do you feel as bad as you look?" Corky eyed him.

"I do," Nick shook out a Lucky Strike and fired it up. Corky nodded at a waitress and she carried over a cup of steaming black coffee and sat it in front of the American. Nick flashed a smile as he took a sip of the scalding brew. It helped clear the pounding in his head.

"Are you going out soon?" Corky looked at him.

"Yeah, don't have much choice about it," Nick shrugged.

"Grace will be back soon my friend. She won't stay away with the government investigators coming. She's a woman who will stand by you," Corky said.

"She will. I know that. She had no idea what she was bringing down on my head," Nick exhaled a cloud of smoke.

"Do you feel as bad as you look?"

"She knows now, and that will make the difference," Corky sipped at his coffee.

"You've got something on your mind," Nick observed. The two men had been friends ever since Nick had first docked at the island and decided to make it his home.

"I do. You're needing some help on yer boat are ye not?" Corky looked at him.

"I could use some," Nick conceded.

"I might have a lad who could use some work but needs to stay out of sight for a bit. Would you be willing to take him on?" Corky asked softly.

"I could use the help for sure. I have a run later this afternoon. You think this boy would be willing?" Nick looked at his friend.

"I think he would," Corky replied.

"Have him down at the dock at noon then," Nick nodded

"Will do. According to Captain Vorlund he didn't have a very restful night," Corky agreed.

"You know his story?" Nick looked expectant.

"Not yet, but I will soon enough," Corky grinned.

"Now that I believe," Nick sipped his coffee while shaking his head.

"Ah Nick, ye know people love to talk to me," Corky chuckled.

"You do have the gift of the Blarney for sure," Nick sighed.

•••

Avery De Long had decided to cut through the jungle to head for the small shack he called home. The sun was just starting to climb over the edge of the horizon and the jungle was a kaleidoscope of green gold and black. De Long was whistling Hoagy Carmichael's Stardust as he slipped along what he hoped was a game trail. He had woken up in front of the Hanging Monkey and wanted to try and make it home before his wife woke up.

A branch slapped him in the face drawing a curse and then something caught his throat. Avery reached up and his questing hand met a vine that was drawing tighter. Avery began to cough and choke as the vine drew tight enough to lift him off his feet. Then hands wrestled him into the tree and sharp teeth began to penetrate his skin. Avery De long tried to scream but all that emerged was a bloody gurgle from the hole in what had once been his throat.

Two hours later Todd Spellman was using the same shortcut. Moving down the path he felt something drip onto his face. Spellman stopped and looked up. Todd Spellman began to scream at what he saw!

•••

Major Smythe frowned as he watched the body being lowered from the tree. It had been partially eaten by whoever had killed it. Cannibals were not unknown on Motugra, but they rarely showed up on the main island. This was something new. He sent a runner to the Hanging Monkey. Corky O'Brian's man Khuna was an expert on the local islanders. Major Smythe was hoping that the native islander might have some idea of who had perpetuated such a horrible crime.

•••

Dark eyes watched from the shadows of the jungle, searching out their prey. They had come for the one who had stolen the Black Diamond from the temple. His life would be the payment for what he had done, for the Dark God demanded no less! What would be even better would be for his blood to be poured on the black diamond in the ultimate sacrifice to the Dark God who will not be named!

•••

Kit Murdock woke around noon, feeling refreshed. He put the black diamond in a box and wrapped it securely before carrying it down to the Hanging Monkey. His Browning Hi-Power 9mm was tucked into his waistband beneath his blue chambray work-shirt. The .38 revolver was holstered on his hip. Murdock entered the Monkey and immediately spotted O'Brian. The Irishman had an open and honest face that Murdock immediately discounted. Oh, he would be honest enough, but if he could figure an angle that would benefit him, O'Brian wouldn't hesitate to exploit it. Kit had known such men before so he was less than afraid.

"Could you put this in your safe, Mr. O'Brian?" Murdock handed him the package.

"I could," Corky affirmed.

"It needs to be kept safe until I can figure out what to do with it," Murdock announced.

"And it will be," Corky promised. "Are you looking for work?"

"I am," Murdock nodded.

"Do ye know yer way around a boat?"

"I do," Murdock nodded.

"I have a friend who needs a hand if you be willing and he will pay you for the work you do," Corky slid a cup of coffee to him. Murdock picked it up and sipped from it.

"I'm willing," Murdock sipped at the coffee again.

"Then I will take ye down to yon wee boat," Corky grinned.

"Wee boat?" Murdock raised an eyebrow questioningly.

"*Fortune's Folly*, owned and operated by me good friend Nick Fortune. She's an old rum-runner that he uses to haul cargo around through the islands. He needs an able-bodied man to help. You fit the bill and you need work. Seemed like a good fit to me," O'Brian shrugged, grinning.

"And that it does," Murdock agreed.

"You and Nick will get along well enough I think," Corky told him.

"I hope you are right," Murdock replied.

"Trust me, Lad."

"Famous last words," Murdock laughed. It felt good he realized. It had been a long time since he had been able to laugh.

•••

Nick Fortune had just fired up the engines when Corky O'Brian hailed him from the dock. A young man stood beside him, stout enough looking. Nick had the immediate impression that the young man would be able to handle himself if push came to shove. He waved them both aboard as he shook free a cigarette from a crumpled pack of Lucky Strikes and fired it up with his battered Ronson lighter.

"Nick, meet Murdock. He's willing to work for ye," Corky shouted over the engines.

"Ever serve on a boat before?" Nick looked at the kid.

"I have," Murdock nodded.

"Time to prove it. I ain't got time to nursemaid you. You prove your worth or I dump you over the side the first time you screw up," Nick said, eyeing Murdock for a reaction.

"I'd expect nothing less."

"He'll do, Corky."

"That he will, Lad, that he will," Corky O'Brian grinned.

"We'll be heading over to Fujitsi first," Nick said.

"Tell O'Connell I said hello. I know you'll be stopping for dinner at The Blustery Duck." O'Brian chuckled.

"I'll let the Aussie pirate know you send your regards. I'm sure he'll turn the air blue in response," Nick shook his head, trying to hide a grin. The feud between Corky and the owner of The Blustery Duck was a long and storied one.

"That he will," Corky chuckled. Corky watched as *Fortune's Folly* pulled away from the docks. He found himself wondering about the package that Murdock had left with him for safe keeping. What was in it?

•••

Grace Thomas huddled in the brush watching as the Japanese fueled a German U-boat. She had not counted on this but it was a story that could make her career and get her editor back in the states to finally take her seriously!

She knew that Jimmy Dolan was waiting on her back on the other side of the island. He had elected to remain and guard the plane just in case there was trouble. Grace frowned, wondering secretly if the pilot wasn't really something of a coward. At least when it came to women!

Grace lifted her camera and snapped photos of the Japanese sailors refueling the Nazi submarine. After she fired off nearly an entire roll she knew she had pressed her luck to the maximum and slipped back into the brush. It took her nearly an hour to make it back to the small cove where the Lucky Duck was waiting.

Dolan looked relieved as she climbed aboard and he fired the engines, quickly backing the Grumman Goose out away from shore and then turning her out to sea and taking off! He would have to caution Nick Fortune about this woman, though he was pretty sure his pal already knew what she was like.

"Do you think the F.B.I. agents have arrived yet?" Grace asked as the Goose lifted into the air.

"I doubt it with the storms we've had. Hell, we couldn't even get up in the air, remember?" Dolan shook his head. Silly women, always forgetting the details. Grace was a bright girl, but she could be a bit on the ditzy side at times. Especially where Nick Fortune was concerned.

•••

Khuna eyed the dead body dispassionately. What intrigued him was the method used to snare the man. It was like nothing he had encountered in his own raids around the Motugra chain. "Well?" Colonel Smythe asked, tapping his foot impatiently. Khuna shot him a look and the Britisher involuntarily took a step backwards, not liking what he was seeing in the native's eyes.

"Killers not from around here. They are at home in the jungle and know how to hide their trail," Khuna rumbled in a voice that reminded one of a bear growling deep in a cave.

"Can you track them?" Smythe asked.

"Of course. You get okay from Boss," Khuna shrugged.

"I have to get O'Brian's permission to hire you to track?" Smythe looked dumbfounded.

"I work for Corky," Khuna turned on his heel and started back towards the village. Smythe watched him go.

The Colonel shook his head. Motugra never ceased to amaze him. The dynamics of the island chain were unlike anything he had ever encountered. The fact that there were still cannibals active in the island chain both fascinated and frightened him. If Khuna were any example, he knew he had reason to be frightened!

"Cut him down and take him over to the coroner's office," Smythe commanded. As distasteful as he found the prospect, he had to make his way to the Hanging Monkey to ask Corky O'Brian for help. Smythe had disliked the Irishman at first sight and it had little to do with the ancestral antagonism between the English and the Irish.

No, Smythe had recognized the Irishman for a crook and as an officer of the law he had a natural dislike for the criminal element. Sure, O'Brian was slicker than most, able to hide his dealings behind a mask of legitimacy, but it was only a matter of time before he would slip up. His kind always did!

And then there was Nick Fortune, one of O'Brian's cronies. Apparently wanted back in the Colonies for murder. He had kept his nose clean in the islands so there was nothing that Smythe could do about him but wait for the Federal agents to come and question him. Smythe shook his head. Nothing would please him more than to shut The Hanging Monkey down for good. Smythe left his men to their work as he walked towards the main street. He felt better as he slipped out of the jungle and onto the street. The sunlight felt warm on his face.

Smythe took a deep breath and let it out slowly, and then summoning his resolve he turned and headed down the street towards the Hanging Monkey. The damn Chimp was perched in its tree, watching him as he came up the walk. Smythe swore that the animal was smirking at him as he turned to enter the doors. Smythe hesitated for but a moment, and then pushed his way inside.

The air inside The Hanging Monkey was cooler, though not by much. Khuna sat near the bar looking bored, his expression unreadable. Miko was behind the bar polishing glasses with a clean cloth. Corky O'Brian sat at one of the tables reading a newspaper. Smythe walked over to stand before him.

"To what do I owe the pleasure of your company Major Smythe?" Corky said without moving the paper.

"I'd like to hire your man Khuna for a few days," Smythe said.

"What did Khuna say?"

"He said I would have to get your permission."

"Khuna," Corky called as he shut the paper, folded it in half and laid it on the tabletop.

"Yes Boss?" the native bouncer replied.

"The Major would like to hire you for a few days. Would you be willing to work for him?" Corky asked.

"Depends on the job," Khuna shrugged.

"I want you to help me track whomever or whatever killed that man in the jungle," Smythe said flatly, not appreciating the situation at all.

"I am interested," Khuna admitted.

"You have my permission, start now," Corky said. Khuna nodded and looked at Smythe.

"Let's go," he said.

"After you," Smythe stepped out of the way, shooting O'Brian a dirty look. He didn't like being played, but at the moment he had no other option than to put up with it. He followed Khuna out of the bar.

•••

"The Colonel, he be trouble Boss," Miko said.

"I know, Miko. Coffee please?" O'Brian replied. The diminutive Chinese bartender carried a pot out and refilled his cup and then went back behind the bar. Corky sipped at the dark brew, thinking.

Khuna had told him about the dead man when he returned to the bar, and about what he had told Smythe. It was an interesting situation, and based on what Vorlund had told him about the trouble dogging Kit Murdock, made him want to pursue it. He took another sip of coffee, wondering where Jimmy Dolan and Grace Thomas were.

•••

Nick Fortune kept an eye on the young man as they made their way from island to island in the Motugra chain. Murdock worked hard and never shirked his duty in any way. In fact, he seemed determined to do more than his share of the work. Nick admired that. Murdock had the makings of a man who would someday do very well for himself if he could only escape the dark cloud that hung over him.

"What brings you to Motugra, Kit?" Nick finally asked, offering the young man a Lucky Strike. Murdock took it and lit it off a book of matches he had pulled from his pocket.

"Bad luck, I reckon. What takes a man anywhere after he's found more than his share of trouble?" Murdock shrugged.

"You saying you found more than your share?"

"I did, back in the jungles of Borneo. I barely made it out alive," Murdock exhaled a cloud of smoke that was quickly carried away on the ocean breeze.

"I've been to Borneo. It's a wild and dangerous country," Nick nodded in agreement.

"But one full of riches if a man is willing to work for them, and fight to keep them once he has them. Except sometimes, the price is too high."

"Sounds like maybe you paid it."

"I am still paying it," Murdock looked out over the blue ocean. The events of the past few weeks seemed so far away out here on the high seas.

"You talking about what happened on the Southern Light?" Nick asked.

"That's only part of it. I had lost everything when my boat capsized when river pirates attacked me. I had heard about a temple deep in the jungle, and an idol that was decorated with a priceless black diamond the size of a big man's fist. I was foolish enough to go after it," Murdock flicked the butt of his smoke over the side of the boat where it sank hissing beneath the blue water of the South Pacific.

"You didn't just go after it. You got out with it," Nick observed, finishing his own smoke.

"Death has been dogging me ever since. Much as I appreciate the job, Mr. Fortune, I hope I ain't brought death to your doorstep."

"You won't be the first, Kit, nor the last. Just know I'll back your play when it comes. You're a first class mate," Nick said, paying the kid the highest compliment he knew.

"Thanks, Mr. Fortune," Kit nodded.

"Call me Captain or call me Nick. That Mr. Fortune stuff is making me feel way too old," Nick grinned.

"Aye, Captain," Murdock grinned back at him.

•••

Jacques Henrique tapped his foot impatiently. Two of his men had taken another boat out after *Fortune's Folly*. Two more were on their way to search Kit Murdock's room above the local watering hole known as The Hanging Monkey. Such a quaint name. He almost smiled as he shook his head. The British would never make sense to him anymore than the Americans did.

The French, his own countrymen, were the only truly civilized people left on the face of the earth. The others were just, he paused in his thoughts, barbarians! Yes, that was the perfect description for them.

Barbarians. Soon though, he would be back in his beloved France, back at his chateau with the fabled Black Diamond as his prized possession!

•••

Du Lac eased the pick into the lock, working both quickly and efficiently as Le Monte kept watch. It would take no time at all to defeat such a primitive lock and gain entry to the room. Except that they were not the only ones there. Yellow eyes watched from the shadows of the jungle canopy just a few feet distant.

The lock clicked and Du Lac pushed the door open. He grinned over his shoulder at Le Monte and slipped inside. His cohort followed him through the door, shutting it softly behind him. Two dark shapes swung out of the shadows to land softly on the wooden balcony that surrounded the building. Silently they slipped up to the door that the two Frenchmen had entered and silently followed them in.

Two muffled thumps and the sickening sound of tearing flesh followed by liquid-sounding gurgles. A few other noises followed, and then the two dark shapes slipped out of the room to vanish once more into the dark canopy of the jungle.

•••

Corky was just finishing his dinner when a loud scream tore through the air like an air-raid siren. He and two men that Khuna had personally trained to act as bouncers during his infrequent absences were out the door and heading for the stairs as a second scream ripped the stillness of the early evening. Corky charged up the stairs his men on his heels.

Two women were standing in front of an open door, looking in with expressions of total shock and horror on their faces. Corky ran up and shouldered them aside, getting his first look inside the room. He recognized the room as the one he had rented to Murdock. What he didn't recognize were the two dead men inside the room that looked like they had been torn apart by wild animals!

Corky O'Brian was a man who had been to war, seen men blown apart on the battlefield, but even that was nothing compared to the horror that now filled his gaze. The hardwood floor was awash in blood. Body parts had been strewn randomly across the floor. What sort of animal could have done this?

"Go fetch the Major! He needs to see this," Corky ordered.

"Yes Boss!" one of his men snapped heading back the way he had come. The other was trying to quiet and comfort the two women who had stumbled onto the murder scene. Corky swung the door closed. He motioned for his man to chaperone the two women past him and down the stairs. He would stand guard himself over the door until Colonel Smythe and Khuna arrived.

•••

"Cap'n we got a boat following us," Kit Murdock reported.

"It's been behind us since we left Motugra," Nick advised.

"You figure it's trouble?"

"Might be, might be totally innocent. No way to tell yet. You keep that pistol handy," Nick told him.

"Will do, Cap'n," Murdock nodded. Nick nodded back, wondering about the boat behind them.

"You know that there are still pirates in these waters?" Nick asked.

"I've heard that. Think those might be some of them?"

"Right now, I don't know what to think."

•••

"Do you think it's safe to do more than island hop?" Grace Thomas asked watching Jimmy Dolan's face. She had an idea that he had been deliberately dragging out the trip back to Motugra, especially since he had really turned on the charm.

"You never know what with all the Japanese pilots in the area. They seem to be trying to carve a bigger niche out of the chain," Jimmy shrugged.

"Jimmy, you are a terrible liar," Grace shook her head.

"Me? A liar?" Jimmy looked flabbergasted.

"Yes. Get us back to Motugra right now or I'll let Nick know about you trying to beat his time!" Grace snapped, her voice cracking like a whip. She watched him flinch despite himself.

"Okay, okay. You found me out. Can't blame a guy for trying though," Jimmy grinned at her.

"I can't. Nick however might," Grace reminded him.

"Yeah, he might," Jimmy heaved a sigh.

•••

The clouds had begun to thicken and Nick kept a wary eye on them. Another storm was the last thing they needed between islands, and there was always the chance it would force them to take shelter on one of the many islands in the chain.

He really wanted to make Fujitsi. At least there he and Murdock would have some back-up. O'Donnell was no Corky O'Brian but the Aussie was a friend. The Blustery Duck would be a safe haven if they could get there. Nick Fortune wasn't sure they would get the chance, though.

The other boat was gaining on them and the Folly just didn't have any more speed to give, not with a full load of cargo. Nick sighed. It was time to fight. He went below and came back up with a Thompson Submachine gun and an M-1 Garand. Nick tossed the M-1 to Kit Murdock who caught it expertly and quickly checked to make sure of its combat readiness.

Nick Fortune nodded to himself. He had pegged the young American accurately. Murdock handled the rifle like an old friend. Nick grinned, they might have a chance after all. "Lay a few shots across their bow!" Nick commanded.

"You got it," Murdock called back. He lifted the rifle to his shoulder and fired three quick rounds across the other boat's bow. The boat came on and return fire came their way. Nick tied off the wheel and ran aft. He lifted the Thompson and opened fire, letting the hot .45 rounds speak for him as they slammed into the other boat. Kit Murdock opened up as well and the other boat veered off, settling lower in the water. Nick Fortune grinned.

"Let's put some distance between us and them," Nick called.

"Aye, aye, Captain!" Kit Murdock called, running to the pilot house. Murdock goosed the throttles. Nick fired a farewell burst from the Thompson before returning to the pilothouse.

"That ought to slow them down a bit," Nick said as he took over the wheel.

"For how long?" Kit Murdock asked.

"Hopefully for long enough," Nick replied as he shook out a couple of Lucky Strikes and handed one to the young American. Nick lit them both, inhaling deeply.

Nick exhaled a thick cloud of smoke from both nostrils. The Kid had trouble on his tail that was evident for sure. Nick wondered how much of it would reach out to touch him.

•••

Jacques Henrique sipped at the glass of brandy he had ordered. He had sent some of his men out after Nick Fortune and Kit Murdock. At this point, he was sitting in the Hanging Monkey, finding out more about the captain of *Fortune's Folly*.

Men in the bar liked to talk and he was regaled by stories of the one-eyed man both real and imagined. The hard part was telling which was which.

•••

Nick Fortune rubbed at his missing eye. He wished that there were someway to deal with the problem. The engine was running a little rough and the seas were getting higher. The clouds were foretelling another storm coming and if they didn't make Fujitsi, then they might well be lost at sea.

"Anything I can do Cap'n?" Kit Murdock asked from behind him.

"Not unless you can change the weather, my friend," Fortune shook his head.

"Can't say that is in my repertoire of accomplishments," Murdock shook his head.

"Gotta say I was afraid of that. We better hope that we can make Fujitsi before it hits. We can ride the storm out there."

He lifted the Thompson and opened fire…

"How long you figure we got?"

"At best about an hour if the current holds with us," Fortune replied.

•••

Motugra Island, South Seas

Khuna had finally eluded Major Smythe and slipped into the jungle that surrounded the town. The wind was blowing and he could taste rain in the air. Another storm was blowing in but this would not last as long as the previous one had. Thunder rumbled above and he would feel the energy in the storm as the lightning flashed and crackled across the sky above.

There were strangers on his island, strange cannibals, and that disturbed him greatly. They had come to Motugra without invitation and he meant to make sure that they learned that was not something that would be forgiven. So far, they had been the hunters. It was time for them to understand that they were now the hunted!

Rain drops began to fall as Khuna climbed into a tree. Despite the storm, it would be far better to hunt from above. His enemies hunted from above and to find them and defeat them he would have to do the same.

•••

Fujitsi, Motugra Island Chain, South Seas

The storm hit just as Nick Fortune and Kit Murdock tied *Fortune's Folly* up at the dock on Fujitsi. Rain hit them in sheets as they hurried up the wooden plank walkway towards the line of buildings that made up the waterfront.

"You called it right, Cap'n," Kit Murdock yelled to be heard over the driving rain.

"Been sailing these seas for a couple of years now, you learn 'em," Nick called back as they headed for The Blustery Duck, another of Nick's hangouts that were scattered throughout the island chain. Both men were getting wet as they moved along the boardwalk.

"You think we left our trouble out at sea, Cap'n?" Murdock asked, staying close on Nick Fortune's trail in the blinding rain.

"No, Kit, I don't. We need to be on our toes," Nick Fortune replied as his eye searched the shadows. He had seen just a flicker of movement ahead at the mouth of an alley between two buildings. Nick drew his pistol and seeing him do so, Kit Murdock did the same. Both men squinted against the driving rain as lightning ripped across the sky above them, bathing the scene in light.

Two dark forms were in the alley and they appeared to be holding weapons. Nick raised his gun and fired, the roar of the report vanishing in the crash of thunder. One of the gun men tumbled to the ground as the second one fired. Nick heard a shot from behind him and the second one hit the ground.

"We gonna check on them?" Murdock asked.

"Let the local constable handle that. We're gonna head on into The Blustery Duck and get a cup of coffee and let my pal summon the cops to check on them," Nick replied, wanting a cigarette badly.

"You think they are tied in with the men on that boat?"

"I do."

"My cloud is still dogging me," Kit shook his head.

"For the moment, Kit, but we're gonna see what we can do about that," Nick told him.

•••

Lancaster "Link" O'Connell was pouring himself a tankard of beer when he looked up and saw a familiar face enter the doors of The Blustery Duck. "Nicky Fortune! Did you finally decide to quit hanging out on Motugra and come stay on a real island?" O'Connell yelled across the crowded room.

"Just here for a visit, Mate! Corky sends his love!" Nick yelled back with a grin. At that point O'Connell began to swear so strong and loud that the barroom fell quiet in appreciation of his knowledge of curse words and the number of languages in which he knew them. When O'Connell ran out of steam Nick looked at him and grinned. "That is exactly what Corky said you would say."

"It would certainly be just like that damned Irishman!" O'Connell shook his head. "What brings you to my fair island old friend?"

"A load of cargo and a black cloud that has been following my young friend here all the way from Borneo," Nick Fortune said as a barmaid placed a cup of hot black coffee in front of him. Nick took a sip and began to tell the story.

•••

Over the South Pacific...

"Damn but that front moved in quick!" Jimmy Dolan cursed as he tried to climb over the clouds. Lightning flashed in front of them, turning the cloud filled sky white.

"We wouldn't be in this spot if you hadn't been trying to beat Nick's time," Grace snapped. Rain pelted the windows as thunder rumbled like cannon-fire around them.

"How long are you gonna beat that dead horse?" Jimmy groaned.

"As long as it takes to get it through your head, Jimmy Dolan. Nick is the only man on Motugra that I have eyes for."

"You tell him that yet?"

"He knows," Grace shrugged.

"Then you haven't told him," it was Dolan's turn to smile.

"Didn't think I needed too. Nick has eyes and more brains than you do," Grace spat.

"Men are funny creatures, Doll, they don't always see the obvious," Dolan laughed.

"Nick sees more than you think, Dolan."

"You really think so?"

"Do you value Nick as a friend, Jimmy?"

"Of course," Dolan shook his head.

"If I tell him what you tried, you'll have lost a friend," Grace said.

"Nick ain't somebody I'd want as an enemy."

"Then you get us somewhere safe and stay the hell away from me," Grace told him, her voice cold enough to give him a chill.

"Fujitsi is the closest island to where we are. We'll put in there," Dolan sighed. Jimmy knew Grace was right. If she told Nick that he had tried beating his time with her, Nick would kill him. Nick had the hots for this girl reporter. Jimmy liked to think he was the guy who could have any woman he wanted, but Grace was one that he couldn't. That hurt in ways he couldn't fathom. It also shocked him, because he had never been turned down so flatly before. That smarted.

"Then land us at Fujitsi," Grace said.

"Yes, Ma'am," Dolan groaned softly.

•••

Fujitsi Island, Motugra Island Chain...

"That was a helluva tale, Nick my boy," Link O'Connell took a swig of his beer.

"Every word of it is true," Kit Murdock supplied.

"I've nary a doubt, Lad," O'Connell told him. "Nick here may be many things, but a liar ain't one of them. We go way back we do."

"You start talking nice about me to the hired help O'Connell and we're out of here," Nick said, grinning.

"Where else on Fujitsi are you going to find such ambiance on such a foul night?" O'Connell grinned back.

"You do have a point there. So can you help me keep an eye on our backs?"

"I can and I will. You and the lad can bunk upstairs tonight. Most of the boys that work for me came from Ireland to get away from the troubles, so they are rock solid and loyal to me."

"Glad to hear it. I think Murdock and myself are both tired of sleeping with one eye open."

"Not something you'll have to worry about tonight," O'Connell assured them.

•••

Motugra Island

Khuna moved from tree to tree, water dripping down from the storm that was assaulting the jungle above. The darkness below the canopy of trees was absolute. The big islander moved using his sense of smell, hearing and touch as he hunted for the interlopers that had killed on his island. The rain could wash out the spoor which was why he had taken to the trees, making his way to the spot where the first body had been found, dangling half-eaten from the branches that interlocked over the trail below.

He knew he had reached the spot when he scented the coppery smell of blood. The branches were awash of it, and beneath that smell he caught another scent. That of an unwashed body that had carried along with it the smell of rancid flesh. Khuna smiled to himself, knowing he had found the trail he needed to follow.

•••

Fujitsi Island, Fujitsi Bay

Jimmy Dolan guided the Lucky Duck down across the bay, the seaplane feeling the jolt of every wave that it jounced across. In the storm, the instruments were useless and he guided the plane by the lights that were only just visible through the pouring rain. Finally they reached the dock and Grace climbed out to tie them up as Jimmy shut down the engines. A few minutes later he joined her, double checking the knots on the ropes that held the Duck in place next to the docks.

"You did good," Jimmy told her.

"Nick taught me," Grace shot back. Then she took her bag and headed up the wooden dock. She knew that the best place to stay on this particular island was an establishment called The Blustery Duck. It was owned by an Australian rival of Corky O' Brien named Link O'Connell.

Jimmy Dolan followed her contritely. He knew that he had made a big mistake in trying to beat Nick's time He hoped that it wouldn't ruin the friendship that the two of them shared, because he was pretty sure that Grace would spill the beans!

The Blustery Duck was warm compared to the storm outside, homey even. Grace breathed a sigh of relief as she walked in out of the rain. She went straight to the bar and ordered a shot of whiskey. It was poured and she quickly downed it and ordered another. The whiskey warmed her up, for which she was glad. The warmth settled in her belly and spread upward. She looked at the bartender. "I'm looking for a man named O'Connell," Grace said.

•••

Nick Fortune was halfway up the steps to the second floor when he heard a familiar voice. He stopped short in mid-step and Kit Murdock ran into him from behind. "What's up Captain?" Murdock asked.

"I need to go back downstairs a minute, Kit. I just heard an old friend," Fortune had a big grin on his face as he turned on the narrow stairs.

"See you in a bit then," Murdock shrugged, trudging on up the wooden steps. Nick Fortune pushed his cap back on his head as he walked back down the wooden steps. It took no time at all to spot the soaking wet woman at the bar who was asking about O'Connell. Fortune crossed the distance in six long strides, people looking at him and clearing a path. He tapped her shoulder and Grace Thomas spun, looking angry and sputtering until she saw his face. Then she shrieked his name as Fortune swept her up in his arms and planted a long and passionate kiss right on her lips.

"I'll take a beer," Jimmy Dolan announced as he pushed up to the bar beside them. Nick broke the kiss and just spent a long moment looking into Grace's eyes. She met his gaze and her left hand with its manicured nails came up to trace the lines of his face.

"I've missed you," Fortune told her.

"What about me, Pal?" Jimmy asked, taking a long slurp on his foam-topped mug of beer. Nick shot him a look.

"Not near so much," Fortune grinned.

"Always the brides' maid, never the bride," Jimmy grinned, shaking his head.

"Pal, I can certainly arrange for you to become a 'bride' to some nice island girl like Moani," Nick told him, still holding Grace close, enjoying the feeling of her body pressed against him.

"Uh, no thanks," Dolan took another drink, nearly emptying the mug.

"Was somebody looking for me?" O'Connell walked out of the back of the bar wiping his hands on a towel.

"A couple more rooms if you got 'em," Fortune told him. Link O'Connell took in Grace and how she and Fortune were looking at each other.

"I bet this is the infamous Grace Thomas, American newspaper correspondent for the islands," O'Connell smiled.

"He's certainly a charmer," Grace smiled, glancing at Nick.

"He is at that," Nick shot the Aussie a baleful look, his one blue eye blazing. O'Connell caught it and backed off.

"I do have a couple of other rooms. Have a drink and I'll get your room ready. Look at this, there's one available right next door to Nick's room," O'Connell smiled.

"Whiskey," Grace called over her shoulder to the bartender.

"Must have been a rough week," Nick observed.

"More than you know," Grace said, shooting a hard look at Jimmy Dolan.

"So did you get your story?" Nick asked.

"I think so, once I get these pictures developed and send them to my boss, I may well have hit the big time," Grace grinned. The bartender sat a shot of whiskey on the bar and she scooped it up and downed it without blinking. Licking her lips she put the shot glass back on the bar. "Another," Grace commanded.

"You sure?" Nick asked her, noticing that Jimmy had made himself scarce after getting his second round.

"I am," Grace smiled up at him, leaning in closer against him. Suddenly the door flew open and seven German sailors crashed into the room, all of them brandishing weapons. "Oh shit!" Grace gasped, recognizing the leader of the men.

"I knew it was too good to be true," Nick groaned, drawing his .45 automatic and firing it, dropping one of the men as the others opened fire. Nick grabbed Grace by the arm and headed around the bar. Bullets chased them across the room as he shoved Grace out the back door into the storm once more. Fortune spun and fired five fast rounds behind him, hearing the rewarding sound of screams. He could hear other shots firing besides those of the Germans. He took Grace by the hand and they stumbled down the rain soaked alley.

They swung around a corner and stopped to get their breath. "Who the hell were those guys?" Fortune asked her.

"My story," Grace gasped for breath. "The Japanese are supplying German U-boats," Grace explained.

•••

Motugra Island

The trail had led Khuna deeper into the jungle. He had traveled through the trees nearly half the way to the volcano that dominated the island. Suddenly something snaked down over his head and tightened around his neck. Khuna grabbed at the vine rope that encircled his throat with one hand and reached above his head with the other, catching the vine and yanking hard on it. There was a crashing sound above him and he leaped as a human form slammed down through the branches. Khuna tore the noose loose and the person on the other end crashed to the ground. Khuna dropped on the man like a rock, driving the wind out of his lungs and cracking a few ribs in the process.

Khuna's knife was out, the blade finding the soft flesh beneath the man's throat and drawing a thin line of blood where it met flesh. "Who are you?" the big headhunter demanded.

"I am Death!" the man spat back, his filed down teeth gleaming in the moonlight.

"Wrong, you are dead!" Khuna smiled as the edge of his blade sliced open the flesh of the man's throat and severed his head. Khuna knew that he had been led deep into the jungle. He also knew that there were at least two killers, not one. Which meant that the other one was back at The Hanging Monkey! Khuna moved rapidly through the trees, hoping that he would be in time!

•••

Corky O'Brian sipped at the glass of Bushmills. The storm continued to rage outside. He was worried. Worried about Nick and Kit, worried about Jimmy and Grace, and oddly enough worried about Khuna.

The big islander had been gone longer without reporting in than ever before. That was very unlike Khuna. Even when he went off on his own extra-circular activities. No, it was definitely enough to worry him. It all had to do with the package that Kit Murdock had left with him, Corky was sure of that.

Corky turned off the lights in the bar and headed for his office. He wanted to put the night's cash in the safe so it wouldn't provide temptation to some light-fingered patron that had concluded the Hanging Monkey might be an easy target. He had just reached the office when he heard a strange noise. Corky turned, taking a step back into the well-lit office. He eased the door closed and walked quickly to the desk where he opened a drawer and removed a Webley .45 revolver.

Corky stuffed the revolver into his waistband and he sat the bag with the money on the desk. Corky moved off to the side of the door and waited. Whoever was in the bar had entered right after he turned off the lights in the main room. They were waiting out there in the darkness. Corky felt the short hairs on the back of his neck raise. He had seen the bodies upstairs, saw how horribly they had been mutilated. He drew the revolver from his waistband and thumbed the hammer back with an audible click.

He could hear movement from the room outside. Someone was making their way across the hardwood floor. Corky raised the revolver as the doorknob started to turn. "Boss, you in there?" Khuna's voice called.

"I am, Lad. Open the door slowly and step into the light," Corky ordered. The knob turned slowly and the door opened. Khuna stepped into the light, letting the door swing closed behind him. Corky breathed a sigh of relief and lowered the hammer on the revolver. "Good to see you, Khuna."

"I can see that," the big islander smiled back. Though it was not evident on his face, he was pleased to see that his boss was still alive. Out in the jungle, he had realized that one of his quarries was leading him away so that the other could go back to the Hanging Monkey to search for whatever they were searching for. That was why he came back after eliminating the first cannibal.

"So what now?" Corky asked.

"We wait," Khuna replied.

•••

Fujitsi Island, Motugra Chain

"That's the big secret?" Nick asked, stunned.

"You knew?" Grace looked shocked.

"Hell everybody in the islands knows," Fortune shook his head.

"The U.S. government doesn't know," Grace said.

"Don't bet on that," Nick shook his head.

"Well the people don't know," Grace shot back.

"Probably not," Nick agreed.

"You've got more than just a story," Nick said, it wasn't a question.

"I've got pictures too," Grace told him.

"I figured as much. Listen, we have to find a place to hide until morning. I don't think they will hang around too long past dawn," Nick Fortune said.

"Hiding is a good idea," Grace nodded.

"I thought so," Nick nodded. Taking her hand he guided her away into the darkness.

•••

Kit Murdock heard the shots ring out from the barroom below and drew his revolver. He was bone tired but ready for trouble. A few shots punched up through the floor, driving him back away from the door. He looked around and noticed the window. "Any port in a storm," Murdock muttered to himself. He grabbed the window sash and heaved it upward, forcing it all the way open. Rain was still pouring down from a night sky that was occasionally lit by jagged forks of lightning ripping across it. There was a thin ledge outside the window, the bricks slick with rain.

Cursing under his breath Murdock climbed out onto the narrow ledge, his pistol tucked into his pants behind his right kidney. He had heard a number of shouts in a number of languages. The doors below burst open and several men flooded out into the rain-soaked night. Suddenly Murdock felt free as an old recklessness washed through him. His lips spreading in a wide teeth-baring grin, Murdock launched himself into space. Several of the men below were fighting each other and were stunned when he fell out of the sky to knock them to the ground.

Murdock pushed to his feet, work-hardened fists pistoning out and back, striking flesh with bone-breaking accuracy, dropping the fighters at his feet. Murdock cleared a path with his fists and feet and then tore off at a run. To hell with The Blustery Duck, he was heading back to the boat where he could get some rest.

•••

Jimmy Dolan hit the floor at the sound of the first shot. The yells, screams and answering gunfire erupted above him. Jimmy scurried around the end of the bar and got behind it. He drained his beer mug. A bullet punched a hole in a keg above him and beer shot out in a golden fountain. Grinning at his good fortune he put the mug under the stream and watched it fill...

•••

Motugra Island, Motugra Island Chain

"I think it's bloody well time we find out what is in that package that Murdock left here," Corky said.

"Especially since death walks in its shadow," Khuna agreed. The big islander looked more sober than O'Brian had ever seen him. It was rather unnerving to see. Then Corky realized why. It was the first time he had ever seen Khuna look remotely frightened by anything.

Corky stood and walked over to the safe and twirled the dial. He had it open in a matter of seconds. The package lay on the shelf, a presence of doom and foreboding hovering over it like a palpable presence. Corky put the money in the safe and picked up the package, carrying it gingerly to his desk. He and Khuna stared down at it.

"Will you open it?" Khuna asked softly, his rumbling voice a barely audible whisper.

"Do I have a choice?" Corky asked, shooting his friend a look.

"I think you should put it back, let the young man deal with it when he returns. Evil shrouds it like a cloud," Khuna shivered. Corky noticed his own arms were broke out in goose bumps. Moving quickly he scooped up the package and put it back in the safe and slammed the door, spinning the dial to securely lock it. Both men breathed a sigh of relief.

"I want you to stay in the bar tonight. I'm going to bunk here to keep an eye on things. I want you here for security," Corky said.

"Yes, Boss," Khuna nodded.

•••

Fujitsi Island, Motugra Island Chain.

Fortune and Grace were below deck on *Fortune's Folly*. She was dressed in one of his blue chambray work shirts while her own clothing dried. Her luggage was still at The Blustery Duck, and Nick's shirt hung around her

Murdock launched himself into space.

petite frame reaching almost to her knees.

"Are we safe here?" Grace asked. Nick Fortune was dressed only in a pair of denim dungarees and nothing else. His dark hair was wet and tousled. A fresh eye patch covered his missing socket, his pistol tucked into his waistband.

"As much as anywhere," Nick replied.

"Nick, the Germans, Nazis if you will, if they and the Japanese are forming an alliance, it cannot be a good thing," Grace Thomas shook her head.

"It isn't. Got to be trouble in the making for the west. You caught me right in the middle of something else though," Nick told her.

"What?" Grace asked.

"I'm helping a kid with a lot of trouble on his back-trail," Fortune replied softly.

"You know what the trouble is?" she looked at him.

"Nope. Don't really care. He needs a friend. That's all I needed to know," Fortune shrugged.

"You are one of a kind," Grace shook her head. She meant it as a compliment and knew that Nick Fortune took it that way.

"I do what I can, Kid," Nick told her, folding her into his arms. He could feel the heat of her body beneath the thin cotton fabric of the shirt, and he also knew she knew it.

"And you did it very well," Grace replied, her eyes a thin slit as he drew her face to his and kissed her lips.

Just then the boat rocked and they both knew that someone had boarded her. "Damn," Grace hissed through clenched teeth.

"Be right back," Fortune whispered, drawing his automatic and heading for the stairs that lead up to the deck.

"Am I ever gonna catch a break?" Grace moaned softly.

•••

Nick Fortune moved softly up the stairs, his bare feet making no sound on the teakwood steps. He could see a light from the pilot-house and he thumbed back the hammer of his automatic, the click barely audible in the storm above.

Nick Fortune moved inside the open door and stepped out onto the deck. A dark shape was in the pilot house. "Freeze, Pal!" Nick said.

"Nick?" the voice asked. Fortune recognized it.

"Murdock?" Fortune asked in surprise.

"Yeah," Murdock's voice was clear.

"How did you get here?"

"Too noisy at the Blustery Duck," Murdock grinned.

"I understand that," Fortune nodded.

"It going to be quieter here?" Murdock asked.

"Long as you don't mind a rocking boat," Fortune grinned.

"I can live with it," Murdock replied.

"Who is it Nick?" Grace called softly.

"Kit Murdock, my deckhand," Fortune replied.

"The more the merrier," Grace rolled her eyes.

•••

Motugra Island, Motugra Island chain…

Jacques Henrique sipped at his cognac. He had decided to make an offer to Kit Murdock when he returned from his voyage on *Fortune's Folly*. Stealing the diamond obviously had not worked. Perhaps it was time to try another tactic.

He had heard of the murders on the island but dismissed them as supernatural fodderal. Yes, he would offer to purchase the stone. He could always take the money back at a later time. Henrique smiled as he sipped his drink.

•••

Moa slipped through the jungle. He had been unable to penetrate the building where the stone was being held, so he had decided to return to where his companion was supposed to lure the one who was hunting them. Tora was not where he had expected. Instead, his companion was tangled in vines, his head severed from his body. His eyes had been gouged out and his tongue had been severed from his mouth.

Anger flashed in Moa's eyes, hot rage built within his heart. The one that had done this would pay, as would the white man that had stolen the eye of Molakai from the temple back in Borneo. He began searching for spoor of the man that had desecrated his companion…

•••

Corky O'Brien awoke from a troubled sleep. His dreams had been haunted by the sense of evil that had permeated the package without even opening it. He felt for poor Murdock, for the lad had certainly been cursed through his possession of whatever was in the package. Corky wished he had never touched it, for now he bore the stain of the evil which permeated it.

The Irishman shivered in the darkness. Cold sweat chilled his body, the sheets of his bed damp with it. Somewhere in the darkness, a Devil stalked the night, he was sure of it. He only hoped that Khuna was sufficient to deal with it...

•••

Fujitsi Island, Motugra island chain...

Dawn was breaking over the island and the storm had finally passed. Nick Fortune was the first on deck to watch the sunrise. He had put a pot of coffee on in the galley and was filling his cup before the sun had cleared the horizon. He walked up on deck. The submarine was gone and he felt fully confidant that the Germans had cleared the area, which was a good thing for Grace.

He had felt the tension between her and Jimmy the night before. He wondered about that. There was something there, something that had hurt Grace. It was something that he would be speaking with his friend about.

Nick fired his first cigarette of the day, watching the sunrise over the South Seas. It was magnificent, even after the storm the night before, maybe because of it. Storms had a way of doing that, making everything bright and shiny and clear again, washing away the dirt and grime that accumulated during dry weather. Back in the Big Apple, the city was never better looking than the morning after a storm.

He put one foot on the rail, smoking and sipping his coffee. This morning the bay was still and smooth as glass. The boat shifted and Fortune knew that either grace or Murdock was awake. He was more willing to bet on Grace due to the discordant shifts in weight that he could feel through the deck. Murdock was a sailor, he could move without causing the boat to shift so much.

"Good Morning, Nick," Grace stepped up on deck carrying a cup of coffee, her blonde hair tousled with sleep, her blue eyes smokey. Her make-up was mostly gone but to Nick she had never looked more beautiful. She was wearing one of his work shirts and from what he could tell, little else.

"Good morning Grace. Gonna be a beautiful day," Nick replied, trying to tear his eyes away from her long slender legs that seemed to go on forever before vanishing behind the long tails of his work shirt.

"I hope so. Do you think those guys are gone?" Grace sipped at her own cup of Java.

"I do. They lit out last night under the cover of the storm. I figure they are long gone," Fortune told her. Grace walked over to him. She leaned in close against him and Nick was very aware of the heat of her body through the thin cotton of the work shirt.

"Can you take me back to Motugra today, Nick?" Grace looked up into his eyes, her body pressed against him and Nick became very aware that his earlier assessment had been right! Nick cleared his throat.

"I can do that," he told her. Just then Kit Murdock appeared from below, making plenty of noise. Grace took a step back and Nick breathed a sigh of relief.

"We eating ashore or should I whip something up in the galley, Captain?" Murdock asked loudly.

"I think breakfast at The Blustery Duck, Kit. Grace, we'll wait while you get dressed," Nick almost whispered.

"See you soon, Nick," Grace winked at him and then she walked to the hatch and disappeared below decks.

"Looks like I showed up just in time, Captain," Murdock grinned at him.

"You did," Nick sighed.

"You don't seem especially happy about it, Captain."

"Pal, I don't know if I am or not," Nick grinned.

•••

"You didn't stick around last night, Boyo," Link O'Connell grinned at Nick as the three stepped inside The Blustery Duck.

"The partying got a little too loud to sleep," Fortune shrugged with a grin, his one eye sweeping the room. "Jimmy still around?"

"Dolan's sleeping it off in the back. Bloody Sod started drinking straight from a keg that took a bullet and put himself out nicely," O'Connell chuckled.

"There's an extra box of Cuban cigars in it for you if you make things exceptionally loud around here when he wakes up," Nick grinned back. He felt Grace shaking with silent laughter and knew that this was exactly the right move.

"Cook will have yer usual out in a few, Nicky," O'Connell smiled and walked away.

"Thanks, Link," Fortune called after him.

"So what is our next move?" Kit Murdock asked.

"We eat," Nick grinned.

"I meant after that, Captain."

"Back to Motugra," Nick glanced at Grace who let loose with a smile that lit up the room.

"What are you saying, Captain?"

"I think it's time we helped you shed your curse. Somebody wants that damned thing. I say you should sell it or give it to them, get this thing off your back," Nick told him.

"Maybe you're right, Captain," Murdock nodded his agreement.

•••

Motugra Island, Motugra Island Chain.

Jacques Henrique presented himself at The Hanging Monkey as soon as the doors were unlocked. The interior wasn't at all impressive. The Frenchman sniffed imperiously as he surveyed his surroundings. He took a seat at the bar and waited until a red haired man emerged from the office, looking slightly rumpled and disheveled. A large, bare-chested Native followed him out, warily surveying the room. The native Islander moved with the sleek grace of a panther and exuded an aura of danger.

"Mister O'Brian?" Henrique asked softly.

"At yer service, Laddie. And you are?" the question was pointed and sharp.

"Jacques Henrique. I am searching for a friend. His name is Murdock and he has something I am interested in. To purchase," the Frenchman said softly so as not to be overheard by any of the other early morning patrons of the bar.

"I will be happy to pass your interest along when he comes back," Corky replied nonchalantly.

"Do you know where he has gone?" Henrique asked.

"I do, but he doesn't want me to be saying. Leave where you're staying and I'll make sure Murdock gets in touch," Corky replied smoothly.

"Make sure that you do," Henrique said stiffly.

"Khuna, I think this bloody frog just threatened me. How would you feel about frog legs for dinner?" Corky called to the big Islander.

"Delicious," Khuna smiled, revealing his teeth, all filed to points for shredding flesh.

"Khuna there, he's a semi-reformed headhunter and cannibal. Still, he's handy to have around," Corky told the Frenchman.

"Semi-reformed?" Henrique gave the man called Khuna a quick look.

"Means I haven't entirely broke him of the habits," Corky chuckled.

"Have Murdock contact me," the Frenchman stood and hurried out of the bar, O'Brian's laughter following him. Corky looked over at Khuna.

"Send two of the boys to keep an eye on him," Corky ordered. Khuna whistled and looked at two of the bouncers. They vanished out the door behind the Frenchman.

Corky watched them go. He thought about getting on the shortwave radio and calling Nick's boat but then decided against it. Nick would be back soon enough and he had no doubt that Murdock would be with him. The kid had what it took to stay in a fix. He had proven that much already. Corky had to admit that he liked the kid.

"We are being watched," Khuna walked behind him and spoke, his lips barely moving.

"Have you spotted him yet?" Corky looked into his coffee cup as he spoke.

"Not yet but soon," Khuna replied.

"Make it quick," Corky ordered. He didn't like the feeling of fear that was gripping him. Evil hovered over the bar like a cloud, had ever since he had handled that damn package last night.

•••

Somewhere on the South Seas…

"How long to Motugra?" Grace asked walking up behind Nick and leaning against him. He could feel the heat of her breasts pressing against his back.

"Couple of more hours," Nick replied, fishing his pack of Lucky Strikes out and placing one between his lips. He took his lighter out and fired it.

"What happens when we get there?" Grace asked.

"You file your story and I help Kit break this curse that's been following him around like a shadow," Nick shrugged.

"What about us, Nick?" Grace moved in front of him and looked up into his eyes.

"What about us, Grace? I love you. I think you know that, but we gotta wait and see what happens when those Feds show up. If I'm still a free man when they leave, we can see," Nick told her, his voice soft and low, barely audible over the clatter of the engine.

"Okay, Nick," Grace smiled.

"What if this story gets you back to New York, Grace? I can't go back either way."

"Then I won't go back either," Grace replied, her eyes meeting his.

"We'll see," Nick exhaled a cloud of smoke that was whipped away by the wind.

•••

Fujitsi Island, Motugra Island chain.

Jimmy Dolan groaned as he opened his eyes. Music was pounding loudly from the bar below. Sunlight streamed through the dirty glass of the window assaulting his eyes with a nearly blinding light. The pilot had the hangover to end all hangovers and he realized it when he slightly moved his head and starbursts of pain exploded behind his eyes.

"Shit," he whispered but it echoed through his skull as if he had shouted. He moved with excruciating slowness, running his hands over his body to determine that he had not sustained any injuries the night before, other than over indulging in a keg of beer that had been shot by the intruders.

It took several minutes but he was finally able to roll to his feet. Jimmy wondered what had happened to Nick and Grace. He had a feeling that the guys doing the shooting had been after her and knew it had to do with the film she had shot on the Japanese controlled island. He wondered if Nick knew about that. Coffee. He needed some and lots of it. He had to get the goose in the air and warn Nick about what he was going up against. Jimmy took a step and toppled forward onto his face. Stars exploded behind his eyes and then blackness swallowed him whole.

•••

Motugra Island, Motugra Island chain.

Moa sat on a branch in the shadows of the jungle, his eyes riveted to the door of The Hanging Monkey. Soon his quarry would return and he would face the vengeance of Molokai! The big Borneo native snarled as he caught sight of the native islander that had killed his partner and sent him to join Molokai in the Underworld!

Revenge was something that would taste sweet as he tore the islander's throat out with his teeth. It would be a battle, but it was one that Moa was confident that he would win. He settled in to watch and wait.

•••

"Shore ahead!" Nick called over his shoulder from the wheelhouse of his boat. He felt the deck shift slightly as Kit Murdock came forward. Grace was down below and he would be surprised if she had even heard him over the clattering roar of the boat's engine.

"So what happens now, Captain?" Kit Murdock asked from behind Fortune's shoulder.

"We get rid of that rock and free you of the curse that has been hanging over you," Nick replied.

"How are we going to do that?" Murdock asked.

"You underestimate Corky. He's figured out by now that the package you left is trouble and I'm willing to bet he already has a buyer for it," Fortune shrugged. He pulled out his pack of Lucky Strikes and shook one free. He offered the pack to Murdock who took one. Murdock stuck them in his shirt pocket and pulled his lighter, thumbing it to life and fired both smokes.

"You think so?"

"I do. We dock in five," Fortune told him.

•••

Fortune's Folly tied up to the dock, Kit Murdock scrambling around like a monkey to make the lines fast. Grace climbed up on deck as Nick Fortune cut the engines.

"Home at last," Grace smiled at him.

"Yes, we are," Nick smiled back. The three of them left the boat and headed up the plank walkway to the boardwalk that would lead to The Hanging Monkey.

"Hey Corky, O'Connell sends his love," Nick called, shoving through the bat-winged doors leading inside the bar. Corky O'Brian released a string of curse words that did every sailor in the place proud.

"Don't sugar coat it Corky, how do your really feel?" Grace called out, and the expatriate Irishman let loose with another stream of descriptive invective.

"I am amazed," was all Kit Murdock could say. Once Corky ran down, he looked at Murdock.

"There is a man interested in your package, willing to pay cash," Corky advised.

"Okay. Get him here," Murdock replied. Corky nodded and waved one of his men over. He spoke for a few seconds and he the man left the bar.

•••

It was early evening when Jacques Henrique put in his appearance at The Hanging Monkey. The Frenchman looked immaculate in his tailored suit. He looked at Murdock and nodded.

"I hear you have an offer," Murdock took a pull from the mug of beer sitting in front of him.

"I do," Henrique nodded.

"So let's hear it," Murdock cocked his head expectantly.

"One million francs for the package. No more, no less, cash money right now," Henrique looked at him.

"I accept. Get your money and I will get the package," Murdock met the Frenchman's gaze unwaveringly.

"Oui," Henrique nodded. He lifted his arm and snapped his fingers and a man appeared with a briefcase. He placed it on the table in front of Murdock. Murdock opened it, took out a random banded stack of cash and thumbed through it. It was real all right. Murdock shot a glance at Corky and Khuna appeared holding the brown paper-wrapped package. The big islander put it on the table in front of Henrique. The Frenchman scooped it up from the table's surface and slid it immediately into his pocket.

"We have an understanding," Murdock said.

"We do," the Frenchman replied standing. He stood and carried the package out the door. Everyone seemed to breathe a collective sigh of relief.

"I am so glad that is over," Murdock slumped in his seat. Nick reached over and gave him a pat on the shoulder.

•••

Jacques Henrique took his seat on the Pan Am clipper to Australia. He had not realized that he had been followed from the bar, that the package gave off a special vibration to those attuned to it. Moa crouched in the baggage compartment. When the plane had lifted off and darkness engulfed it, he slipped out of the luggage compartment and made his way forward. He was on the trail of the one who now carried the mysterious black diamond...

The End?

NOTES ON BLACK DIAMOND, BLACK DEATH.

The Motugra Island Chain is a fun place to play. That being said, as a creator of this particular corner of the world, I like to keep things interesting. My initial outing in Tales from The Hanging Monkey was just a straight up and fun adventure romp. For this second volume I decided that I wanted to do something different, a cross between mystery and outright horror. I had another character that would fit in perfectly as the catalyst for this tale and that was Kit Murdock who had hunted diamonds in Borneo.

Murdock is not a regular character here in Motugra, but his current ownership of a black diamond stolen from an ancient temple deep in the jungles of Borneo set the story up. Because the tribe who worshipped that dark god want the diamond back and had sent two of their members to get it back. They stalk Murdock on shipboard after he leaves Borneo and then when Murdock lands on Motugra, they arrive as well to continue their hunt.

During the writing of this story, a co-worker and I were in a conversation about something, I forget what exactly when he uttered the phrase blustery duck. It stuck in my head and that night after I got home and started working on the story, Link O'Connell and his bar on the neighboring isle of Fujitsi were born and the bar called The Blustery Duck which plays a part in the story was born and will likely show up again. The Motugra Islands are expanding and I look forward to spending more time there with Nick Fortune, Grace Thomas, Corky O'Brian and the rest!

•••

BILL CRAIG – is the author of more than eighty novels and numerous short stories. A single father and caregiver for his own father, he works customer service to support his writing habit. Craig taught himself to read at the age of four and started penning his own stories by age six, all with an adventure theme. He writes in a diverse range from adventure and new pulp to mystery to children's stories to poetry. His burning ambition is to break Walter B. Gibson's record for the most words written in a year. He is currently working on his next Decker P.I. mystery, his next Hardluck Hannigan adventure, and a serial title with four stories running through four books to complete four novels titled Two-Fisted Adventures.

"My ex-wife likes to say the reason I can work on so many different things at once has to be because I am secretly ADHD, but I think it has more to do with the fact that the voices in my head just won't let me rest until I tell their stories. As a writer, I can say that without risking a visit from the men in the little white coats and the jacket with the really long sleeves!"

PROPHECY OF THE FIRE LORD
by J. Walt Layne

November 1937

It was beneath dark skies that Nick Fortune brought the forty foot rumrunner *Fortune's Folly* into Motugra harbor. Motugra and its sister islands were currently neutral territory and he eyed the multitude of different flags the ships in the bay sailed under.

He crossed the deep water port at seven knots, unconcerned for the wake he was creating in the deep water port. At the eastern end of the harbor, he gave the wheel a hard roll a-port and eased the throttle down by half as he entered Nelson Cove. The cove had been named by Fortune and his friend, Jimmy Dolan, whose Grumman Goose seaplane, already gently bobbed on the rolling waters. The two men had discovered the tiny inlet together and for months argued over naming it. The dilemma was whether it should have an American or British name. Fortune voted for Yankee Cove. Dolan wanted something that identified with the Union Jack. Nelson's Cove was a compromise of the Lord Admiral Nelson and Baby Face Nelson. Both men identified personally with the names and the title stuck.

Fortune turned the wheel so the boat would lie in, bringing the stern of the small ship in to the dock first. He cut the engine and hurried down to the starboard gunwale to throw a line to the dock hand and secure the *Folly* for the coming storm.

Once the thick line was secured to the bollard, Fortune secured all hatches and portholes. In his cabin he drew the cord on his oilcloth sea bag and started to hoist it to his shoulder when he realized he'd forgotten it. He dropped the sea bag, leaning it against the bunk and hurried to the footlocker.

Lifting the heavy lock from the hasp, Fortune hoisted the lid and searched for it. A golden bottle of Tortuga 'Black Pirate' Rum and a small mother of pearl box waited patiently among the lifejackets. Running his finger over the pearl box, he opened it and smiled widely: inside a pair of blue gold and black diamond earrings flashed in the light. He snapped the box shut and slipped it into the left breast pocket of his shirt. He eased the bottle into his sea bag and then locked the chest.

Thunder rumbled and lightning shattered the sky as Fortune walked along the dock. He drew his rain slicker close around him as the sky released a sheet of bitter rain. The black afternoon sky was quickly shifting into a dark and miserable night. He pulled his hood low against the gale. Shielding the good right eye, the left was covered by a black leather patch. He hunched his shoulders against the rain and the weight of the sea bag. Without so much as a backward glance, he hurried his way up the dock.

At the mouth of Nelson Cove a Nazi U-boat broke the surface and slowed, blocking entry or exit from the cove. When the storm began to unleash its real fury, at its darkest and heaviest, a small boat, hull number DB 1234 ferried a handful of men and supplies toward shore. By the time the storm broke, the men and their equipment had disappeared.

•••

The mood in The Hanging Monkey was raucous. The barkeep and proprietor was Corky O'Brian, a former boxer. The big Irishman held court at the bar with a couple of sea dogs and Jimmy Dolan. The place was crowded with sailors a group of whom were clapping and stomping as a scurvy old seadog belted out a bawdy old seaman's shanty. The waitress, a Chinese beauty named Miko, rolled her eyes as she slunk between the laden tables. A woman of mystery and intrigue, this was old hat to her.

No one noticed Khuna as he ascended the stairs from the trap door behind the bar. The pub's number one bouncer, Khuna was native to the island and a descendant of kings; he was a quiet man who cast a powerful shadow. More than once he had mused as to what his ancestors would have thought of his job: they would have been appalled.

He heaved the half-barrel of beer from his shoulder and sat it upright on the floor. Like a ballerina, he stretched his body, his foot closing the trap door while he reached for the tap spud. After prying out the plug, Khuna hammered in the spigot before lifting the barrel and placing it on the keg stand. He opened the tap when Corky turned around with two empty steins and closed it when they were full.

At the same time, Miko tucked a tip within the swell of her breast and swished away from the drunken sailors, her cobalt-silk dress rustling against the beer-soaked floors. Her toned arms flexed as she lifted a tray of fresh beer steins from the barrelhead. With the tray resting on her shoulder, she expertly picked her way through the maze toward the back of the barroom. The sailors, though rowdy and excited, parted like the Red Sea for her.

At the back of the bar, a group of dark characters sat crowded around a table in a large alcove. Two were arm wrestling; the winner slammed a fist against the jaw of the loser, both men laughed and raised their steins. Four men at the center of the gathering were arguing the merits of several long bladed knives, among the blades were a kukri, a scimitar, a Fairbairn fighting knife, and an old serpentine blade with a handle made of a human fibula. At the head of the table an old sea dog sat low over the table having a secretive discussion with two swarthy men.

As she neared, a tanned arm snaked around Miko's waist. Indifferent, she smiled and turned to the man as she had done countless times in her waitressing career. It was all part-and-parcel of working at The Hanging Monkey.

"Hey, darlin' why don't you and I settle down under a banana leaf and you punch me out a couple'a slanty eyed little chimps?" he growled, his hand lowering over her tight backside. He gripped it painfully.

Smiling wider, she shook her head. Her accent was intentionally thick, her exaggerated English poor, "You no likey China girl, no makey monkey business."

Hoping that was enough to sway the man, she attempted to pull away. The man fumbled with the waist of her skirt, quickly sliding his hand down her bottom. Miko dropped her tray and screamed.

Her scream alerted Khuna, who leapt to her rescue. Seizing the foul man, he held him off the ground, the tips of the man's shoes scraping the floor. A slew of profanity surged across the table as his comrades came to his rescue. The effort was pointless; the bouncer effortlessly grabbed them, banging their heads together. The eerie hush of sudden silence washed across the bar.

The third man glared at Khuna, eyeing the pile of sailors heaped at Khuna's feet. Slowly, he began to sing a bizarre rhyme. In the quiet, it was ghostly and grotesque:

"Up and down the Barbary Coast,
the rackers hold a secret:
on Motugra Isle, at the edge of the world,
the Fire Lord's whip'll crack your soul!
An' now ye know the Dead Men's secret."

"What's that blarney?" Corky rumbled at Khuna, who recoiled, waving him off.

Not one to be waved off, Corky pushed through his patrons to Khuna's side. What he saw made his blood run cold: A faded map upon on a weathered sheet of vellum lay on the table. To Corky's horror, hair follicles edged the hastily shorn hide.

"Well I'll be deviled. That map's drawn on..." Corky trailed off flabbergasted.

"Who it's drawn on, be a more likely question," cackled the one armed sailor, punctuating with the bone handled Kris. "That'd be right lad. It's the map of The Prophecy." The grizzled, one eyed barnacle of a man rumbled.

Corky laughed at Khuna's superstitious reverence and swore. "Fools, The Prophecy you speak of was a witch's tale invented to keep children in their beds and men vigilant over the island. The old witch said it was to please the Matriarchal Goddess Kanaloa.

"You speak of Sha-hae-La. My mother said she was a Futsetta." Khuna's voice trembled in reverence. He glared at the old man and Corky. "But the old men, and my grandmothers... They knew. The old kings and queens, they honored the gods." He growled and turned away.

"Blarney," Corky spat.

But the old sea dog scratched his chin with a deformed claw of a hand, growling, "Pox on ye blarney. That gimpy jungle monk, knows what I'm talking about, don't he?"

The words had no more left his blasphemous mouth when Khuna's blade, called Death's Whisper sang through the air, shaving off the horrid man's left eyebrow. Remarkably, the eye patch was left unscathed. The remaining men flew to their feet, but were quickly halted by Corky's voice which thundered over the storm outside.

"Back to your grog or out in the gale!" he ordered.

The men looked to their leader who sidled up to Corky. "You spec we gonna let your man off?"

"You will or you're out." Corky jabbed a thick, freckled finger into the man's chest.

"I wouldn't be doin' that if I were you!" one of the thugs bravely voiced.

Corky shrugged. "You're right, Shamus. Maybe I'll just go cry in my petticoat." He grinned at the man and turned away.

"Don't you turn your back on me!" the big man roared, spittle flying off his lips.

"As you like," Corky spun and shot a stiff-armed right into the big lug's jaw. The man dropped to the floor, knocking three of his mates aside like bowling pins.

"Not another word or you're all out of here and into the blow." Corky warned the bunch. He turned on Khuna. "Now you tell me what the hell is going on, Boy-o."

Khuna nodded and followed Corky stiffly back to the bar. When he finally chanced to look up, his boss and Jimmy Dolan glared back at him. Squeezing what looked to be a black glass tooth suspended by a leather thong around his neck, he returned Corky's glare.

"Motugra is an island of gods and kings, once peopled by a warrior race that worshiped the Fire God, Pyrotiki. But the people grew weary of being ruled by a hundred generations of cruel despots and rose to overthrow the tyrant who threatened to bring down the wrath of the Fire God who lives in the soul of Mount Motugra.

"The rulers handed down relics of these feudal times through the ages, including crown jewels of blue gold and black diamonds, and the shaft of a whip that belonged to Pyrotiki. The Prophecy states that one day an outlander with powerful magic would appear and attempt to unseat the final heir of the kings. If the heir prevailed Pyrotiki would cleanse the land and oceans of invaders. If the outlander was victorious, with the power of a god at his disposal he would rule for all eternity."

"Blarney!" Corky growled.

Dolan's eyes widened. "Surely you don't believe that. Do you?" Khuna's answer was muffled as the heavy entrance door swung open and momentarily the gale ventured within.

All eyes trained on the dark figure who slammed the door closed and rested against it. Streams of water dripped off his coat staining the wooden floor like blood. The man turned and slowly made his way to the bar. Lowering his sea bag to the floor, he pushed his hood away and adjusted his captain's hat.

He grinned at Dolan. "You fellas look like you just saw a ghost."

"Nick!" Dolan said, smiling with relief. Enthusiastically, he slapped Fortune's back, only to pull away with a soaked hand. Shaking the water to the floor, he indicated to Corky. "Corky, set us up."

Fortune held up a hand as Corky moved for a bottle of gin. "I brought you something from my latest run." Digging into the sea bag, he pulled out the bottle of Tortuga Rum.

Corky beamed. "I've not seen the black pirate in a long many years! Thank you, Mr. Fortune!"

"Blimey, Cork. Don't preach it a sermon! Pull its cork and let it catch its breath before we put it out of its misery. It's likely been in that bottle thirty years." Dolan chided.

"I know exactly what to do with it." Corky said, kissing the bottle and whirling away.

Fortune settled onto a stool as Dolan asked, "What the news from outside?"

"Outside" was island vernacular among the transplants and meant anywhere but Motugra or the other local islands.

Fortune sounded tired beyond his years. "It's bad Jimmy. The Germans and the Japanese are spoiling to fight everybody but each other. If they get that one going, it won't be safe anywhere."

"No worries mate: Motugra's the Switzerland of the South Pacific." Dolan said, raising a pint glass of dark beer to his lips.

"Yeah everybody's neutral until the wolf is at both doors and banging on the windows. Then it's too late." Corky said as he set three tumblers next to the uncorked black pirate on the slab.

"Gracie says the Germans hit Spain and they are trying to get Mussolini to back them, but the garlic eaters are knee deep in Tunisia." Dolan said, noticing that he had Fortune's total attention at the mention of Grace Thomas's name.

Fortune turned his focus to the glass of rum Corky was pouring. For a moment, they drank in silence, but it became too much for Dolan to stand and he placed his glass on the bar.

"Look Nick, you need to go and talk to her. They way you two parted the last time had her torn up for weeks. I'm not sure why, but that woman loves you."

Fortune refused to meet his friend's gaze, but the weathered crease in his brow told the tale. The truth was, Gracie constantly weighed on his mind. His thoughts turned to the mother of pearl box in his pocket.

"Where is she?" he asked.

"Given the weather, I'd say she's in her rooms." Dolan finished downing the drink.

"What if she won't see me? We pretty much said what there was to say the last time." Fortune said, savoring notes of regret.

"Boy-o, a woman frets more on what you don't say than what you do in the short term, and then vicey-versey as time drags on." Corky offered. "T'ain't fit for a bowl of fish or the fisher a' men, but If I was a man wonderin' 'bout his best girl, I'd damn sure drag my arse out to see about her. Yep, that's where I'd be, Skipper."

Fortune finished his glass and reached for his sea bag, his fingers fumbling to pull the drawstring tight. Without another word, he excused himself, donning his hood before slinging the sea bag onto his shoulder and heading out into the storm.

•••

Heavy rain pounded the corrugated tin roof of the tiny bungalow and rattled the gate of the makeshift bamboo fence. The small trees and plants bent at an awkward angle as the gale hammered away.

Safe inside, Grace Thomas ignored the storm and tapped away at her manual typewriter. Though it wasn't particularly cold, she had lit a fire in the small stove to ward off the chill and it made the small place rather homey. Her attention was momentarily diverted as the desk lamp flickered. She reached for the box of matches that sat alongside the oil lamp. These storms were a constant in her life and she was well prepared.

No sooner had she lit the wick and placed the student shade and chimney back in place, when the electric lamp flickered one last time and died.

"Just in time," she said to herself, and pulled the oil lamp closer to the typewriter.

The familiar sound of footsteps on the boarded walk rose above the storm. Holding her breath, she waited, and jumped when three sharp knocks sounded against the door. When she made no reply, three more knocks came in rapid succession.

"A moment please," Grace dug into her desk drawer, her fingers closing around an emergency candlestick. Twisting it into the brass candleholder, she lit the candle and moved through the dark room. Reaching the door, she stood on her tiptoes and opened the peek.

"Yes? Who is it?" she called and listened intently. Whomever it was knocked again, hard.

Grace frowned, releasing her hold on the peek. As the incessant knocking continued, she threw open the plank door and confronted the dark figure.

"Just who is knocking at my door on a night not fit for a drowning duck?"

The figure threw back the hood of his slicker. It was Nick Fortune.

Soaked despite his raincoat, he pleaded with her. "Gracie, I'm sorry. I just got in. I looked for you at The Monkey, but you weren't there."

Grace looked uncertain and for a moment, Fortune thought she might slam the door in his face.

"Nick Fortune," she hissed. "Get in here. You have some explaining to do."

He stepped inside and Grace locked the door.

"You will be lucky if I don't give you a piece of my mind." She complained and stared at the man who fidgeted before her. "Put your sea bag in the hold and get out of that wet thing. Hang it in the mudroom." She ordered, turning away from him.

Fortune did as he was told and walked the familiar route to the mudroom. Upon returning, he found her sitting on an ancient horsehair sofa.

"Jimmy says that you told them that the Germans attacked Spain," Nick said, standing uncomfortably in the middle of the room.

She regarded him coolly, her lips pressed thin. "Is that why you came to see me? Because you want to talk about Jimmy Dolan, Nick? Or Hitler, or Mussolini, or grain markets or butcher hog prices?" She was irritated with him.

"Well no, but …"

"Well?" she demanded.

Nick scratched his neck in irritation. He wanted to make up with her and get some sleep.

"Look, the last time, we said some pretty rotten things to each other. I didn't want to leave on a sour note, but you made it fairly clear that you didn't want …"

"Nick, I never said anything about what I did or didn't want. I said a great deal about what I wasn't willing to accept. I deserve a little respect. You tell me how I am supposed to react when I walk into a club and find you sitting with some slinky burlesque girl in your lap and all your buddies half drunk?"

She was getting angry and Nick couldn't help but notice how beautiful she was when she was angry. "Yes, you deserve more respect than that. Yes, it was wrong of me to allow that to happen, let alone persist if I'd known you were so determined that we were going to be an item."

"What makes you think that I'd want to be an item with a man who... A man who…" she hissed.

"I know you're mad. You have every right to be. If the shoe was on the other foot, I'd have been just as upset as you are. I have deserved everything you have said, I was wrong."

"Nick Fortune, if you think for one minute that I can be charmed with your honey tongue!" She gave him a very cross look.

I brought you something." He held up the mother-of-pearl box. "Not that you'd be interested."

She drew up her mouth into a bitter scowl.

Nick gave the box a disappointed shake, allowing its valuable contents to rattle and slipped it back into his shirt pocket. "You were saying?"

She eyed his shirt pocket. "I was saying that if we were in fact going to be an item then I deserve much more respect than finding you with some hussy. Before you disappeared I felt things really heating up, I was falling for you Nick. And you knew it. We both did."

"Was that before or after you couldn't consider a man like me for being an item?" Nick sighed and glanced around. "D'you have anything to drink?"

A flicker of care crossed Grace's face and she shrugged. "I can make tea. I am out of coffee. There's booze. I also have a bottle of Cabernet that I was saving for dinner."

Nick feigned a smile. "I'd hate to rob you of your fancy grape juice. I'm pretty boozed up, so how about that tea?"

Grace smiled and got up. She gave him a stern look as she walked toward the kitchen and stopped in the doorway, "You're nowhere near out of trouble mister."

"Oh, yes. I know. Understood," Nick said firmly, around a smirk.

Grace said something but he didn't hear over the din of the rain. He heard the squeak of the hand pump and then a cupboard door.

While she was out of the room Nick slipped the mother of pearl box out of his left breast pocket again and opened it. He imagined how the blue gold and black diamond earrings would look on Grace. At the sound of her footsteps, he closed the box.

Grace set a small tray on the coffee table and poured tea into two heavy mugs. "Okay I'll bite, what'd you bring me?" She offered him her best girly smile.

He allowed his gaze to roam over her petite figure. "Grace, I know you're unhappy with me. But I didn't bring you a gift to make amends. I thought of you when I saw this." He hesitated. "A beautiful woman should have beautiful things."

Nick held the box out to her. Her fingers were cool as they grazed his palm. She turned the box in her hand, admiring the polished black wood and the delicate pearl inlay.

"It's beautiful, Nick!"

Unsnapping the gold catch, she opened the lid. Tears welled in her eyes as she regarded the treasure within.

"Oh, Nick…"

•••

In the wee hours of the next morning, Nick walked the muddy mile to his bungalow overlooking Nelson Cove. The storm had passed and the night was alive with sound. The wet heat had succeeded in bringing out the bugs and frogs, bats trilled, male rock apes battled somewhere in the distant jungle. Slapping at mosquitos, Nick pushed his way through the dense foliage, arriving in a wet mess.

Stomping the mud from his shoes, Nick paused at the door, fishing for the key and hardly noticing the small outboard sounding in the distance. Then he heard the young man's voice ring across his property.

"Haben sie, eine zigaretten, bitte?"

"Germans?" The language was foreign to the islands and Nick found himself creeping to the large tree on the corner of the small lot. He peered through the darkness and was surprised when the glow of a cigarette illuminated two German soldiers.

"What the hell are they doing here?" Nick stepped backward to the safety of his home. He hurried to open the door and closed it carefully behind him.

"These islands are neutral territory," he meditated out loud and hung the rain slicker on a peg.

"But for how long, Mate?" chanted a voice from somewhere within the dark.

Nick whirled, drawing his Browning Hi-Power from his belt.

The lamp cord was pulled washing the small home in light and revealing Jimmy Dolan lazing on the sofa.

"Jimmy! Cripes, I almost let the wind out of you!" Nick exclaimed. "How'd you get in here anyhow?"

"I left The Monkey right after you. I was going down to the Goose when I heard an outboard, like for a skiff or a little Rodney. That'd be fine, but it was coming in not going out, and I heard it come and go twice as I walked along." Dolan explained.

"That's a bit odd." Fortune agreed.

"You think that's a bubble off, there's a U-boat at the mouth of our channel," Dolan growled.

"How'd you get in here?"

"Are you sure? I mean, why, what do they want?" Surprise and anger shot through Nick. It was a dangerous combination.

"I don't know. I've been wondering that all night," Dolan said, standing up.

"You've been sitting here all night, in the dark, wondering why there are Nazis just outside the front door?"

"Well I've also been wonderin' where you keep the booze and if there's anything to eat. I used the crapper." Dolan sounded uncharacteristically surly.

Fortune grinned. "As long as you made yourself at home."

"I figured you'd be out for the night and I wanted to get out of sight quick, it was here or the shanty." Dolan chuckled.

"No booze in there since that night you and that little nymph from Christchurch..." Nick grinned as he pulled out the bottom drawer of a wooden file cabinet and pointed to the bottle of scotch.

Opening his sea bag, Nick dumped a full laundry bag on the floor. He handed Dolan a slab of cured meat, followed by wheel of waxed cheese as wide as a hand and twice as thick.

"Productive trip?" Dolan asked, opening his jack knife to help himself.

Fortune set a mailbag near the door and removed the last item: a heavy brown leather pouch that jingled with money as he set it on the desk.

"Fairly."

•••

By late morning, all evidence of the German presence was gone without a trace. After careful consideration, Nick and Jimmy searched the dock and found nothing; not even so much as a cigarette butt. Their dock hand, Koni, had left after securing *Fortune's Folly's* lines the prior evening. When they told him about the submarine and the skiff, he looked at them as if they were putting him on.

•••

It was 2:00 a.m. and The Hanging Monkey was near closing. It was the emptiest it had been in days; its sole customers Jimmy Dolan and some ginger gal with pouty lips and nice gams. Miko sat in the corner counting her tips and ignoring Corky's ramblings about some bare knuckle brawler he'd beaten in his youth.

Used to being tuned out by Miko, Corky sighed loudly and began to batten the shutters when a group of men walked into the bar. Two stationed themselves near the door while another pair took seats in the rear corners. The leader, accompanied by two thuggish lieutenants, walked to Dolan's table where he sat nearly cheek to cheek with the sweet-talking girl. His arms about her waist, she tousled his curly mop of blond hair.

The man cleared his throat and waited. Jimmy was about to kiss the young woman when the bespectacled little fellow spoke in German.

"Danke Miss. Das wird alle sein."

The little minx puckered her lips at Dolan and gave his hair one last toss as she stood up.

"What's this? What's going on? Where are you going?" Jimmy complained, standing to follow, but the spectacled chap stepped in front of him, his lackey shoving Jimmy back into his seat.

"Bloody hell!" Dolan cursed.

"All right there, Jimmy?" Corky's brogue rumbled from behind the bar. The giant Irishman withdrew a coach gun from under the bar and laid it atop the slab.

The wiry little fellow gave Corky an unnerving grin. "You might want to think carefully about your next action Mr. O'Brian. We simply want to charter the use of Mr. Dolan's airplane."

"Get out of my pub!" Corky roared.

The little fellow's smile faded. "I am Professor Gothimmel, from the University of Mainz. I am here, legally. I am only searching for an island shaman. I want to ask about the island's theological system and artifacts. Perhaps we would like to buy items of a certain nature for the university collection."

Corky wasn't buying it. "I want you out of here, now."

"Very well, then. Mr. Dolan, my man will fetch you when we are ready for you to take us aloft." Gothimmel directed.

"I haven't agreed." Dolan grunted.

"Mr. Dolan, don't be silly. This is your singular opportunity to volunteer. If I have to ask you again, it won't be nearly as polite." The little man screwed his lips together in a fake smile. "You would be wise to accept my offer. We are going to pay you generously for your time, provide fuel, and cover expenses for any maintenance or other necessities." The little man hissed as his two attendants encroached.

Dolan eyed them suspiciously, "If you're trying to hire a seaplane and are all legal and above board why do you need your two attack dogs?"

Gothimmel simply smiled that same hollow, mirthless screw of lip.

Dolan was on the hook and he knew it. Gothimmel motioned to his entourage and they gathered quickly. "Very well, Mr. Dolan, we will be leaving within the week. My man will notify you when it is time."

The man turned on his heel, leaving the bar, once more, empty. Corky carried the shotgun in the crook of his arm and barred the door as soon as it closed. "Bloody hell, Jimmy what are you going to do?"

"Looks like I'm fixed. You know how these blokes do business. They ask, but it isn't really a question," Dolan lamented.

"Little wonder how they found you," Corky groused, pouring a pair of shots.

"Aye, that strumpet's knickers are embroidered with a swastika," Dolan said and they both laughed deeply.

•••

Nick had asked Grace on a date and she had accepted. Dinner took place at a quaint garden café called Cha-Cha where they were carefully attended by two young waiters. They were well served; their plates kept heaping with fresh seafood. When finished, they eased back in their chairs and watched each other in that knowing way that couples in love do. Finally, Grace broke the silence.

"I was in the telegraph office this morning to send my columns to The Post and Tribune. A man was complaining that a parcel he was expecting from New Zealand hadn't arrived. I overheard the clerk tell him that the pilot hadn't made the weekly trip. Isn't that Jimmy's run?"

Nick glanced around. "Corky was in a huff about something the day before yesterday. He mentioned that Jimmy had to fly some Germans to look for artifacts on the upper islands."

Grace's golden hair fluttered in the breeze. Somewhere, a macaw called. She sat up quickly.

"What? Again, what about looking for artifacts? Did you say German?"

"Corky was fighting mad, said the fellow, Gotheimer or whatever his name is, is nothing more than a skeleton with skin stretched over him, with fiery eyes and a voice like a razor against a strap."

They were silent as they pondered the meaning. Suddenly, Grace choked on her wine. "Gothimmel, Edmund Gothimmel?" she sputtered. Nick patted her back through the aspiration.

"You okay?" Nick asked, reaching to help her and she waved his hand away. "Yes, that's him: Gothimmel. What's wrong? They came to see me about chartering a boat and paid upfront for the fuel. They're covering expenses and basically paying a king's ransom for pretty basic fare."

"Oh, Nick. You can't. We need to go see Corky and hear the rest of it," Grace insisted.

"Why not? I can use the money," Nick said, striking a very blasé tone.

"Because, Nicholas that man is vile… We're going to see Corky," She said, exasperated.

•••

"Bleedin' Nazi Occult Buggar!" Corky rumbled. "You two had better steer clear of that."

"A bit late for me I'm afraid. They've already hired me to escort them to the far end of the island. From there they want to explore the dead volcano."

"You will not!" Corky rumbled, drawing the attention of Khuna, who had been conversing with a thick-necked islander.

Upon Nick's objections, Grace threw up her hands and stood, nearly bowling Khuna over in the process.

"See if you can talk some sense into him," she ordered and huffed away to the powder room.

A smile cracked the corners of the bouncer's mouth. "Why is Grace catching fire?" he asked.

"Nicky here is taking our German visitors to look for tiki trinkets at the volcano," Corky said with a frown.

"Pyrotiki," Khuna exclaimed and rattled off a string of oaths in Polynesian.

Confused, Nick and Corky tried to follow the complex language. As Khuna finished, Corky's expression changed to surprise and settled with at anger.

"What now?" he cried. "Prophecy? I thought that was a wives' tale!"

Khuna's expression didn't change. "I must go see Moki."

"Pog ma hon!" Corky swore, pounding a fist on the bar.

Khuna shot Corky an angry look; the fierce warrior from within springing forth, and Corky shifted uneasily.

"Moki is Tohunga, a wise man," he spat, "and he will advise my people what to do."

"Whatever you say, Boy-o," Corky saluted Khuna who turned away and headed for the door.

"What's gotten into him?" Nick asked over his shoulder as he watched the heavy plank doors swing wide in Khuna's wake.

The sentiment was seconded by Grace who had returned. "Gee-wiz! Where's Khuna going in such a hurry?"

"Oh, just some bloody, juju witch doctor nonsense," Corky growled and wiped the bar.

"What?"

"Well, it's real enough to him, just as this Gothimmel is real enough to both of you," Nick explained.

"Pot of shite pudding if you ask me!" Corky growled at Nick, as Grace shot him a frustrated look.

"You're not seriously considering taking their offer, are you? That's like supporting the devil himself!"

"There's no better way to see what these people are up to and keep my eye on Jimmy."

His point wasn't lost on Corky who fumbled with a new cigar deep in thought. Biting the end off, he pointed the thing at Nick. "You may have a point lad, but don't expect any of us to like it."

"Especially not me," Grace seconded. "If you must do this, be careful and keep an eye out for what's really going on."

"That's my girl, always looking out for her next story," Nick groused.

"Yeah, I just hope it's not your obituary," Corky concurred.

•••

The knock at the front door made Dolan's stomach drop. Exhaling the cigarette smoke slowly, he reached for the door and hid behind the small crack as it opened.

"Yes?" he asked, tentatively.

One of Gothimmel's thugs grunted in a heavily tinted German accent, "Ready your aircraft. The doctor wishes to leave in one hour." Without giving Dolan a chance to reply, the fellow simply turned and walked away.

Dolan closed the door and made his way in a daze to the edge of the small table. His fingers mechanically closed around the morning-old cup of coffee. But his hand was shaking, and instead, he opted for the bottle of whiskey. Not bothering to pour a cup, he gulped several mouthfuls before returning the bottle.

He lit another cigarette and packed a duffle bag with a change of clothes, an extra box of cartridges for his revolver, and other necessities. He pulled on and secured a shoulder holster, then slipped the Colt Police Positive from beneath the pillow on the unmade bed. He grabbed his leather pilot's jacket and pocketed a pair of brass knuckles.

Dolan trudged along the path that led to the dock in Nelson Cove like a prisoner walking the last mile after his final meal. Instead of physical guards marching him, he was seized in the apprehension of the unknown.

On the dock, he found Professor Gothimmel and his pair of heavies waiting. Gothimmel was dressed in khaki field clothes, boots, and a hat made of woven grass. Nick stared at the professor's getup a moment to long and the man asked, "Is there a problem with my clothes?"

Nick fought to keep a straight face when he replied, "Not a thing professor Challenger."

"Droll, Mr. Dolan, you have a singular wit," Gothimmel hissed.

The professor's comrades, clad in business casual attire, oxford shirts, belted wool trousers, and hard-soled shoes stood at his side. It would have looked like a simple safari, had they not been carrying MP-38 submachine guns.

"If this is a treasure hunt, why do you need the bloody machine guns?" Dolan demanded and Gothimmel flushed.

"It is sometimes necessary to motivate people into providing the help I require." His brittle smile did nothing to ease Dolan's concerns. "Don't take me for a fool Mr. Dolan. Are you not armed, yourself?"

Instead of answering, Jimmy opened the plane's fuselage door and allowed the thugs to load their baggage and then board the Goose.

When Gothimmel was settled into the copilot's chair, Jimmy asked, "So where are you hiding the rest of your expedition?"

When they'd finished, he ran through the preflight checklist and prayed for a reason not to take off.

Gothimmel gave that unnerving chuckle. "That is hardly your concern, but if you must know, my men accompanied an advance party on foot two days ago to set up camp near the volcano."

This sparked a dozen further questions, all of which Jimmy decided to keep to himself. Instead, he focused on setting the flaps, opening the choke, and pulled the throttle to the start position. Cementing a leather helmet to his head, he clicked on the two way radio, and was startled when Gothimmel immediately turned it off.

"Let's keep this a private expedition, shall we?" the cadaverous man asked.

Jimmy shot him a burning look and depressed the contact switch.

The big rotary engine, coughed once, sputtered twice, and roared to life. Throttling up, he taxied away from the dock, cut a sharp left and then a sharp right. Louder and louder the engine roared like a cyclone as he raised the throttle to FULL and the plane surged forward, cutting through the water, and gaining speed.

The plane ate the distance to the natural spur sea wall, isolating Nelson Cove from the main port and open sea. The tree and rock covered arm grew ominously closer as Jimmy waited for the cold little man to flinch.

As the distance narrowed to less than one hundred yards, Gothimmel began to fidget nervously and Dolan heard one of his henchmen complain to the other.

Squirm, you buggars, he thought to himself as Gothimmel swallowed hard.

"Mr. Dolaaan…" Gothimmel exclaimed, groping for something to hold on to as Jimmy pulled back hard on the yoke.

The Goose leapt from the water and screamed skyward, slowing against the drag of the steep climb skyward. It cleared the treetops so narrowly that Gothimmel made eye contact with a falcon perched in the topmost branches of a large cedar tree. The bird turned its head way around and screed angrily.

Dolan eased the yoke forward, leveling the Goose so that it accelerated and turned into a stomach churning roll to the left. This succeeded in orienting the aircraft north as well as proving his point to Gothimmel that he was in control. However, he was not prepared for what happened next.

Amidst the terrified screams from the men in the back seats, a cold, hard muzzle of an MP-38 pressed hard against his cheek. Gothimmel's scraping voice rose calmly above the din of the engine.

"Thank you, Mr. Dolan. You are indeed an adequate flyer. If there are any more such displays, you will find that my men are more than adequate marksmen."

Dolan obeyed in contemptuous silence and followed the jagged coastline at a safe distance. He focused on the comforting ridgelines and saddles set into the vegetation. Once in a while, the dense jungle gave way to crystal blue mountain lakes. Under different circumstances it would have taken his breath away.

Forty minutes later, Mount Motugra loomed into view. An ash plume curled toward the heavens and Jimmy gently banked around it, descending to five hundred feet. Circling the volcano, he pointed to the mist shrouded cone of the lesser, long dead Pyrotoko volcano. The aspect of Pyrotoko was eerily like a giant moss covered skull. The Goose descended through the mist, crossed the cape and began to circle for a landing. As he brought the plane around, Jimmy noted long, dark shape of the U-boat submerged less than a mile offshore.

The Goose came in low over the water as Dolan slowed the airspeed. A slight press on the left rudder pedal and the seaplane's attitude was nearly perfect. He adjusted the flaps to a full quarter upright and pulled back slightly on the yoke. The nose ascended slightly and the rear of the pontoon runners broke the surface of the water, dragging the plane down gently. Dolan released the flaps and taxied the plane toward the shoreline.

He brought the plane to a halt in mere inches of water, a dozen feet from three beached skiffs with no hull numbers or markings of any kind.

"Very nice, Mr. Dolan," Gothimmel seemed impressed.

"See you when you get back," Dolan said, with a two-fingered salute as the men behind him pushed open the fuselage door and exited.

"On the contrary, you will be coming along with us to ensure that you will be available on my command!" Gothimmel chuckled. The words had no sooner been spoken when the pilot's door was flung open and Dolan was jerked from the cockpit.

•••

Khuna sat comfortably on a grass mat, his legs crossed underneath him. He eyed the plumage of smoke the small fire in the stone pot emitted and watched Moki, the Shaman, drop a bundle of herbs onto the flames. An aromatic smoke began to rise and Khuna closed his eyes. He listened to the Shaman and his apprentice chant their haunting song.

When the song concluded, Moki settled onto the grass mat across from Khuna, and picked up a palm leaf. With it, he began to bathe Khuna in the smoke. With great ceremony, the apprentice served a traditional ceremonial meal and drink that would not be consumed.

Moki bowed low and started speaking some invocation then beckoned to the heavens. Three times this was repeated and at the conclusion he blew three long blasts on a conch shell.

Facing Khuna, Moki shook his head in sorrow. "I know why you have come. You live a modern life among the white people and work in one of their hostels. You do not keep to the old ways. But you do not observe the decadence of their modern life. You are the last generation of the great warrior sept. You should take a wife and have many sons, continue the line of your fathers," Moki said, reverently.

Khuna shot the shaman an angry look as he continued. "Your white friends are in danger. You have come to ask the spirits about the prophecy of the Fire Lord, Pyrotiki."

Khuna grunted in affirmation. The shaman wasn't off the mark, but Khuna wasn't impressed. Nothing the man had said thus far had been anything but common knowledge among the islanders.

Khuna nodded in frustration. "I think my coming here was a mistake." He started to get up.

"There are outlanders in our land whom your white brothers say are very bad. Men who want to steal our magic and enslave the Fire Lord to make war on the people," Moki said slowly as the smoke washed over him.

Khuna settled back onto his folded legs.

"You do not keep to the old ways. What do you care if what you say comes to pass and the people are slaves of the Aryan Devil? Why do you seek Moki's words when you have not taken your rite of passage; when you have not done your duty to your people? Why now do you come? Why would the spirits want to help the people, when their own Alii-Amoku (tribal leader) has turned his back on them?" Moki accused.

Khuna did not fold to guilt easily. He jutted his jaw in defiance.

"You are the shaman of my father's people. You commune with the spirits. I don't come to you to tell me about the feelings of ghosts. A ghost doesn't feed my mother. It will not hunt, or spear fish. A legion of smoke bears no arms against my enemy. If your familiar spirit will not tell of the prophecy of Pyrotiki, I will ask him when I meet him." Khuna jumped to his feet.

"Where do you go?" Moki asked.

"If your grandmother's spirit won't defend my people, then I will. I will do it on my own. I do not need your Kolohe-Konane (mischief games). If I am to be a king as you say, then I will do it with my own hands, not because Moki's ghosts say so," Khuna thundered, storming off the grass mat and into the night.

•••

Nick Fortune was dozing in a hammock in a corner of the yard when the heavy sound of boots thumped against the boardwalk leading to his front door. Two German soldiers accompanying an older man noisily gathered at Fortune's door. Silently, he reached for his pistol and slipped from the hammock.

"You should take a wife and have many sons…"

As the older man tried the doorknob, Fortune stepped behind the group and growled, "What's your business here?"

The soldiers spun and pointed their MP-38's at him. The older fellow addressed Nick.

"You must be Fortune. I am Werner Hess, an associate of Doctor Gothimmel. Please ready your watercraft immediately."

The man was deceiving: his mouth smiled, but his eyes did not. The two soldiers lowered their weapons and followed him like sheepdogs as they retraced their path back down the boardwalk. Nick holstered his pistol as the sound of their steps echoed into the night.

Nick's thoughts turned to Grace as he trudged down the dock. He knew his departure would bring about another unhappy ending that Grace didn't deserve. He also knew that the best way to protect her was to break it off clean and not let the Nazis see them together.

Automatically, his gaze shifted to where Dolan's Grumman Goose should have been docked. A pang of guilt washed over him as he recalled their last conversation, but he beat the feeling away by justifying this trip. He would find Dolan regardless of what Hess and his toy soldiers had in mind.

Despite his rationalizing, it was with a heavy heart that Nick stepped aboard *Fortune's Folly*. The six steps to the wheelhouse felt like scaling a mountain. After stowing his sea bag in a cabinet, Fortune turned the key to start the generator. As the small diesel plant coughed to life he switched on the running and deck lights.

In the engine room the eight-cylinder in-line diesel engine rumbled to life and Nick took comfort in the familiar hum as he checked the transmission. With everything running along perfectly, it seemed Fortune's only issue was his unwanted guests.

Hess arrived with a dozen local laborers dressed in a mix of traditional clothing, more modern clothing such as dungarees and denim work shirts they were accompanied by half a dozen soldiers most of whom didn't look old enough to serve.

Two of the cadre had been with him at Nick's bungalow. The younger soldiers were under the authority of that particular pair who kept close to Hess, who looked ill from the moment he stepped aboard *Fortune's Folly*. He held the rail in a death grip as he walked along the deck toward the cabin.

"You there," Fortune commanded, leaning out of the wheelhouse window, pointing to two soldiers and gesturing to the lines securing the boat to the dock, "cast off!"

The fresh faced young men in their pressed uniforms looked to their superiors for direction. Nick was about to yell again when Hess himself angrily yelled something to them in German and they scrambled to untie the lines.

Nick shifted the transmission into first gear, turning the wheel to port and increasing the throttle one quarter. *Fortune's Folly* slipped away from the dock and Nick steered toward the mouth of the cove at the end of the short channel.

When the boat entered the channel Nick eased the throttle forward, the speed of the boat increasing substantially. The laborers seated on deck talked amongst themselves, here and there one of them gestured at the young soldiers, most of whom were struggling to maintain footing as the boat pushed against the resistant water. At first Nick thought to apologize, but decided that it wasn't necessary: unwanted passengers should have brought their sea legs.

Nick shifted the boat into high gear and the boat lurched as it entered open water. Again the soldiers were nearly spilled. Hess was nearly green as he scrambled to the rail to lose the contents of his stomach.

A mile from shore, Nick rolled the wheel to port and steamed north. Dawn broke, casting an eerie shadow over the demon landscape of the dead Pyrotoko volcano. A black storm cloud stretched as far as the eye could see over the land. It seemed to reach down from the heavens and touch the plate glass surface of the deep.

"Dead calm," a voice said behind Nick, who looking over a map. Nick looked up, suddenly equating the voice and its owner. He was surprised to see Hess had made it off the deck and up the stairs to the wheel house.

"Never good: a seaman's life is turmoil; turmoil ashore and turmoil at sea. There's turmoil over his head if not below his knees," Nick said, trying to sound afoul, which wasn't much effort, all things considered.

"It looks bad to the west," Hess offered, seeming to make an attempt at conversation. Nick nodded and glanced at the dark western sky.

"We're running along the front right now. We can't go far enough or fast enough to outrun it. This boat is heavy and fairly steady, but in a big storm, I stay in close and find a place to button it up if I have to. I'm never in enough hurry to trade my life for a few hours time."

Hess seemed to appreciate that and the conversation turned to the boat and workings. For the better part of an hour, he asked questions about navigation and driving the boat. Nick was surprised by the man's curiosity and answered his questions cautiously.

Not long after the last of his questions were answered Hess left the wheelhouse when one of the soldiers called to him from the deck. Nick didn't speak German, but putting together the urgent tone and the repetitive nature of the summons, Nick knew that there was only a short list of things that could be so important to them, none of them good for him.

On deck one of the soldiers peering through a pair of field glasses pointed to a place just beyond one o'clock off the starboard bow. Nick took his own field glasses from the shelf near the captain's chair and scanned the area where the young soldier had pointed.

At a distance, the recognizable insignia of a black eagle and swastika adorned the conning tower of a submarine. A bright light flickered in a pattern that Nick recognized as Morse Code. He didn't recognize a great number of words in the transmission, but Kreig, and Boot 1234 stood out.

War boat 1234? These guys might be scientists, but they're not from any university.

Nick made no effort to slow the boat when one of the soldiers reached for the large spotlight and swiveled it around to return the message. He couldn't see the outgoing message and had no confidence that he wasn't in danger. Considering their leader traveled in the company of soldiers armed with MP-38 submachine guns and two men carried an oiled canvas bag marked MG-42, Nick was on his guard.

Hours later, under a late morning sky, Nick pointed to a group of small boats. Many of the laborers went to the port rail and waved to the fishermen casting nets from their punts and spear fishing from kayaks.

Nick recognized the rustic dugout canoe of his friend and sometimes deckhand, Faipa. The big islander looked out of place standing in the center of the small boat with his young sons perched at either end with spears. He was hauling in a loaded net, bracing a foot against the gunwale to avoid capsizing the boat and dumping his sons into waters known to be the hunting ground of sharks and killer whales. As the boat passed, Faipa threw up a hand and waved; Nick waved back and turned his attention to the rising breeze.

Nick watched the dark clouds of the storm in the distance reach into the dark water's plate glass surface and pound it into a jagged chop. Within the hour, a torrential downpour was upon them.

•••

Grace was furious. She stood on the porch of Nick's bungalow, pounding on the door. She peered through a dirty window, into the darkened rooms within. Nick was not there. Slapping at the door once more, she turned and strode down the path to the dock in Nelson Cove. Angrier yet when both *Fortune's Folly* and Dolan's Grumman Goose were absent, Grace stormed off in the direction of the Hanging Monkey as thunder rumbled across the darkening sky.

Corky had just turned the sign and lifted the bar from the door when Grace flung it open and surged into the bar.

"Where is that scoundrel Nick Fortune? Tell me, Corky!" She yelled.

It wasn't often that Corky was caught off guard. He wasn't prepared for the surprise attack.

"How am I t'know where your lad's got off to?" he blubbered. "If'n you came off to him mad like a bulldog chewin' a wasp, I don't blame him for bein' scarce!"

It was all Grace's nerves could take. She burst into tears burying her head into her hands.

The door behind the bar opened and the warm nutty aroma of coffee cut through the stench of flat beer and cigar smoke, it was accompanied by the smoky allure of frying bacon. Miko exited Corky's apartment, her arms laden with a coffee pot and white stoneware mugs. She shot Corky a look like that could kill as she set the cups on the nearest table and began to fill them with coffee.

"Miss Grace," she announced loudly, "don't listen to him. He's a man; what does he know of love?"

The heavy plank door swung open admitting the chill breeze of warm salt air. A rail thin old man in field clothes and knee-high riding boots entered with some difficulty, followed by his manservant. The black man was stooped in his back and appeared stout though bent. He carried a large valise and sleeved rifle in one hand (the obvious tools of his master's trade), and pulled a large wheeled steamer trunk behind. Neither of them drew attention. They took a corner table in the rear of the joint where the room and entrance could be observed.

Grace sank into a chair and began to sob. Corky laid a hand on her shoulder.

"Now ya wee bean, I'm sure he's not off being a lout. You know that he and Jimmy both were shanghaied into workin' for that Nazi druid."

"Nazi druid?" The white stranger's discounting Texas drawl sliced through the quiet.

Corky looked up from the sullen Grace, "Bloody right. Gangly ghost he is with a cold smugness about him. Gothimmel's his name. Travels in the company of two stiff hoodlums and soldiers so young their faces have barely seen a razor."

"What do you know about him?" the Texan asked his voice suspicious.

Corky gave Grace's shoulder a squeeze and looked at Miko, who gave him the nod. He walked to his guests.

"We know what they said. But we also know they pressed two of our friends into service against their will. They say he has something to do with the occult, but I think that's a lot of bollocks."

"Sounded like bear scat to me too, the first time I heard it. But that hell rat that's running Germany right now is spoiling to fight the whole world. If Gothimmel's here it's because he thinks there's some jujube bead or Tiki head that'll help that effort." The fellow held Corky's gaze with ice blue eyes.

"I'm Irish and I've heard enough fairy shite to fill a copper pot. Our friend Khuna went off to see the witchdoctor and hasn't come back. He's wicked sharp as islanders go, and doesn't hold with all that ghost-in-the-fire-hole nonsense. But something got him going," Corky explained.

All the while Corky talked to the hunter, his valet listened intently. As their conversation came to an end, the Texan averted his gaze to his valet who continued the conversation. "They've been very successful at keeping this quiet and maintaining the illusion of academic interest. Where they're slipping is in their increased use of military transports and soldiers to motivate assistance. Do you have any idea where they're working? We need to find them and stop them at all costs."

"Blimey, who are you people?" Corky asked in disbelief.

The valet gestured at the Texan. "He is Greg Duquesne, big game hunter, adventurer..."

"Thief, liar, and stud!" Duquesne cut him off. "'fore I got gored by a bull and laid low in the bottle for too many years."

"Yeah, but he climbed out of there, got back on the horse and when his country called, he showed up to work." He gave the Texan a look of intense respect.

Suddenly, the valet sat up to his full height and revealed that he was tall and very fit. "You can call me Alcatraz, Traz if you must. We've worked together a fair number of years," he explained.

"Can I get you gentlemen anything?" Corky offered, trying to digest the plethora of information.

"Breakfast would be good. We don't usually get a decent breakfast," Alcatraz said with a grin.

Duquesne eyed the bar and inhaled deeply. "That coffee smells fine. I'd like some of that and breakfast. I don't suppose you have biscuits and gravy back there anywhere?"

Corky grinned. "No but Miko there'll make your omelet fit for a king!"

"Sounds good to me," the Texan drawled. He gave the exotic beauty an appreciative appraisal. "Looks purdy good, too," he said smoothly as she set a coffee my in front of him.

She smiled at his harmless banter, "You're very sweet for an old man."

"The older the fiddle, the more lively the bow," Duquesne said with a mischievous grin. A blush burned its way up her neck and flushed her cheeks.

•••

Deep in the jungle, Khuna watched the Nazis from his hiding place in the shadows until the party reached the base of Mount Motugra. As the laborers made camp for their captors, Khuna slipped away to the cave leading to a cavernous underground shelter. Generations of old had weathered the storms of nature and other tribes in the shelter and it was well known to the locals.

Khuna had camped at the site many times over the years. The jungle was full of edible plants and game of all sizes. Knowing what to look for made for traveling light and the ability to provision along the way.

Just inside the cave's entrance a number of torch staves were piled along with a bundle of punky wood. With a flint and steel Khuna struck a torch alight and walked into the darkness. At some point in the history of the cave, his people had used the lower level as their spiritual place. Moki had been unable to provide any solid answers and Khuna had not been surprised. The old shaman rarely answered any questions head on.

Khuna moved slowly, feeling his way along the right side of the elongated ellipse-shaped wall until it curved abruptly inward. The hair on the back of his neck stood as he stepped down into the lower level. The sulfurous copper smell of blood caused his tongue to curl: something had recently been butchered.

He covered his nose and mouth against the foul smell. "By Tu, I will know!" he growled, entering the spiritual chamber. The light of his torch reflected brilliantly off the polished obsidian walls. Khuna moved the torch until he found two other staves wedged into the rocky crags of volcanic glass. He lit them both, surprised by the amount of illumination provided.

His surprise turned to disgust as he noticed the small koa wood bowl upon the altar. There was no need to inspect the bowl or the wrapped parcel at the foot of the shrine to understand what had happened. He swore in a slew of Creole; a combination of English and Polynesian.

Khuna thought of Moki, the Shaman and grew angry. At first it was easy to believe that the wretched fool would sacrifice a child to prove his medicine. He did not find the traditional dagger made from a marlin bill, or the alii lei O mano, a hacking tool of wood with shark teeth set into the blade. Even the manner of presentation was different from what his grandmother had told him about the supplication rite to please the angry god who lived in the earth beneath the mountain of fire.

Standing there in the chamber, seeing the remains of the savagery that had occurred, the words of the prophecy came back to him:

An outlander will come with powerful magic and unseat the kind and enslave the people. If he awakens Pyrotiki the power of the Fire Lord will be his for eternity.

When Khuna left the chamber his blood was boiling. He wanted to go directly to the group of soldiers and kill them to the last man. But the man whom he felt sure was responsible wasn't with them. The palest of the white men, the one they all yielded to was not among them. He'd find Gothimmel and his men at the long dead volcano near the northern tip of the island. He knew they would search out the resting place of Pyrotiki. He would reckon with that fellow soon enough, but first he would make returning to the death chamber impossible.

•••

Nick Fortune was marched into the camp that served as Gothimmel's base of operations by four of the soldiers.

"You will wait here until we are ready to leave," one of them said in a post-pubescent rasp. Two of them shoved him onto a log next to Jimmy Dolan.

"I see this party's drawn the finest flies," Fortune quipped.

Dolan chuckled, "I see they've let you keep your Browning."

"Yes. It doesn't figure that they wouldn't disarm a prisoner," he agreed.

"They didn't take my Smith, either. I think Gothimmel would consider it rude to solicit help from a prisoner. He leaves us our arms, but curtails our liberty," Dolan griped.

"Well, you have to admit that it's a fool's gamble to face down those submachine guns with two pistols," Fortune admitted.

"Peace through superior firepower," Dolan agreed.

"I don't think that's the worst of our problems!" Nick gulped as two of the soldiers opened the long canvas duffle and revealed a pair of MG-42 machineguns and a score of rolled belts of ammunition.

"Blast! You could be right, mate," Dolan agreed.

"What kind of professor needs soldiers and machine guns?" Nick asked.

•••

Khuna carried bundle after bundle of green banana leaves, palm fronds, dry limbs, and dead dry grass into the cave. He packed the small chamber and the main room of the cave and as dawn broke, lit the browse in several places. The flames spread quickly toward the back of the cave and into the passage to the lower level. Almost immediately thick smoke began to billow from the cave.

Within minutes, a flurry of activity stirred in the camp. Cries of, "Feuer!" and "Vulkan!" spread amongst the soldiers sent to investigate the source of the smoke. Khuna was startled when three soldiers suddenly ran into view.

They stood in awe of the smoke and flames funneling from the opening. The leader split the two: ordering one to stand watch and the other to return to camp. Instead of attempting to put out the fire, he began to walk the trail south. Within seconds, he had disappeared into the jungle.

The young soldier turned his head toward the jungle and his eyes widened when he saw the big islander. Before the young man could react, or make a sound, Khuna's huge fist slammed into his head with the force of a falling tree.

The soldier's finger tensed against the trigger of his gun and he fired several rounds as he dropped to the ground. Khuna ran after the older soldier.

•••

The dead quiet of the morning hung as eerily as the mist around Pyrotoko. Soldiers marched the laborers into an opening in the rock. Each man carried mining equipment, lamps, torches, picks or shovels.

Gothimmel and his attendants stood by a table beneath a canvas awning where a number of artifacts were being cleaned and cataloged. A number of artifacts such as blessing statues, fertility totems, and items of peaceful theological significance were discarded in a rickety crate. The only items Gothimmel regarded with any sense of reverence seemed to be those of an ominous nature.

He appeared unhappy and constantly referred to it under his hand to keep it from curious eyes. Finally, he opened the letter-sized book and laid it on the table. The hand drawn illustration was of a short staff or ornately carved club or kali stick. It was carved into the shape of a sea serpent or some type of dragon with an open fanged mouth breathing fire at one end and a whiplike tail on the other.

One of his attendants stopped mid-stride and faced Mount Motugra. In the distance he detected wisps of black smoke in the ever present mist. Unsure, he traced the trail, and was sure he saw a soldier running toward him. But the man disappeared as a shadow passed between them.

Unable to believe his eyes he blinked several times and took a second look. Glancing at the dark sky, he grew alarmed at the gathering clouds and alerted the nearest corporal to organize a patrol to reconnoiter the trail. Wary of the professor's wrath, he hoped his concern would be justified by the patrol.

Gothimmel wasn't a big man, but there was something absent that made him very cold.

The professor looked up from his journal as the patrol disappeared into the jungle. Angry at not being informed as to why, he began to call after them, when he was interrupted by a young sergeant who ran out of the belly of the volcano.

Breathless, the man yelled, "Herr Doktor! Bitte komm schnell haben wir etwas gefunden!" Immediately, he ran back inside.

Gothimmel pocketed the journal and hurried after the soldier.

•••

Greg Duquesne awoke in the V of a large gum tree. It wasn't yet light, and he judged from the morning chill that it was somewhere between false dawn and first light. He surveyed his surroundings and listened to the sounds of birds, insects, and other creatures. The early morning was alive with the sounds of creatures all telling a story.

He slipped down from the tree and moved quietly away from the massive trunk. The penetrating moonlight was minimal under the jungle canopy. He inhaled deeply. The slight breeze alerted his senses to the typical scent wafting from the low canopy. The scent of decomposing plant material, damp earth, and animal scat hung on the air. As he moved along, the estrous urine of some small mammal stung his nostrils. Then, there was something else.

Duquesne took a knee in a depression just to the side of the disused jungle trail and was surprised to see the marks of traffic. An impression of a bare foot was pressed into the mud. Beside it, were the tracks of sandals and military boots. He also smelled the pungent odor of feces, belonging to someone who didn't eat a Polynesian diet.

Hearing a strange noise, he raised his Model 1903 Springfield Rifle and looked through the telescopic sight. Visibility was poor due to the lay of the terrain and multiple light angles, but not so poor that he couldn't see the line of soldiers snaking their way along the trail.

Judging from the ease of their movement it was plain to him that the old trail he was following intersected a more active one. They joked and made a surprising amount of noise for three men. Duquesne recognized their Mauser rifles. These were infantry men: unlike the others who would rely on the spray of bullets emitted from their machine guns, these soldiers would be competent marksmen. Their aim would be deadly.

Duquesne figured they were a roving patrol, whether they acted like it or not. He continued to study them as they moved further south along the trail. When they finally dropped out of sight, he moved along the old trail toward the intersection. He settled into the black shadow of a massive tree covered in a long mantle of lichen. From his cover position among the huge roots of the giant tree, he could observe the intersection of the old trail and the newer one.

He waited in relative silence listening as the jungle noises in the distance began to grow quiet. He assumed that the patrol was returning from their sweep.

A macaw perched directly above Duquesne, suddenly erupted into chatter. It unnerved him, but he knew better than to scream aloud. Expertly, he raised the rifle and looked through the scope in an attempt to find the source of the movement that had alerted the bird.

A rifle shot cracked across the rolling hills.

"ALARM!" someone screamed and the soldiers sprang into alert.

The hurried shuffle of booted feet and young loud voices called out in German, flooding the area as the patrol runs into the small clearing at the intersection of the two trails. Duquesne knew that they would attempt to secure the area and more of them would follow.

Duquesne made a final hurried scan. A flash of motion trailed by a wisp of long black hair crossed his scope and he withdrew like he'd been bitten by a snake. *Was that even human?*

A branch broke behind him. "Halt! Teufel Hunden," an angry voice growled.

Duquesne knew he was found. He lay the rifle aside and turned, thinking of the Colt riding in the shoulder holster beneath his left arm.

•••

Gothimmel was about to enter the dead volcano when he heard the shot. He stopped short and turned to his lieutenants. "Wer Schuss?"

"Der schutz," the closer of the two said.

"The guard? They must have found something!" Gothimmel exclaimed in German. "Send a detail." He turned to the other. "Find out why there were shots fired."

The fellow turned and called to a squad of soldiers who were sitting around a fire barrel. The first to stand was Stahlhammer. A brawny man, he was always the first to volunteer, however, he never seemed to enjoy the fact. The others quickly followed his lead, imitating Stahlhammer's disdain for Gothimmel and his lieutenants.

Dolan watched the interaction between Gothimmel and Stahlhammer. Everyone yielded to the pair of sadists, the lieutenants whom the professor used like a pair of attack dogs to do his bidding. Neither he or Fortune recognized the insignia on Stahlhammer's uniform, or the half dozen men who followed him, but it was evident that neither he nor they were impressed with Nazi science.

Dolan gave Fortune a nudge. "You might want to watch this mate," he whispered.

•••

Duquesne stood slowly, holding up his left hand and pointing with his right to his rifle. The man tensed as he moved. Keeping his movements slow, Duquesne continued to back up until his captor exhaled, making the hair on his neck tingle.

"Halt!" the soldier ordered, his tone uncertain; a mark of immaturity.

The safety on the rifle clicked and in that split second, Duquesne prayed for forgiveness and turned, bringing his right hand across his chest. As his shoulder brushed the muzzle of the rifle barrel, he squeezed the trigger of the Colt.

The rifle and the soldier fell away as Duquesne turned to cover him, raising the .45 as the report still echoed. He turned the 8mm rifle over with the toe of his boot. The safety was in the fire position. He exhaled sharply as a tremor of pain washed over him, radiating from his old wound.

With hardly any time to reflect, the soldiers from the intersection clearing appeared, shouting at him in German. It wasn't his first rodeo. He knew they were ordering him to drop his gun. He wouldn't be so lucky this time and he raised both hands. Before he could turn, an explosion of movement careened toward them.

•••

Khuna launched himself from the tree limb. The soldiers never saw him coming. In a flash the first one lay dying. The second was in shock, knowledge of a mortal wound taking his breath away. The third had spun down and away, but death's whisper had already sung her song, the man struck a fighting stance only to see his entrails spill out before him.

The blade of the knife sang through the air as Khuna sheathed it. He turned toward the hunter who was in awe of what he'd just seen. He knew from the man's reverent nod that they were on the same side, and cut from the same roll of cloth. The deaths of these men were tragic, but necessary.

Khuna knelt near the roots of the tree and stood watch as Duquesne gathered his weapons. There were no others in the vicinity, but it was not a relief. He had to make it into the old volcano and find Pyrotiki's tomb before the white shaman, Gothimmel could defile it.

"I reckon we're both headed to the same place, maybe for the same reasons. I'll find some high ground and make the way safe," Duquesne offered.

"I must get to Pyrotoko. If the white shaman unleashes the Fire Lord, soldiers will be a small problem compared to the power of an evil man in control of a vengeful god," Khuna whispered as the jungle sounds ceased, alerting them to another unseen presence. They shared a final look and the two hunters disappeared into the jungle in different directions.

•••

…he squeezed the trigger of the Colt.

An hour later Gothimmel stood in a small subterranean room in the bowels of the dead volcano. The laborer who summoned him stood by a wall of chiseled stone blocks that felt very warm to the touch.

"What have you found here?" Gothimmel demanded.

"We search for more tiki. But down here we find nothing; just the wall," the fellow said in halting Polynesian-accented English.

The professor ran a hand over the surface of the ancient stone blocks. He felt the radiant heat and stepped back to appraise the height and breadth of the block wall. "You will get excavation equipment, picks, shovels, and a bar to pry with. You must open this chamber!"

"You must not!" an elderly laborer pleaded, "This is the tomb of a God whose anger was felt on the land and in the sea. With his flaming whip he created Motugra and the chain islands by raising fire from the sea!"

Gothimmel extended a hand toward the smaller of his henchmen. The man passed him a Luger 7.65mm pistol. He cycled the toggle to charge the pistol.

"Why do you think we want it?" he chuckled cruelly and pulled the trigger. The old man fell dead at the feet of the other laborers. "Does anyone else wish to object?"

•••

Nick Fortune saw Gothimmel and his lackey's return from the volcano. Something in the man's demeanor had changed. People were giving him an extra wide berth.

"Heads up, Jimmy!" he warned, "Something's up."

Dolan sat reclined against a log, his hat low over his eyes. He didn't move a muscle as he mumbled, "I'll be ready mate."

An hour later, Nick and Jimmy were sharing a canteen of warm canned water and talking about their best chance of escape when thunder rumbled from somewhere underground. Chaos ensued as a cloud of superheated air and gasses vented from the entrance of the volcano. Seconds later, a screaming, writhing abomination of a man ran headlong from the opening, straight for the professor, who stood transfixed. The horrific, crazed man dropped at his feet as a shot rang out over the camp.

•••

Gregory Duquesne cycled the bolt of the M-1903 Springfield and scanned for his next target. Two soldiers, one with binoculars and another loading an MG-42 were not yet a threat. Scanning onward, he watched as the powerful islander, who came to his rescue, disappeared into a cleft in the east face of the rock. Duquesne wondered how such an enormous man would fit into such a tiny space.

Returning to the task at hand, Duquesne shot the four soldiers pursuing a group of laborers escaping into the jungle. His ears were suddenly filled with the sounds of rushing wings, angry animal chatter, and the mechanical stutter of an MG-42. As he scanned and located the crew serving the machine gun, Duquesne felt the eyes of the spotter on him. The feeling that he'd made eye contact via the scope was almost unsettling.

The fellow pointed emphatically, directing fire to his position, when a .30/06 caliber bullet tore through his head. It entered just beneath the septum, ripping loose muscle and bone, nearly severing his head. The gunner held his nerve and directed fire to the last position his assistant had marked. Duquesne's next shot silenced the machine gun and the gunner.

Gothimmel bolted for the entrance of the volcano, a group of his men hot on his heels. Before Duquesne was able to react, a rain of bullets splintered the wood and shattered the rocks around him, forcing him to withdraw into the shelter of the jungle.

•••

Khuna exhaled sharply as the cloud of steaming gasses erupted underneath him. The stench of brimstone was nearly unbearable and he choked back a cough. He steadily made his way into the depths of the volcano, recalling the passages from playing there as a boy. Only, the openings were much smaller than he'd remembered and the passage downward slower and more awkward than he intended. A section of the old vent passage had given way and the tunnel now connected directly with the main passage.

Though the open passage made it easier for a man of Khuna's size to traverse, it made it impossible for him to hide. He moved as quickly as he could, a shard of volcanic glass occasionally reminding him to tread carefully.

As Khuna reached the location of the tomb, he was taken aback by voices. He listened intently, but it was impossible to derive any meaning from the muffled words. Instead of hiding, he opted for action and leapt into the tomb of Pyrotiki.

Khuna raged like a cornered tiger, tearing through two soldiers as if they hardly existed. The third raised his gun only to have his arm torn from the socket. The fourth meekly tried to cover himself with an ancient sharkskin shield.

Khuna's blade sliced through the shield from top to tip, severing the cowering man's hand in the process. He grabbed the man by the shirt and slung him into the passage.

The tomb was silent with the exception of Khuna's heavy breaths. He wiped his brow and leaned against the wall to catch his breath.

"Well, here you finally are!" Gothimmel's voice cut into the silence like a well-honed knife. "It is unfortunate for you, that I was here first. I have already taken what you dared to consider yours!" He smiled smugly at Khuna and brandished an ornately carved koa wood staff.

"Ahee hoko ho I o'u kou mana!" He shrieked and grinned with glee as energy emanated from the staff. The tip of the dragon's mouth glowed cherry red, but instead of exiting the staff, it reversed and flew down the base of the dragon's tail. Gothimmel screamed in pain, dropping the whip of Pyrotiki at Khuna's feet.

"Ahi haku ho I o'u kau mana, kela ia'u hiki ho'ola malama po'e kanaka!" Khuna said with deep reverence as he knelt to pick up the whip.

•••

When Nick saw Gothimmel run into the camp, cradling his left hand and screaming orders, he drug Jimmy Dolan to his feet.

"I think it's time for us to go."

"It's about bloody time! Let's get the hell out of here!" Jimmy exclaimed, and the two bolted toward the tree line.

One of the soldiers yelled after them, but they refused to turn around. Instead, they ran smack into the returning squad of commandos led by Stahlhammer.

The commandos forced them to return along with a prisoner who kept rambling on about being a noncombatant and conscientious objector. One of the commandos gave him an extra hard shove and he literally fell into Nick and Jimmy. The man's grip was like steel.

"So much for the brilliant escape," Dolan quipped.

The prisoner answered in an intelligent and confident voice, "Don't worry, this is almost over. Just be ready."

The commandos marched them to the center of the camp where

Gothimmel was receiving medical attention and dictating orders. Gothimmel spoke as he watched the medic wrap his hand.

"I thought I was clear when I retained your services, that any attempt to terminate your employment was punishable by death."

The Nazi looked upon the third prisoner with disgust. "Alcatraz Brown, surely you are in the islands on holiday. Your country has not yet declared an affiliation, so your presence here could be viewed as an act of war. Not that we are concerned with any nation that would grant commissions to persons that barely count as citizens."

Traz grimaced. "The beauty of the idea of America is that freedom is for every one. She also grants us the right to defend that freedom from tyrants and maniacs."

The larger of the henchmen produced a Luger, but as he brought it to bear, he was leveled by the granite fist of Stahlhammer. The commandos raised their weapons, taking aim at Gothimmel and his people.

"Sergeant! I demand that you execute this prisoner," Gothimmel ordered. "You!" he turned to another of the commandos, who looked to Stahlhammer for affirmation.

Realizing the betrayal, Gothimmel paled. "Berlin will hear about this, you will be sent to Spandau. Who do you think you are?"

"Gunnery Sergeant Scott Stahlhammer United States Marine Corps. You and your men are suspected of war crimes and you are my prisoners."

Just then a company of German soldiers poured into the camp, surrounding Fortune, Dolan, Alcatraz Brown, and Stahlhammer's commando squad. A dozen of them drew in close. The muzzle of at least one weapon was pointed at every head.

"No, it appears that it is you who are my prisoner, Sergeant." Gothimmel's tone was once again sadistic and his voice as brittle as slate.

Stahlhammer and his men placed their weapons on the ground. The German Soldiers were tying the hands of the commandos when the ground started to rumble.

•••

Several small objects pelted the ground, followed by a baseball-sized chunk of smoldering brimstone. The soldier, pressing the muzzle of his pistol against the back of Stahlhammer's skull was struck by a red-hot stone the size of a golf ball, which stuck to his flesh and began to burn through. The solider screamed in agony, dropped his pistol and beat at his sizzling flesh.

One after another of them were hit by burning stones, and some sliced or impaled by flying volcanic glass. A hot wind swirled around as the bindings on the commando's hands burned to ash. Awestruck, Gothimmel stood gape-mouthed as his minions fell in the writhing agony of burning flesh.

Without hesitation Stahlhammer and his team secured their weapons and rushed Fortune, Dolan, and Alcatraz Brown to cover. Somewhere behind them someone called out. As they reached cover behind the boulders and large tree roots, Fortune stared back at the camp and could not believe what he saw.

Khuna was suddenly in their midst as if he'd been placed there by a lightning bolt. The startled soldiers took up firing positions. Khuna raised his arms skyward, the whip an extension of his right hand. With a twist of his wrist, a thong of fire whirled overhead, which he flicked, driving the soldiers back. As others raised rifles to fire, Khuna turned the fire lord's whip on them, slicing through them with a fiery crack.

An infantryman running in from the flank fixed the long bayonet to his rifle and charged. He was inside, low and stepping into the thrust when Khuna sidestepped, drew the long knife and cleaved deeply along the man's breastbone penetrating nearly to the spine. Whipping the blood from the blade he struck a fighting stance, and gave the whip a sidearm flick, decimating a machinegun emplacement.

Hot and terrible winds rose and he whirled and flicked the whip over head. Ear-splitting thunder rumbled across the sky and lightning tore it wide open. A vortex of superheated air began to swirl around Khuna. The great and terrible power emanating from the whip responded to Khuna as if he were its master.

As rain poured into the flaming funnel cloud and lightning struck attacking soldiers, Khuna roared in the old island tongue, "In the name of the Fire Lord Pyrotiki, I banish you from the time of my people on the land and in the seas." With a final flourish he brought the whip down, cracking the fiery tip at his feet. The ball of thermal energy exploded outward with the sound and fury of a hellish bomb.

Every German soldier carrying a weapon was reduced to ash. Gothimmel's two lieutenants were impaled by foot long shards of volcanic glass. As the haze and smoke dissipated, Gothimmel cowered at Khuna's feet.

"Go!" Alcatraz commanded, and Stahlhammer and the commandos moved in. Khuna tucked the whip staff into his belt as the commandos seized Gothimmel and hauled him to his feet.

Astounded, Fortune and Dolan stood before Khuna barely able to voice their thanks. The large man was emotionally spent and could only nod his welcome.

Gregory Duquesne joined Alcatraz Brown and they watched Stahlhammer and his men march Gothimmel toward the beach. He cleared his throat and Fortune and Dolan politely excused themselves.

For a moment, Traz tried to read the big islander and found it nearly impossible. "You know that weapon would be of great assistance to the cause of liberty in Europe, and there's a war brewing in Asia as we speak."

"No. I will return it to Pyrotoku. The power is too great for any man to control. It belongs in the soul of Motugra," Khuna nodded, and walked toward the volcano.

With nothing more to be done, Traz shook hands with Nick and Jimmy and followed the commandos to the beach.

"Well mate, I could use a drink!" Dolan sighed and surveyed the scene. He was grateful to see that the Nazi presence had all but disappeared.

"I have to find a way to make my disappearing up to Grace," Nick complained as they started toward the beach.

"I'll have a drink for you while you take your medicine. Personally, I'd rather stay here!" Dolan jabbed and Nick gave him a shove.

The End

LOVING TALL TALES

This was a marvelously fun and easy story to write... I tried to write a fast moving story with an interesting twist. I have always been interested in the history, mythology, and superstitions of various regions. So I thought it would be interesting to make an artifact related to an enigmatic old wives' tale and make it the McGuffin for the story, sought after by an evil, sadistic Nazi occult scientist and the last heir to the monarchy of a proud line of island warriors...

Adventure stories have a certain romance about them, strange goings on in exotic locals. Difficult to describe relationships, and high drama interactions with love interests abound. I did my best to impart all of these things into the tale and still leave room for the mystique of ancient culture.

If I had to describe The Prophecy of the Fire Lord in one sentence it might go something like – An unapologetic tall tale. As usual I hope that you enjoy the story, happy reading.

•••

J. WALT LAYNE – lives in Springfield, Ohio. He is a veteran of the US Army, a married father of three, and a voracious reader. A prolific writer, he is the author of Frank Testimony a legal thriller set in Bedford, Mississippi in the 1950s. He is also the author and creator of The Champion City Series of pulp detective stories to be published exclusively by Pro Se Press (March 2013). He has written a laundry list of articles for Backwoodsman Magazine and is the former Op-Ed columnist for The Albany Journal (Albany, Georgia). You can catch up with him on Facebook as Author J Walt Layne.

In His Own Words – "I love the craft of telling a good story. I try to breathe real life into the characters and their surroundings. I try to put seemingly ordinary characters, some as humble as can be, in extraordinary circumstances. I don't like to compare my work to that of other writers. It is a comparison of apples and oranges. To say one author's story isn't as good, or is better than another's is a matter of opinion and perspective. For an author to indulge in such is an act of vanity alone.

"I'm both self published, and published traditionally in a variety of media – news, blogs, magazine, short stories, novellas, and novels. Fiction and non. The worst thing any author can do, and especially those who have achieved success is to discourage the efforts of others. While no one's success is guaranteed, we must all help each other the best we can."

THE STAR OF THE SEA

By
Don Gates

Morning sunlight streamed down in heavy dusty shafts, spottily illuminating the cave through the cracks and holes in its roof. The chamber had a naturally formed inverted bowl shape to its ceiling, and several passages led off into darkness in multiple directions. In the center of the domed central chamber was a strange altar: it was formed from what appeared to be dead coral that seemed to grow upward from the rock floor itself. It twisted and turned in its sinewy shapes and almost seemed to be an animated form that had been suddenly petrified amid its writhing, frozen forever as if in a photograph. It was grotesque, as incongruously ugly as the object that sat upon it was beautiful.

It was a rough sphere of what appeared to be solid gold; the orb was about the size of a medium cantaloupe and was shot-through with clear crystal growths. These crystals emerged randomly from the dull golden skin of the object, and the overall appearance of the thing was one of a weird natural beauty. It didn't sit on the altar as it seemed to be lovingly cupped or held by it, as if the altar itself had a reverence for the bizarre spiky shape.

Alton Treadaway stood before the altar and wiped the sweat from his brow yet again: the sweltering heat and smothering humidity of the islands was amplified in here, and he was soaking wet from perspiration, rivulets of which were coursing down his unshaven face. He considered the thing on the altar in front of him and wondered exactly just what it was. His employer was paying him more than handsomely for this retrieval, more than three times what he normally charged for his services, but there was something about the thing before him, something that was telling him to walk away and forget about money.

There was a sound, a rustling from deep within one of the cave passages, and Treadaway swung up his flashlight and revolver to confront the darkness there. There was nothing revealed, and after a moment or two of tense waiting he lowered his weapon.

He turned back to the domed chamber and shined his flashlight around. There were some strange markings on the walls, some weird kind of glyphs he had never seen before in his experiences as a tomb-robber and treasure-hunter, and he'd seen a lot in his time. They bothered him, those symbols, written in a hand that was definitely primitive and more interested in producing the markings' message than with maintaining a calligraphic uniformity or sense of artistry. On the floor there were murky pools of unclean-looking water, and he wondered briefly how deep those pools were.

There was another rustling sound; a kind of dull scraping off to another side and down another tunnel, and Treadaway's skin crawled. He cursed himself for being so jumpy, even as he resolved to grab the object and get the hell out of the cave.

Treadaway reached out and paused momentarily as his hand brushed one of the crystals. There was a strange moment of light-headedness that made him shudder. He shrugged it off and grabbed the jagged sphere. Lifting it from the weird altar, he held it up in a shaft of sunlight, marveling for a second at the way the light rainbowed out from it more sharply than from any other prism he'd ever seen. Another rustling in the cave broke his trance and threw him into action; he stuffed the object into his bag, and after buckling the canvas pouch shut he threw its strap over his head and shoulder and broke into a run.

The treasure-hunter threaded his way back through the cave the way he'd entered, trying to make as little noise as possible as he ran. His steps echoed in the halls of the cave, echoing even louder in his head. His flashlight beam bounced on the walls and floor ahead of him as he made his way to his exit. Treadaway's palms were slippery with sweat: the pistol he gripped in his other hand felt like it could slip from his grasp at any second, but there was no way in hell he was going to holster it now. The dampness on his neck felt cold, slimy. He risked a glance over his shoulder and saw nothing pursuing him, yet his flight-reflex was still in full effect. In fact, he began to run harder after seeing that empty blackness behind him. The sunlight of the cave entrance was visible ahead, brightening as he approached it.

And then he was through: Treadaway crashed through the bushes and foliage outside the cave's mouth, stumble-running down the little hill that the cave's entrance jutted from. He slowed when he reached the bottom, trotting to a stop where he stooped over panting for a few moments. Treadaway felt safer in the dappled sunlight of the jungle outside. He straightened and looked to the mouth of the cave, and when nothing followed him out he thrust his gun into the holster at his waist. He removed his cap and wiped at his sweaty forehead, his grizzled face broken into a grin. He laughed at himself for jumping at shadows and sounds and acting like a scared old woman. Treadaway's employer had already given him the first half of his payment and was on his way personally to Motugra to collect the object from him. The other half of Treadaway's fee was as good as his.

Saluting the blackness in the mouth of the cave, Treadaway replaced his cap and drew again the ancient map from his bag. He carefully handled the ancient and crumbling parchment as he got his bearings again. In a few moments, Alton Treadaway began to retrace his path back through the jungle and back to the beach.

•••

Jimmy Dolan caught himself snoring and jerked awake. Rubbing his eyes and cheeks, he cast a sleepy eye again at the tiny island not too far away. The gentle sway of the waves had rocked Jimmy's Grumman Goose seaplane, the *Loosey Goosey*, where it was anchored offshore and it had conspired with the boredom and oppressive heat to lull him to sleep. The previous night had been a late one at the Hanging Monkey bar, too, and this early-morning job wasn't agreeing too well with Jimmy's slight ghost of a hangover.

Jimmy ran a sleepy hand through his curly blonde hair and checked his watch: he'd been asleep for about a half hour or so by his reckoning, and had been anchored in that spot waiting for over two hours. Looking around at the deep blue of the South China Sea, Jimmy wondered how much longer he'd be out this far from Motugra's main island. Nobody ever paid Jimmy to take them this far out unless they wanted to get lost… or unless they wanted something found. Treadaway's reason for coming out here wasn't Jimmy's business at all, only his fare's money and he was content not to think too much on the matter.

Jimmy lit a cigarette with a steel Zippo lighter stamped with a horseshoe. He'd borrowed the lighter earlier that morning from his friend Corky O'Brian, owner of the Hanging Monkey bar back on Motugra's main island. As he exhaled the smoke from his Lucky Strike he made a mental note to return it later that evening. Swinging his gaze back to the tiny island that had been his fare's destination, he spotted something white bobbing on the waves. After a few moments' watching it grew into the

Loosey Goosey's tiny rowboat, with his client rowing the oars steadily and occasionally looking over toward the island he'd just left behind.

"All done?" Jimmy called out when Treadaway reached the seaplane. The other man simply grunted and nodded, and Jimmy helped him climb out of the little boat. The two men pulled it aboard and stowed it, and wordlessly Treadaway climbed into his seat in the back and strapped himself in.

Jimmy glanced at the weather-beaten countenance of his client and a sour look crossed his face. He didn't care for the guy, who was downright rude and non-communicative. Jimmy understood that he was providing a service for his customer, but the guy could have at least been a little friendlier with him. This one was all business and there was no conversation coming from this customer at all.

"Ah well… money talks," he mumbled to himself as he strapped himself into the pilot's seat. In a few moments the Goose's twin engines began to cough into life and soon it was roaring into the sky, wheeling back to turn toward the main island of the Motugra chain.

•••

As the *Loosey Goosey* approached Motugra's harbor, Treadaway looked down from his passenger window and scanned the vessels docked below. He frowned: there was no sign of Clay's yacht. He frowned: his employer had yet to arrive, and so he'd have to stay another night at the island's little flea-ridden inn if he didn't show up by nightfall. Treadaway shrugged inwardly. He had stayed in much worse places in his life; Motugra's inn felt like the Ritz compared to some of those holes. He laughed to himself.

Treadaway's laugh choked as he spotted uniformed figures waiting on the dock along with Jimmy's mechanic, Jake Sloan. They were looking up as the plane passed overhead, and something in Treadaway realized they were waiting for him. He knew it, felt it in his blood; he'd been waited for by the law enough in his life to recognize it instinctually.

"Shit," he muttered, and followed that by an increasingly colorful string of oaths, curses, and blasphemies. Treadaway hastily unbuckled his safety belt and leaped to his feet, snatching up his canvas bag. He looked toward Jimmy, who hadn't noticed his passenger had gotten out of his seat. *Everything will be okay for me once Clay gets here*, he thought. He only had to hide the object that he'd stolen from the cave until his employer showed up in Motugra.

As Treadaway thrust his hand into the bag and grabbed the gold-and-crystal artifact within he glanced again into the pilot's cabin of the seaplane. Jimmy was being radioed from the ground and was reaching for the microphone. He'd have to act fast.

Treadaway snatched up an empty supply bag from a utility rack on the wall. Opening the flap, he pushed the weird orb down into the bag, along with the ancient map that had led him to the object's resting place on the island. Yanking the draw-string shut, he hastily replaced the supply bag in the rack and beat a retreat back to his chair. Treadaway drew the belt across his waist just a second before Jimmy replaced the mic and glanced back at his passenger.

The passenger in the back was sitting there, where he had been the last time he'd seen him. If Jimmy didn't trust the guy before, he damn sure didn't trust him now, not after the transmission he'd received. Colonel Neville Smythe, the British official that was Motugra's next best thing to a policeman, and his boys were waiting for the passenger down below. Jimmy surreptitiously unsnapped the holster strapped to his right thigh and drew his revolver. He set the gun in his lap. Just in case.

Jimmy circled the *Loosey Goosey* out past the bay and dropped it gently to the waves. Setting it gently down in the water he did his best to keep his passenger in his peripheral vision as he taxied it to the dock. Colonel Smyth and three of his men waited with Jake the mechanic as the seaplane approached, and Jimmy cut the engines to coast the rest of the way in. The Goose gently bumped the dock and Jake hopped onto the craft to secure the mooring ropes.

Jimmy turned in his seat as he removed his headphones. "I dunno what you did, mister, but it looks like you got a welcoming committee waiting for you."

"Yeah, looks like," Treadaway grunted. His accent was Australian. He seemed strangely calm for a man about to be arrested.

The Goose's door opened and Smythe and his officers entered the cramped cabin.

"Alton Treadaway?" Smythe addressed the passenger, who sighed and nodded. "We've received word via telegram that you are wanted for the theft of historical documents. We've been tasked with holding you until your accuser and the document's rightful owner arrives. She should be getting here within the next day or so. In the meantime, you are the guest of Motugra's most hospitable jail cell. Please come along with us, sir."

Treadaway looked at Smythe and his men for a moment, and Jimmy thought the Australian might go for his gun, despite the fact that he'd be up against four pistol-toting cops (as well as Jimmy and his revolver) with nowhere to run. But desperate men do desperate things, and it seemed like it could happen.

And then it passed. Treadaway's shoulders slumped a little and his hands came up and he stood. And he smiled.

"Go ahead," he said. "I'll need a place to stay anyway until my ride off this island gets here, and I'm likely to catch something if I stay another night in that bloody hotel of yours."

Smythe jerked his head toward the dock. "Oh, you'll like it just fine, lad: four-star accommodations." Smythe's men removed Treadaway's gun belt and supply bag and searched him, then they manacled him and helped him out of the *Loosey Goosey* and onto the dock. Smythe himself stayed behind and climbed into the pilot's cabin and sat down in the copilot's seat next to Jimmy.

"Strewth! It's going to be a hot one today, eh Dolan?" the Colonel said as he dabbed at his brow with a handkerchief. Jimmy nodded. Smythe looked out over Motugra's bay for a few seconds and turned to the pilot.

"As I told him, our man back there's wanted for stolen documents. A map of some kind, I believe. He didn't have it on him just then. You didn't notice him using one out there, did you?"

"Nope," Jimmy answered. "The guy got my name from Mortimer Collins when he came to town. He grabbed me last night at the Monkey and asked me if I'd fly him out to one of the little islands at the edge of Motugra. He flashed the necessary cash under my nose so I took the job. Met him here this morning and he showed me on the map of the islands which one I had to get to, but that was it. He left the plane alone by rowboat and was gone for a couple hours or so, then came back and that was it. I don't know what he was doing out there, and I really don't want to know. It's none of my business. But as far as what you asked about a map, there was none beyond the one of the islands I mentioned."

Colonel Smythe nodded and studied Jimmy for a second. It was well known that a lot of the money that got made on Motugra wasn't always a hundred percent honest, but Jimmy was well liked by many and overall a decent fellow. Smythe nodded and rose, content for now.

"Well, if you remember anything else you let me know, eh Dolan? I'll be away from the island for a few days but you can tell one of my men if you need to. You know where to find me, and I'll know where to find you." He winked at the pilot. "Keep yourself cool, flyboy."

"Will do," Jimmy called to him as he exited the Goose. "You too, Colonel."

Jimmy yawned and stretched in his pilot's chair and began to wonder if he should take a nap right there in the Goose. He felt like he could.

•••

The rest of the day passed lazily on Motugra. Apart from the arrest and imprisonment of Alton Treadaway in Motugra's little stockade, there was relatively little that happened that day. Jimmy got his nap, though it was at home in his room at the hotel and not in the cabin of the seaplane. Jake Sloan performed his routine maintenance of the *Loosey Goosey* at its spot in the harbor. By the late afternoon, Jimmy was up and about again and signs of life were slowly increasing around Motugra's social-center, the Hanging Monkey.

The bar, a bamboo and clapboard structure by the waterfront, was *the* main hangout for Motugra's regulars, as well as anyone looking for a drink or entertainment on the main island (though there was very little planned entertainment: every once in a while a singer with a guitar or ukulele might show up, but most of the time the entertainment came from watching the patrons themselves). Outside the double-doors of the Hanging Monkey was a little stand of palm trees and to one of these clung a little monkey, a denizen of the surrounding jungle that liked to watch the comings and goings of the bar's customers. Jimmy tipped his cap to the monkey as he passed him on his way into the bar.

"Isn't it time you named your little fuzzy pal outside, Corky?" Jimmy said as he slid onto a stool at the bar. "He's here all the damned time, so you might as well face it: he's yours, and you just gotta name your pets."

Behind the bar Corky O'Brian swabbed the countertop with a towel. The Irish expatriate and former boxer wore one of his customary flower-print Hawaiian-style shirts and one of his usual wry grins.

"Now look here, Jimmy: the damned thing gave this bar a name and it's a name I'm not changin' anytime soon," he said with his thick brogue. "Let's say I did name the lil' beastie and I call him 'Sammy' or somethin' like that. Somebody overhears this and word gets around and spreads and before you know it this bar becomes known as 'Sammy's'. Do you really want this bar to be called 'Sammy's', Dolan?"

"No, but I've heard it called much worse things," Jimmy said with a laugh.

"I should name the monkey after you, Jimmy. He looks like he could be one of your relatives," Corky chuckled. "Hey, did you remember that Zippo of mine?"

Jimmy made a pinched face. "Ah, hell, it's back in the Goose, Corky. I'll grab it for you tonight." He knew what was coming, and he threw up his hands. "I know, I know, it's…"

"It's my lucky lighter. I got it when…"

"When you hopped the freighter to Motugra. You've had it with you ever since and had nothing but…"

"The best of luck, aye. I need my lighter back, Jimmy. My lucky lighter means more to me than just lightin' my Luckies. It's a personal talisman, it's a part of me, it's…"

"Alright, dammit, I'll get it for you later. Just lemme sit for a while and relax, carrot-top." Jimmy ordered a beer and sat back to watch the crowd.

Grace Thomas, the pretty blonde newspaper journalist from America, was sitting with famous big-game hunter-turned-lush Gregory Duquesne and his servant Otis "Alcatraz" Brown at their table. She was attempting to interview Duquesne about the mysterious events that resulted in the explosion onboard a ship called the *Vienna Queen* not too long before. Grace was getting flabbergasted: Duquesne was far more interested in spinning a yarn about a rhino hunt he'd taken part in back in his glory days. Brown, ever the faithful servant, looked on with a bemused twinkle in his eye.

Meanwhile a trio of drunken German sailors warbled a tune together in a corner table, while the crew of a tramp steamer out of Singapore played a card game at a nearby table of their own. One of the steamer's sailors bumped one of the Germans and there were words exchanged in each man's native tongues. It looked like the situation was going to come to blows until a massive hulking figure stepped out of the shadows at the side of the room. It was Khuna, Corky's bouncer and a local Motugran warrior. Khuna was short but built like a linebacker: one look at the menacing wall of muscle and the look in Khuna's eyes was all it took. The card game swiftly began again and the German sailors simultaneously jumped back into their song as if it'd never ended. Khuna moved on.

It was, of course, business as usual on a Saturday night at the Hanging Monkey.

"I heard you had some problems with a guy this mornin'," Corky said as he handed Jimmy his beer. "The guy had to be handcuffed and beaten down before bein' dragged away by Colonel Smythe's boys?"

Jimmy was taking a long pull at his cold beer, and nearly laughed it out of his nose. "No, hell no, nothing like that," he chuckled and wiped his mouth with the sleeve of his jacket. "No, he didn't go kicking and screaming. The guy was just wanted by the cops for stealing something, a map I think. Somebody saw the guy go off with me to the outer islands this morning and tipped the cops off, and they were waiting on the dock when we got back."

"What were you doing all the way out there?" a voice rumbled behind Jimmy. He turned to find Khuna standing there behind him.

"I don't know," Jimmy responded, "The guy just paid me to take him out there and to wait around for a couple hours while he poked around on one of the islands. Wasn't really my business, I was just the cabbie." He took another sip of beer.

Khuna shook his head slightly. "You shouldn't be messing around out there. There're things that weren't meant to be 'poked around' at. Your man stirred up a hornet's nest, and the hornets are likely to come here."

Jimmy and Corky exchanged glances.

"What the hell does that mean, Khuna?" Corky finally asked.

"Maybe nothing, maybe something. There's something in the air here and has been since this morning. Something very old and something very not-good." Without a further word, Khuna moved on back out amid the Hanging Monkey's slowly-growing crowd of patrons.

Jimmy and Corky looked at each other again and laughed quietly.

"He's so damn spooky sometimes," Jimmy whispered.

"Aye, and you're lucky: you don't have to work with 'im," Corky replied before moving along the bar to take a new customer's order.

•••

Nightfall had come to Motugra. Torches were lit around the little town and especially near the Hanging Monkey, which was doing a bang-up business now. Cool winds were blowing in off the sea and giving the lingering heat of the day some much-desired relief. The water down at the harbor was stirred up by the breezes, and the waves crashed against the rocks and piers there. Out in the moonlit bay, the sound of a channel marker-buoy's bell clanged intermittently as it bobbed on the frothy waters.

Jimmy Dolan emerged from the Hanging Monkey's open door, laughing and waving to someone inside the raucous establishment. "I said I was gonna get your lighter and I'm going to get your damn lighter!" he called into the bar, and someone else inside laughed, more than a little drunkenly.

Jimmy walked along the boardwalk and away from the bar. He'd had a few more beers and had a nice buzz going on, but didn't feel too out of it and the cool night air helped reinvigorate his head. He took in a deep lungful of sea air and continued on his way. Jimmy wanted to get Corky's lighter before it got any later and he got any tipsier. He walked out onto the dock and to where the *Loosey Goosey* bobbed up and down on the water.

Opening the door to the plane, Jimmy entered and made his way to the cockpit. Corky's lighter lay in the moonlight on the console, and Jimmy picked it up and regarded it. "'Oi needs me lucky charm, Jimmy, an' ye can't have it'," Jimmy said to himself in a bad parody of Corky's Irish brogue. Then chuckling to himself he tucked the lighter into his pocket.

As he made his way back through the dark passenger cabin of the Grumman Goose, Jimmy felt with his fingers along the interior wall of the plane. As he reached the supply rack, his hand slipped past the first aid kit and his fingers touched a shape that he didn't recognize.

Jimmy turned toward the rack and felt with his fingers at the canvas-covered shape. He knew the *Loosey Goosey* like the back of his hand, and the shape inside the supply bag was extremely foreign to him. He lifted the bag from the rack and hefted it, noting the shape again and the weight of the object. *What the hell is this?* he wondered.

Exiting the Goose with the sack, he closed up the hatch and made his way along the pier until he was under the pool of light cast by the single lamp there. He knelt and opened the bag and reached down inside.

A weird cold thrill passed through him as his fingers touched the object within, and Jimmy felt his scalp tingle. He almost jerked his hand back, but instead he wrapped his fingers around the thing and pulled it into the light.

The bizarre gold-and-crystal orb shimmered and gleamed dully under the light of the pier. Jimmy turned it this way and that, examining the way it caught the light, reflecting and refracting it like nothing he'd ever seen before. He shook his head: it must have been just a sound on the wind, but he could have sworn he'd heard the object humming softly.

Jimmy could feel another object in the bag too, a flat thing much smaller and more brittle than the weird sphere. He reached down into the bag and pulled it out. A paper, some kind of old and thick parchment. It was folded into quarters, and he unfolded it in the light to reveal an ancient map. One section of the map's illustration showed the crudely-depicted islands of Motugra, including one that was circled and identified. It was, of course, the island that Jimmy and Alton Treadaway had visited just that morning.

The larger section of the map depicted the island itself in greater detail and showed a maze of little hills, short valleys, and the walls of ancient ruins. It showed a cave jutting from one of the hills, and Jimmy knew that's where the object, whatever it was, had been stored there: along with a diagram of the cave there was a sketch depicting the item and a weird altar that it sat on. The text on the map was very sparse and hard to read, and Jimmy realized at last that it wasn't even in English.

Jimmy was taken aback by the strange finds in the bag, but he knew that it had to have something to do with his Australian fare from that morning: obviously this was the map that Smythe was asking about. Jimmy stuffed the artifact into the bag along with the map and pulled the drawstring shut. The stockade and tiny headquarters of Colonel Smythe's officers were at the other side of town, but he knew someone was there all night, especially when they had a prisoner in lock-up as they had one now.

Tossing the bag over his shoulder, Jimmy began the walk to the police station. He began whistling softly to himself as he walked and was feeling pretty good about himself for being such an honest citizen, but not so good about himself being such a sap: the thing in the bag was probably solid gold and those crystals… could those have been *diamonds*? The thing could be worth a mint, and here he was taking it to the cops. Well, it was stolen property anyway, so he was doing the right thing and bringing it back to the cops to be given to the rightful owner when she showed up. Then again, only the map was reported as being stolen, so maybe the ball-thing was up for grabs. Maybe he should just take the thing home before he delivered that map. Hey, finders keepers and all that stuff was the rule of the playground as kids, and it still applied in the world of adults. If nobody *asked* about the golden object, then he didn't have to *tell* anybody about finding it.

•••

As Jimmy stepped beyond the last of the harbor's lights, he found himself in a big pool of deep shadow. The nearest lights of the town were still in the distance to his right, while the warm tiki-torch glow outside of the Hanging Monkey was in the opposite direction, back past the lights of the harbor. To Jimmy's left was the seawall and past it he could hear waves crashing themselves onto the rocks down below.

He stopped there as he walked through that big dark expanse. There had come to him a weird sensation, something Jimmy felt more than anything, a non-sound that he found himself straining to hear. There was a sudden impression that he was being watched; stronger than that feeling was the sense that he was being *hunted*. He glanced to his left and thought that he glimpsed something as it dropped suddenly behind the other side of the seawall.

Panic gripped Jimmy as he realized that he was unarmed and his pistol was back in his room at the hotel. He broke into a run, trotting away from the seawall now and toward the lights of the police station and stockade. He felt like a scared little kid but the feeling that was insistent. He listened to it: he'd never felt like this before, and he damn sure didn't feel like sticking around to keep feeling it. He ran harder.

And ran into someone…*something*.

Jimmy bounced off of a wall of muscle encased in thick, rubbery skin and fell onto his backside. There was a split second that he was grateful to have encountered someone and was going to apologize for running into them, but the smell hit him next: open graves and open sores, rotting meat and something like a dead fish in the sun. Jimmy looked up at the inky shape in the darkness, and it was almost human and yet all wrong. It took a step toward Jimmy and breathed, and the sound was a weird rustling noise like dead leaves rubbing against each other.

Jimmy's hand found a handful of dirt and he flung it up toward the thing's head. It hissed and stumbled back a second and Jimmy leapt to his feet. He grabbed the canvas sack and prepared to swing it like a weapon toward the shape.

The thing was lightning-fast: it rushed Jimmy and swiped out at him with its claws. The first strike raked across Jimmy's stomach and chest and it tore fabric and drew blood. Jimmy managed to lean back as the second claw-swipe whistled through the air that his head had occupied a split-second before. Jimmy couldn't recover from the dodge because the thing was striking out again already, grabbing his wrists in its clawed and slimy grip. It forced Jimmy's arms out to the sides and its head lunged toward Jimmy's. He dimly caught the flash of teeth.

And then something whistled through the air and connected with the back of the thing's head with a thunk. The thick skin on its back protected it from the blow. It roared in anger and released Jimmy and turned away from him toward a newcomer in the darkness. It struck out at the other shape, and the man there grunted in pain as its claws connected. The creature began to strike out again with its claws but there was another whistle as the newcomer swung his weapon again.

The blow struck the creature in the shoulder, and a small shower of

And ran into …*something.*

gore and blood exploded from the wound and splattered Jimmy. The thing hissed and tried to lash out again at its combatant but another blow from the weapon struck it in the side. The other man in the darkness was striking out faster now, and the foul-smelling thing had been slowed by the rapid-fire attacks that met it.

The thing turned and fled, scrambling away from the area of combat on all fours, running with a curious and frantic gait toward the seawall. When it reached it, the weird shape bounded over it higher than any man ever could and disappeared. A moment later there was a splash beyond the seawall and the rocks below as it landed in the harbor.

A hand reached out of the darkness and gripped Jimmy's. It hauled him to his feet and Jimmy found himself facing the broad features of Khuna.

"I told you, Jimmy: stir up the hornet's nest, and the hornets are likely to come here."

"That was a pretty big friggin' hornet!" Jimmy shouted breathlessly, adrenaline still pumping through him. "What the hell was that?!"

"I don't know, and you're welcome." Khuna had walked to the seawall and rested his tribal weapon, a broad-bladed wooden club fitted with shark teeth around the edges, on his bleeding shoulder.

"Hey, thank you, I mean… I don't mean to come off as rude but…" Jimmy fumbled but couldn't help himself. "What *was* that thing?"

"Don't know," Khuna repeated, "and I don't want to know. Are you okay?"

Jimmy checked himself, remembering the scratches the thing's claws had dug into his torso. "Yeah… yeah, just some minor cuts is all, I think. How'd you spot that thing?"

"I saw you come back come back up from the docks, and saw something jump over the seawall. A few something's actually." Khuna looked around for more.

Suddenly a man's scream ripped through the darkness. A panicked sound, it was followed by the sound of rending metal and rock. The sounds came from the stockade.

•••

Jimmy and Khuna broke into a run and sprinted toward the sounds. A second scream was cut short and then there was several seconds of ghastly silence, followed by a shout from another voice. Then gunshots, and yet another scream erupted from that second voice.

Ahead, the lights of the Motugra police station and jail loomed closer, and a crowd was heading toward the station from the nearby bungalows and buildings. The people advanced on the scene, then there was a cry of fear and horror from several of the women, and the crowd stopped advancing.

As Jimmy and Khuna neared the station, the dim form of something running into the jungle on all fours was glimpsed at the other side of the building.

"Khuna!" Jimmy cried.

"I see it," the tribal warrior grunted, and sprinted past the pilot and into the darkness of the jungle beyond. Jimmy stopped.

"I can't believe the crazy bastard's following it," Jimmy muttered to himself, before trotting to the side of the stockade to see what the crowd was confronted with.

Jimmy skidded to a halt. A section of the jail's wall had been torn down: metal barred window, bricks, all of it. On the ground outside the jail, in mangled heap, was Alton Treadaway's body. Jimmy recognized the clothes that his client had been wearing that morning, but he couldn't have identified him by his face because Treadaway's corpse *had no face.* A jagged wound replaced the front of the man's head, and through the red gore bits of broken skull shone through. Treadaway's face had been bitten off.

Jimmy's face winced in disgust, and he turned his head. Then he saw inside the building and there lying on the floor of the cell was another dead body, this time a uniformed member of Smythe's crew of policemen. This body had fared somewhat better and had only suffered a broken neck. The corpse lay still on the floor, the head twisted around at in an unnatural angle.

Jimmy turned away and moved into the crowd, which was edging closer to the bodies. He listened to their jumbled conversations.

"Oh God, what happened?"

"His face, what…?"

"Somebody call Dr. Bryce!"

"Where the hell are the other cops?"

"Didn't you hear? That was it, the night-shift was just him. Smythe had to take all of his men away to an emergency in…"

"Colonel Smythe's not around?"

"No, he said he'd be back in around two days."

"Somebody get to the telegraph…"

Jimmy's mind raced. No cops on Motugra? The weight of the strange artifact hung on his shoulder, the bag digging into it. He had a strange feeling that the map, and the item that it had led Treadaway to, had everything to do with the things that assaulted him and had killed the two men. It was bad luck, bad news, and he wanted no more part in it. The rightful owner of the map would be coming the next day, but what about in the meantime? Jimmy wanted to get rid of the things or at least hide them, and fast. Where could he put them? Someplace secret and safe...

"Hey Jimmy," Corky O'Brian said, startling him out of his panicked reverie. The Irish barman stood before him in his dirty apron. "What the hell's goin' on around here?"

Jimmy opened and closed his mouth without a sound when he saw his friend. Relief had washed over him and he needed to tell someone but he couldn't speak about it in public.

"Not here," he said.

Corky understood. He nodded. Turning toward the direction of the Hanging Monkey, Corky motioned Jimmy to follow him.

•••

The Hanging Monkey was empty of all patrons when Corky returned to it with Jimmy. The customers had all rushed out when the screaming started, just as the others in the little surrounding village had done. Most of the townspeople were still milling around and discussing the events, their drinks at the bar forgotten. Many had come back to pay their tabs, and now the Monkey was officially closed. Miko the Chinese barmaid was cleaning up the place after giving some first aid to Jimmy, who hadn't spoken yet of what he and Khuna had encountered in the darkness. He wouldn't speak, not until he and Corky were completely alone. Khuna had come back to the bar not too long after it was officially announced as closed. He told Jimmy that he had found a trail of blood left by whatever had attacked the men at the station. The trail had wound through the jungle and had ended at the edge of the water. The Motugran warrior advised Jimmy to watch out for himself and left not too long afterward.

"He's still spooked," Corky said as he poured Jimmy a healthy shot of bourbon. "Drink up, it's on the house."

Jimmy nodded and gratefully swallowed the shot, savoring the bourbon's smoky burn as it trailed down his throat and warmed his stomach. He looked around for Miko.

"She's gone, so don't worry: we're alone. Now spill it," Corky told him, filling his own shot glass. He only drank after-hours. "What th' hell is goin' on out there, Jimmy?"

And Jimmy told him, beginning with the recap of Alton Treadaway's hiring of Jimmy's service that morning, onward to the arrest at the docks and through Jimmy's discovery of the map and the weird object in the plane. He told Corky of the walk through the dark, the strange creature that nearly killed him and Khuna's rescue, which lead into the event at the stockade and the deaths of Treadaway and Colonel Smythe's constable.

Corky shook his head at last. "What th' bloody hell…," he said, pouring shots again for the two of them. "So where's the map and the other thing now?" He hadn't noticed the sack that Jimmy had been carrying.

Jimmy lifted the bag and set it on the bar with a heavy thunk. "Wanna see it?" he asked Corky. The Irishman stared wordlessly at Jimmy for a long moment before he shrugged and nodded.

Jimmy removed the map and the artifact from the bag. Corky examined the map first, and then turned his attention to the spiky gold and crystal sphere. He too felt the weird thrill pass through him when his fingers first brushed it and he yanked his hands back.

Jimmy nodded. "Yeah, you felt that too, huh?"

Corky looked at the pilot for a second then picked up the orb. He held it up to the light, looking at the light play across it. "It's a weird little thing, isn't it?" he said. "Whatever it is… er, what is it?"

Jimmy grunted a short humorless laugh. "Wish I knew. Maybe we'll get answers when the map's owner shows up." He looked at Corky. "I'm not keeping this thing, at least not on me."

"Where is it goin, then?" Corky asked, still entranced by the object. He stopped and looked at Jimmy, who raised his eyebrows hopefully. "Oh, no," Corky began to protest.

"Yes, Corky, please."

The barman shook his head, beginning to slide the orb back into the sack. "No. Uh-uh. No way, boyo."

"Aw, c'mon Corky! Please. You gotta stash it for me. Nobody will know where it is, not until it's time to turn it over, *if* it even needs to be turned over. It'll be okay, and it shouldn't be for too long. Things should be a bit clearer once the owner gets here. Colonel Smythe says she should be here tomorrow," he said, before he added a mumbled "Hopefully."

Corky shook his head and looked at the clock: dawn was just around the corner. "The sun's comin' up, Jimmy. You've been up too long, and you're not thinkin' straight. There's no way in hell I'm keepin' this thing."

Jimmy drew a wad of cash from his pocket. "I know what you charge to keep stuff down there, Corky. I'm willing to triple it. C'mon, I'm asking you as a friend: hang onto it. Just for a bit."

Corky regarded the money with his hard blue eyes. He sighed and shook his head a fraction. Jimmy grabbed Corky's hand and pried it open, forcing the money into it. "Please," he said.

"Ah, don't beg, dammit," Corky said. "Yeah, you're my friend, and you're also a triple payin' customer so I'm takin' yer money." He stuffed the wad into the pocket of his Hawaiian print shirt.

"Thanks, buddy," Jimmy said gratefully. He picked up the map from the bar and put it into the pocket of his leather jacket. "I owe you one."

"Shut up and get outta here before I change my mind," the Irishman told him gruffly, waving his hand irritatingly. "The bar's closed, go home and get some sleep."

Jimmy walked to the door and opened it, a shaft of graying light seeping into the bar. The salt-air of the sea cleared his head a little and the coming sunrise was helping to dissipate the memory of the nightmare he'd faced out there in the darkness not that long before.

"Hey," Corky called to him, and Jimmy turned back. "What about my lighter?"

Jimmy scoffed. "Oh yeah. I don't think it brought me any luck today." Reaching into his shirt pocket, he pulled out the Zippo and tossed it to Corky, who caught it and grinned. "Looks like maybe it only works for you."

Corky laughed and pocketed his lighter as Jimmy left the Hanging Monkey.

•••

There is an ancient mariner's rhyme that goes *"Red sky in morning, sailors take warning; red sky at night, sailors delight."* True to this poem, the bloody red sunrise that dawned over Motugra that morning was followed by a tumultuous storm that railed against the islands. Fierce winds threatened to rip the little buildings and huts of Motugra's village to shreds. Palm leaves and branches were hurtled through the air, and the waves of the harbor were topped with angry white foam. The storm lasted into the afternoon when it finally began to die out slowly.

When the tempest finally ended calm was returned to the island, but with the calm came a strange new visitor. A gleaming white yacht sailed into Motugra's port in the late afternoon. The yacht was a top-of-the-line pleasure craft and was in stark contrast to the rusted tramp steamers, weary ships of war, and tiny dilapidated fishing boats that were anchored and moored in the waters of Motugra's bay.

The stern of the yacht was decorated with the vessel's name in simple gold lettering along with a strange and intricate occult symbol: the *Sea Star*.

After anchoring in the port, crew members began to disembark from the craft: a crew of roughnecks in grey uniforms and with the looks of hardened killers. Among them was the yacht's owner, as incongruous among his crew as his vessel was among the utilitarian ships it was docked alongside. The man was in his mid to late fifties, silver haired and smooth skinned, and everything from his mannerisms to the cut of his expensive suit bespoke of his wealth and bearing. Around his neck and hanging on the outside of his suit was a gold amulet of an ancient esoteric symbol, the same that adorned the *Sea Star*'s rear section. The man fanned his face with his white Trilby hat as his crew went about their docking procedures and studied the surrounding port and the village beyond. The look on his face was equal parts interest and distaste.

Once the yacht was secured and checked in with Motugra's port authority, the yacht's owner and two of his crew members walked to Motugra's little hotel.

Approaching the front desk, the dapper man doffed his Trilby to the native Motugran girl behind the counter.

"Good evening, ma'am," the man said in a voice that drawled like Mississippi honey, "My name's Lucius Clay and I'm looking for a friend of mine that's staying here, a fellow by the name of Alton Treadaway." He smiled, and though his face was tanned and youthful for his age, there was something cold in the expression.

The receptionist blinked a few times. "I'm sorry, Mr. Clay," she said, taken aback by the request. "But unfortunately Mr. Treadaway is no longer with us."

"I see," he replied. "Well, will you kindly direct me to the hotel that he's staying at now, please?" The smile again.

The receptionist swallowed. Lucius Clay scared her, and she wanted to get rid of his presence as soon as possible. "That's not what I meant, sir," she said. Then she told Clay about the events of the night before.

As Clay listened to her, his smile slowly faded and something moved behind his dark eyes. The receptionist felt more than ever like she was speaking to someone who was wearing a mask.

When her tale was over, there was a solid fifteen seconds of silence. The receptionist shifted in her chair, and the creak of it sounded like thunder in the vacuum.

Finally, Clay nodded. "I see," he said at last and replaced his hat atop his head. "Well, that *is* unfortunate. I suppose I'll need to speak to the authorities about this. Uh, tell me ma'am," he said as he rested his elbows on the desk. "Has anyone collected Mr. Treadaway's belongings from his room, yet?"

"No sir," the receptionist said, fighting the urge to lean back away from Clay. "With the authorities away from the island right now, we're keeping everything as it is until they come back."

"I don't suppose my friends and I could take a quick look around his room, then? Just a little peek?" The smile came back.

"I don't think that…"

"Oh, come on now," Clay insisted. His two companions shifted closer to the desk. "Surely a little look wouldn't hurt anyone? And nobody would ever know."

Clay's hand produced a wad of money as if by magic, and the receptionist took it hurriedly. "Room number three," she told him; she handed him the key and was careful not to touch his hand.

Clay nodded and kept the smile frozen on his face. After he tipped his hat to the girl he and his crewmen left for Treadaway's room.

When they were gone the receptionist let out a breath that she didn't know she had been holding. She felt like she'd just dodged a bullet.

•••

"Find it."

In the late Alton Treadaway's room, Lucius Clay stood in the center of the floor with his hands in his pockets as his pair of men went to work. With speed and thoroughness they began rifling through drawers, under the bed, dumping the contents of Treadaway's luggage out on the floor. Clay watched them with a cool detachment: beneath his stony exterior he was seething with expectation, anticipation, and anger that events had happened in a different way than he had planned. Tense minutes ticked by while Clay's men searched for Treadaway's find, for Clay's eagerly-awaited prize.

Nothing turned up.

Defeated, Clay's men looked at the mess they had made of the tomb robber's belongings. They avoided their master's eyes.

Finally, Clay sighed deeply closed his eyes for a few moments. He opened them again and told them "Put it back, all of it, carefully."

As he watched them repack Treadaway's things, Clay pondered his next course of action. He'd come so far to go back empty-handed. Motugra couldn't be that big, could it? How many islands were there in the area? He had seen enough of the map to be able to guess where the island was, but he hadn't seen the map of the island itself that would lead to the shrine. If Treadaway hadn't had a chance to find the relic, then it was still out there, somewhere. Maybe a local could help find it for him.

Clay's eyes landed on a yellow slip of paper that was sticking out from under a lamp on the bedside table. He lifted the lamp and pulled out the paper, and unfolded it.

The yellow sheet was telegraph paper, and it was blank. Clay turned it over and found writing. He read the words by the light of the setting sun that streamed through the blinds: "*Jimmy Dolan, the Hanging Monkey bar.*"

Clay's eyes looked up from the paper. "Boys, after we're finished here it's time for a drink," he said.

•••

The meaty fist whipped out again and collided with Jimmy Dolan's face. The pilot's head snapped back from the punch, and he felt a tooth come loose from his jaw in a coppery-tasting wad.

Jimmy's head lolled to the side in a daze. He would have fallen down completely if Clay's thug hadn't been standing behind Jimmy holding his arms behind his back. The other henchman, the more muscular of the two, twined his fingers in a handful of Jimmy's mop of blonde hair and lifted his head as he drew back for another punch.

"That's enough... for now," Lucius Clay said as he got up from the chair in Jimmy's little hotel room. "I need to talk to the boy, not bury him."

After searching Treadaway's room, Clay had assigned one of his men from the yacht to break into the locked-up police station and stockade and search through the deceased treasure hunter's confiscated belongings. Meanwhile, Clay and his men had taken a walk to the Hanging Monkey to look for Jimmy Dolan, whom they had claimed they wanted to hire. They didn't find him, but they did find others who knew Jimmy. The Irish owner of the bar had claimed to not know where the man was and regarded Clay with suspicion, but other patrons of the bar weren't as close-lipped. It was from them that Clay had learned that Dolan was a pilot, and through conversation it had come out that Dolan was indeed the man who ferried Alton Treadaway out to the remote islands at Motugra's edge. They knew nothing else of the events except for the fate of Treadaway and the lone officer on duty at the station, but they did know where Jimmy could be found usually during the day (besides the Hanging Monkey): down at the dock with his plane and his mechanic, Jake Sloan.

They had immediately left the bar to talk to Sloan, who hadn't seen Jimmy all day but knew his friend was always on the lookout for a job showing visitors around or carrying cargo. He had been eager to give Clay the address of the pilot's place of residence: the very hotel they had been to earlier in the day. They then had returned to the hotel later in the evening, when the streets of Motugra had thinned and there was less chance of being spotted by any passer-by.

Through swelling eyes Jimmy now watched Lucius Clay as he approached him. As soon as he'd seen Clay at his door he knew the man was up to no good, and when the man's talk had begun to drift toward Alton Treadaway and the map Jimmy knew he might be in for trouble. At first Clay had tried to pass himself off as the owner of the map, but he didn't know that Jimmy already had been told the owner was a woman. Jimmy had tried to get rid of the men but they forced their way into his room. He had immediately gone for his gun but Clay's thugs had been faster than he had been. They had swarmed and disarmed him and beat him into submission before Jimmy had a chance to defend himself.

"I told you before," Jimmy moaned, "I don't know anything about any damn map. I took the guy out to his island but I didn't see anything he had with him."

"Listen to me again, good sir," Clay told him in his thick drawl. "The map is missing from the late Mr. Treadaway's belongings. You were the last person he was with before he was incarcerated. My men have checked the station for Treadaway's things, and there wasn't a map among them. This all means that if anybody has the map, it's you. That map leads to something that I want most badly. I want it. I want that map. I *need* that map. Where is it?"

Jimmy thought of the weird object he'd found with the map aboard the *Loosey Goosey*. This had to have been what Clay was ultimately after, and he didn't know that Treadaway had already found it. Nobody did except for Jimmy and Corky. He had the map still, of course, but couldn't let this guy find out that Corky had the object itself. He didn't care if Clay got the thing or not, he only wanted to make sure he didn't go to the Hanging Monkey and start any trouble to get it. Corky wouldn't give it up and Clay wouldn't stop without a fight. There would be violence and bloodshed and who knows who would be hurt when the fists and bullets started flying?

Jimmy fixed the man squarely in his sight and inhaled. He spat a mouthful of blood and the loosened tooth right into Clay's smiling face.

"There's your map, 'kind *suh*'," he said, mocking Clay's accent. He smiled a bloody grin.

Clay slugged Jimmy in the gut, then again and again. Jimmy coughed and wheezed and his eyes went wide with pain. Clay had a hell of a punch; Jimmy hadn't seen that coming.

Clay himself pulled Jimmy's head up by the hair, and swung a haymaker that connected with Jimmy's jaw with a crack. Jimmy's eyesight swam and dimmed at the edges a second before he toppled into darkness and went limp.

Lucius Clay straightened up, smoothing his suit and tie. "Tie him up," he told his men. "Look for the map here among this little rat's things. I don't believe that crap he tried to feed us."

The henchmen did as they were told and trussed the unconscious pilot up before hitting his belongings. They trashed his little hotel room in minutes, being as thorough as they had been when they searched Treadaway's room, but nowhere near as careful to hide traces of the job. Clay stood by and watched, absently fingering the strange amulet around his neck.

"Got it," one of the men announced, and he held up the folded parchment. He had found it in one of the pockets of Jimmy's leather jacket.

Clay snatched the map from the thug's hand and unfolded it eagerly. His greedy eyes scanned the map. Clay was gleeful; a huge smile split his face in two. He was back on the trail.

"Back to the *Sea Star*, boys. Bring him along, too," he nodded at the inert form of Jimmy Dolan. "We could use him yet."

Lucious Clay and his men made their way back to Motugra's harbor, where his gleaming white yacht bobbed on the waves. The crewmen had hidden Jimmy's body in a large sack and they had no trouble bringing him aboard the *Sea Star* while avoiding any suspicion in the growing darkness of the night. Once they had Jimmy secured the crew got under way with haste and guided the swift luxury boat out of the bay and out to the moonlit sea.

•••

Clay's yacht had just barely been driven out of sight when a shadowy figure emerged from the waters of the bay near the pier. In the darkness, the shape turned its head back and forth. Sensitive eyes saw clearly in the dark tropical evening.

In the distance, the shadowy figure spied the Hanging Monkey bar. It was closing for the night, the last of its patrons walking or weaving away from the place and waving to the owner inside. After a few more minutes a hulking native Motugran and a small Chinese woman exited, and the owner locked the door behind them after bidding them a good night.

As the figure in the shadows watched, a second shape detached itself from the darkness of the bay and moved off toward the darkened bar.

The first figure followed stealthily in the gloom.

•••

Behind the bar in the Hanging Monkey was a door that led to Corky O'Brian's little apartment. He emerged from this door now with beer in hand, having been roused from his after-work relaxation. He cocked his head to the side and listened: over the sound of the record he'd been listening to he thought he'd heard a noise from down below. He couldn't be sure. Corky had once had a problem with rats in the storage area and was hoping that they hadn't returned.

After listening for a few more moments in silence he turned away, convinced that it was just his imagination. Another noise, louder this time, came to his ear and made him stop in his tracks. He shut off the phonograph and he could still hear the sounds in the basement. Something definitely *was* moving down in the storage area, and it was much bigger than a rat.

Corky went back into his apartment and came back with a Colt .45 automatic in one fist and a flashlight in the other. As quietly as he could, Corky knelt and lifted the concealed trapdoor in the floor behind the bar. As he did so he found himself wondering: if someone *was* really messing around down there, how had they gotten in? The trapdoor behind the bar's counter was the only real entrance to the basement. If someone were to break into the basement they would have to have used that trapdoor, otherwise they would have had to have sawed through wood and pulled away rock in order to get in. Corky hadn't heard any sawing or a jackhammer, so they couldn't have gotten in that way, right?

Bracing himself, Corky lifted the trapdoor and came down the stairs and into the basement as fast and as quietly as he could. There were a few crates he could see on the floor in the gloomy light from above, and something was moving around in the pitch-black corner beyond the crates. Whoever they were they were over by where he had stashed the gold and crystal orb for Jimmy Dolan.

Corky crept up behind the shape and switched on the flashlight, aiming his .45 as he called out. "All right, you'd better have a damn good reason t' be pokin' round here in the middle of the—" He froze.

In the bright circle of the flashlight he could see what he took to be a crouching person wearing a grayish green rubber suit of some kind. The person whirled and stood up to their full height, and Corky realized it was no person at all.

The thing towered at nearly seven feet tall, its head brushing the ceiling of the basement. Its skin was rubbery and glistened in the light like a fish's. It had long, strong arms and legs that ended in clawed and webbed hands and feet. Growing from its torso, where a man's ribs should be, grew a smaller pair of vestigial limbs that ended in flippers. The thing stood upright like a man, but it was no man. The scaly head was flanked by a pair of fan-like gills; its eyes were as black and dead as a shark's and its wide mouth was full of multiple rows of sharp crescent shaped teeth.

"Gah!" Corky let out a startled shout at the sight of the creature, who responded with a challenging roar of its own in return. It approached the barman with its arms held wide, claws glittering in the flashlight beam.

Corky aimed his Colt at its head but the thing lunged and swatted the pistol from his hand. Corky was already moving back and reaching out to his side, toppling a pair of barrels down into the creature's path. It slowed its approach, but only for a second and it leaped over the barrels toward him.

Corky's boxing instincts kicked in and he threw a roundhouse punch into the creature's face. It collided with the thing's skull with a thudding blow that staggered the creature, and Corky lashed out again, swinging his flashlight toward the thing's skull like a club.

The creature swung up an arm. It happened so fast that Corky didn't even see it. The arm struck Corky's own and the flashlight flew out of his hand to spin away into the darkness.

The creature pounced on Corky and threw him to the ground, pinning his arms down on either side of his head as vicious teeth snapped out at him. The thing's head lashed out again and again at Corky's face and throat. He was dodging the attacks with his head and trying his best to use his legs to push back against the thing on top of him but it was no

Corky…came down the stairs into the basement…

good. Whatever it was, it was much more powerful than he was. Corky's eyes bulged as the creature's mouth bent down again, thick saliva running down from all those wicked looking teeth poised over his face.

There was a sound, a weird hiss as something whistled through the air. It struck the side of the creature and the beast howled in pain and rage. It leaped off of Corky and spun around to face the darkness of the basement behind it, blood flying from the wound in its side.

Corky sat up: he could see someone in the dark there beyond the weird sea-creature. The newcomer crouched in an exotic fighting stance. *Khuna?*, thought Corky as he remembered the story of Jimmy's rescue. No, too small. The fighting stance, then... was that Miko, the waitress with martial arts skills?

The monster and the newcomer in the shadows sized each other up for a moment, then leapt at each other in unison.

The two figures met in mid-air, and a furious bout of combat began. In the dimness of the basement, Corky couldn't make out much of the shapes as they fought but he could see the weird sea creature lashing out with his claws while the smaller figure ducked and weaved to avoid them. Gouges were slashed in a barrel of Corky's private stock of whisky and a part of him grimaced to see the liquid splashing out of the slices the claws left. As Corky got to his feet the smaller combatant had ducked the attack and lunged around the creature's side, stabbing out with a weapon of some kind: was that a *sword*?

The beast howled again in frustration and spun to face his quarry but they had already leaped again, diving forward and through the space between monster's legs. They rolled and sprang to their feet behind the creature, bringing that blade down again and stabbing into its rubbery flesh.

Corky was moving now, rushing toward the still-lit flashlight in the corner. The sounds of combat, of whistling claws and blade and the pounding of fists and feet, thundered in the little darkness of the basement. Corky snatched up the flashlight and swept it around the floor, looking for his dropped pistol. This had to stop; he had to find out what was going on.

There in the corner near the weird golden orb was the glimmer of Corky's .45 and he snatched it up, just as a pained gurgled scream ripped out from an inhuman voice. Spinning with the flashlight, Corky brought up the Colt to aim at the vicious fight.

•••

With a click, the basement storage room flooded with light. In the wall up near the ceiling of the basement Corky could see where the creature had torn a ragged hole in the rocks and wood so it could get inside, and the dark night was visible through it. On the concrete floor the grey-green body of the sea monster shuddered a final time and stopped moving, dark blood bubbling and oozing from several deep stabs and slices in its flesh. There was a leather-booted foot resting on the creature's back, and Corky's eyes traveled up the foot and its connected leg, up to its owner.

His scalp tingled in a weird thrill, something he hadn't felt since his first boyhood crush back in Ireland: a quiet and demure farmer's daughter that had lived down the road from his family.

The woman that stood before him was nothing like the girl Corky had been in love with back then. Clad in a dark green trench coat over a slim black skirt slit up to her hip, this woman was as beautiful as she had been tough and lethal during combat. Raven black hair, as straight as a razor, hung down around her shoulders. The woman's bangs were cut straight horizontally just above her eyebrows, and the effect framed her pale white face with an almost ghostly effect. Sharp, well-defined cheekbones and ruby red lips added to her beauty but the main attraction was her eyes: luminously pale blue and large, they were hypnotic eyes that beckoned him to the mystery behind their gaze.

The woman's gloved left hand was on the basement's light switch; her right hand slid her barely glimpsed sword into the scabbard at her hip beneath her coat. The sound was a low hiss with a terminating metallic click that almost seemed to echo in the new quiet of the room.

"Are you alright?" the woman asked him with a hint of a Gaelic accent. "Did he hurt you anywhere?"

Oh, God, you're even Irish, Corky thought. *That's it, you* are *perfect.*

Corky dropped his aim. His arms were slack. He did his best to remain composed, feeling tremendously exposed and vulnerable to this woman the way he'd felt exposed and vulnerable to that thing she'd just killed.

"I'm alright," he said, nodding. "Thanks t' you, of course. I thought I was done-for until you showed up, Miss..."

"LeCain," the woman answered. "Moira LeCain, and I'm glad to have arrived when I did. No offense, but you looked like you needed the help..." She trailed off a bit, and Corky stared blankly at her before he got the hint.

"Oh! Corky: Corky O'Brian," he introduced himself, perhaps a little more enthusiastically than he would have preferred. "Nice to meet ya!" He grinned as he stuck his hand out to shake her gloved hand in return but blasted himself internally. *Cool down, you fool! Yer actin' like a twelve-year-old boy.*

"Mister O'Brian...," Moira began.

"Corky, please, Miss LeCain," he corrected her. He was hoping she'd tell him to use her first name as well. She didn't.

"Corky," she said, "I don't mean to be rude, but time may be of the essence and we haven't got much time do dawdle. I need to get right to the point. I came here to claim something but I see I may be too late and there may be someone ahead of me. I need to ask you: do you have the Star of the Sea?"

"I'm sorry, I don't follow you." Corky scratched his head.

"It's an ancient artifact," Moira explained patiently, holding up her hands to demonstrate as she spoke. "Roughly this large, a golden ball with crystalline protrusions."

"Ah, that! Yes, I do," he told her, and enthusiastically bounded over where the object lay in the corner, hidden behind some boxes. It was half out of its bag where the creature had been pulling it out, and he snatched it up and brought it to the mysterious woman.

There you go again, like a puppy! he scolded himself. *You know nothing about this thing, and nothing about her at all.*

Corky watched Moira's amazing eyes light up at the sight of the Star of the Sea, and she gently took it from his hands. She turned it over and over, looking at its myriad crystal facets and surfaces, each seeming to shine with its own light.

Corky watched Moira as she gazed at it in silence, smiling to herself dazedly. Finally, he broke the silence (even though he felt as though he could have watched her like that forever).

"Miss LeCain," he said gently, "I don't mean to pry, but what *is* this thing? It's been causing quite a bit o' commotion lately."

Moira looked up at him, her trance seemingly broken. "It's a long story, and there's some business I have to take care of first. Has anyone else, besides you, touched it or had it in their possession?"

"Yeah," he began. "First there was this treasure hunter..."

"Alton Treadaway?"

Corky looked at her with a puzzled expression. "Yes, but how...?" He snapped his fingers. "The map! You're the owner."

Moira nodded. "Yes, it was my map. Mr. Treadaway stole it from me, and obviously it led him right to the Star. Where is Mr. Treadaway now?"

Corky chuckled. "In a drawer in Motugra's morgue," he said, "an' there ain't much left of him to talk about." He jerked a thumb at the sea creature's corpse on the floor. "One of those fishy bastards got their hands on him and a poor member of Colonel Smythe's finest while he was locked up in the stockade."

"I see," Moira responded soberly, picking up the canvas bag and stuffing the relic back inside. "And how did you end up with the Star in your possession? Did anyone else have it between Treadaway and you?"

"Yeah, a pal of mine by the name of Jimmy Dolan. He took Treadaway to the outer islands and found where he'd stashed the thing on board his seaplane before he got arrested. After he found it he was attacked and nearly killed by one of these things, too. Maybe it was the same one that got Treadaway an' the same one you, er, perforated in here tonight?" Corky grinned in a way that he hoped was charming.

Moira shook her head, her straight jet hair fanning out gently about her shoulders. "I hate to be the bearer of bad news, Corky, but this isn't the only one. There are more out there."

"How many?" Corky asked, his grin fading.

Moira smiled, and Corky melted a little inside. "A *lot* more, I'm afraid. The Star of the Sea, they covet it. It was perverted by their purposes, and ever since then they are drawn to it. And they're also drawn to anyone who's ever *touched it.*"

Corky shuddered, and the feeling made him recall the weird tremble and light-headedness he felt when he touched the relic. Jimmy said he'd felt it, too. *What the devil's going on?* he wondered.

"It's a long story," Moira said, as though she had read his mind. "We need to find your friend Mr. Dolan. He, and you, are in grave danger right now." She put the Star of the Sea back into the canvas bag and closed it up. She turned to leave the basement.

Corky snatched the bag from her. "Look, until I know more about what's goin' on, until I know if Jimmy's alright, I'll be hangin' on t' this thing."

The woman glared at Corky momentarily with her shining eyes. Corky held his ground.

"I'm sorry Miss LeCain, and I'm sure you're meanin' well, but I promised Jimmy I'd keep it for him and I mean to do just that. For now."

Moira's look softened and she nodded. "Very well," she said. "For now." She turned and rapidly ascended the steps to the Hanging Monkey. Corky was left behind, staring at the monstrous corpse on the floor.

"But what about this guy?" he called up to her. "We gotta move him."

"Leave him," Moira's voice called from the bar. "We've got no time to lose."

Casting a last glance at the corpse, Corky went up the stairs, grumbling. "I hope th' damn thing doesn't start to stink before me an' Khuna can get it out o' here."

•••

Corky ran to Motugra's little hotel with Moira LeCain in tow. The ex-boxer was beefy and fit and a good runner, and yet he had the weird feeling that the Irish woman with him could have run past him and left him in the dust if she hadn't needed Corky to lead the way for her. There weren't many people out and about in town at this hour, and the little roughly graded streets were deserted and empty save for the two of them.

When they got to the hotel Corky knocked at Jimmy's door, hoping it would be opened by his groggy friend. Corky had an apology ready to go, but there was no answer to the knock and Corky's heart sank.

Corky tried the knob and it turned. He opened the door the rest of the way, his Colt cocked and ready in his hand. In the corner of his eye, he saw Moira reach beneath her coat to loosen her short sword from its scabbard.

The door swung inward to reveal Jimmy's apartment. The pilot's belongings were strewn about the room, drawers were pulled from his dresser and Jimmy's mattress and box spring were pulled from the bedframe completely.

Corky whistled. "Jimmy's not usually the best of housekeepers, but this's a bit much," he said. "Lord, please tell me one o' those things hasn't been here."

"They haven't, I can tell," Moira reassured him. "Someone was here, someone *human,* and they were looking for something."

"Your map, no doubt," Corky said. He picked up Jimmy's brown leather jacket from where it lay on the floor and reached into the interior pocket where he had seen the pilot deposit the map early that morning in the Hanging Monkey. It wasn't there, and it wasn't in any of his other pockets, either. "Whoever it was, I think they got it," he said sadly. "And they got Jimmy."

"Maybe they didn't. Where else could he be?" Moira asked him.

"At this time of the night? Usually here, maybe down by the docks with his plane. Maybe Jimmy's grease monkey Jake's seen 'im."

The two left Jimmy's apartment.

•••

Jake Sloan hadn't seen Jimmy Dolan since earlier that day. The pilot hadn't had any jobs and as far as Jake had known he had spent most of his day at his room at the hotel. Jake told Corky and Moira that his friend and boss had seemed a bit spooked when he saw him, and Jimmy had chalked it all up to being tired. The mechanic also said Jimmy had spent a lot of time nervously looking at the waters of the bay.

"Is Jimmy in some kinda trouble, Corky?" Jake asked, pushing his cap back on his head to scratch his balding head.

"I don't know, Jake," the barman responded gravely. "There might have been a few folks looking for him, or for somethin' he had, and they might not'a been all that nice."

Jake's face lit up a little. "Hey, I just remembered somethin': there was a guy here lookin' for Jimmy today. He said he wanted to hire him for something. I, er... aw hell, Corky, I gave him Jimmy's address."

"Who was this guy?"

Jake was sheepish. "I didn't catch his name but he was kinda strange, like. He was really tan, older fella, nicely dressed. Had a couple of guys with him in uniforms..."

Jakes description of Lucius Clay sparked Corky's memory. Moira stepped forward in front of Corky. "This man you talked to, Mr. Sloan, did he speak with a Southern American accent? Did he wear a strange medallion?"

Jake nodded. "A star of some kind, yeah. He did. You know him, miss?"

Moira's face clouded and she nodded solemnly. "I'm afraid I do, yes. Thank you, Mr. Sloan." The mysterious woman turned away abruptly, her black hair whirling about her shoulders, and she stalked away down the dock and back toward the town.

Jake stared after the woman's sensuous but purposeful stride. "Corky, who *is* that?"

"I'm still findin' out, lad, but remember: I saw her first." Corky lightly slapped Jake's pudgy stomach with the back of his hand and grinned. "Don't worry," he followed with more seriousness in his voice, "We'll find Jimmy. Hang in there." Corky turned and hurried to catch up with Moira.

"Wait up, Miss LeCain," he called to the woman ahead. *She's barely walking, how the hell is she going so fast?*, he wondered. "You know something, something you're not tellin' me."

"I do," Moira said to him as he fell into stride beside her. "The man who was after your friend, the man who is after the Star of the Sea, is very dangerous."

"Yeah, I remember the guy now. He was at the Monkey today lookin' for Jimmy."

"His name is Lucius Clay. He's after the very artifact that you're carrying in the bag. No doubt he thinks it's still on the island that Treadaway took it from, and he may have your friend Jimmy with him, though I shudder to think of why. Perhaps as a sacrifice."

"A sacrifice?!" Corky blurted.

"I will explain everything, but right now we're going to need as many trusted allies as you can muster. We need to get to that island, and we need to stop Clay."

"I can get my bouncer and my barmaid to help back us up."

Moira looked doubtfully at him.

"Don't worry: they're more help than they sound" Corky assured her. "They're not your average bar-staff. Transportation's goin' t' be more of a problem right now. At times like this I'd turn to Jimmy and the *Loosey Goosey,*" Corky laughed bitterly. "That's out of the question right now, o' course, and there's no other pilot that I'd trust around here."

"What about boats?" Moira asked him. "Are there any fast watercraft around here right now?"

Corky smiled.

•••

Nick Fortune stood in the doorway of his cabana. The Italian smuggler had been sleeping deeply when the knocking at his door had roused him from a pretty good dream (and good dreams were rare to Nick Fortune). His right eye squinted sleepily at his visitors. The empty socket of his left eye was covered, rather haphazardly at the moment, by his black eye patch.

"Now what the hell do you call *this*?" he mumbled. "Are we going on an adventure, kids?"

At his door were Corky and a mysterious black-haired girl with bright blue eyes that nearly glowed in the dim light. Behind the two of them stood little Miko the barmaid and Khuna. Khuna and Corky wore pistols at their waists; Miko wore something dark and form-fitting while the hilt of a sword could be glimpsed beneath the mystery girl's trench coat.

"We don't have time for small talk, Fortune," Corky began. "We need a ride out to one of the outlying islands. Can you take us?"

Nick scowled at them incredulously. "Are you kidding me, Corky? Do you know what time it is? It's…" He checked his wrist for a watch that was back on his bedside table at the moment. "Er, it's pretty damn late, is what it is. Isn't Jimmy in town right now? Let him take you." He started to close the door.

Corky's hand came out to stop the door from closing. "It's Jimmy we're worried about, Nick. He's in trouble and if we don't get to him soon somethin' bad's gonna happen to 'im."

Nick rubbed his scalp, ruffling his brown hair. "Oh jeez, what'd he do this time?"

"Nothing except his job, with a mild side of curiosity," Moira LeCain said to the smuggler as she fixed him with her eyes. "Your friend... *friends...* need your help, Mr. Fortune. Please. Won't you assist them?"

Nick looked at Moira for several seconds, his head cocked at a slight angle. "Alright, but it'll cost you double my normal transportation rates" he finally said. "Lemme get dressed. Wait out there." He shut the door.

Corky gawked. He'd been prepared to butt heads with Nick Fortune over this. The three men, Corky, Nick, and Jimmy Dolan, were most often friendly with each other but they each had been in competition before over a woman in the past (and usually the woman in question was Grace Thomas, the journalist). Nick was stubborn and not always quick to help the other two men when they were in trouble, but he rolled over almost immediately at just a few words from Moira LeCain. It was like she'd put some kind of whammy on him.

The beautiful Irish lass smiled briefly at Corky, and he returned the smile. She still made him puddle up inside, but his head was struggling with the fact that he knew so very little about her.

The door to the cabana jerked back open suddenly and Nick Fortune stepped out. Around his waist he wore his own Colt .45, and he placed his captain's cap firmly on his head. "Alright," he muttered, "let's go bail the kid out of trouble."

•••

The *Fortune's Folly* was much faster than she looked. The old rum-runner knifed across the moonlit water of the harbor, carefully following the channel-marker buoys until reaching the mouth of the bay and open water. As soon as they were out in the clear and open sea, Nick Fortune told his passengers to hang on and he threw the boat's throttle forward, launching them toward their destination in the tropical night. A map of the islands was pinned to the console and Moira and Corky had marked one of the tiny islands at the edge as their goal.

Once underway, the passengers settled in for their ride. Khuna took a spot near the bow, while Miko took a position at the port side opposite Nick's spot at the wheel.

At the stern of the boat, Corky sat beside Moira LeCain and watched her long black hair glitter darkly in the wind behind them. Gathering his courage (and chiding himself again for his unusual shyness), Corky cleared his throat and spoke up over the roar of the engines.

"Miss LeCain, we've got a ride ahead of us, and I just have to find out: just *what the hell* is going on here?"

Moira turned her pale face to Corky, and the moonlight illuminated a bright smile. "Corky, it's a long story…"

"I know that, an' you've said it a few times now," Corky interrupted, "But it seems to me that we've got some time ahead of us." He smiled. "There's nothing but time and water between us and the island where we're goin', so now would be a good time to tell your long story."

Moira looked out to sea and ran a hand through her black hair. She drew a deep breath and exhaled it, then turned back to the Irishman.

"Once upon a time," she began, and Corky couldn't help but smile again, "legend tells of a kingdom of mer-people, who lived under the sea since the dawn of time. The people of the kingdom flourished for thousands of years, being blessed with long-life and vitality, and gave rise to myths and legends around the world."

"Mermaids?" Corky scoffed.

"Yes, and mermen," Moira nodded. "I told you it's a legend so you can choose whether or not to believe it but it's a part of the story."

Corky leaned back and was silent, gesturing for Moira to continue.

"The legends say the people of this kingdom had a magical gemstone they kept within one of their temples, a jewel of raw crystal and gold that came from the stars themselves. The power from this crystal protected their city and helped to nourish the people who dwelt there. It fueled their magic, and for this reason it was coveted by the Abyss Dwellers: horrible sea creatures that dwelt in a deep crevasse on the ocean floor near the mer-folk's city.

"The Abyss Dwellers were even older than the mer-folk. It is theorized that they have ties with the Deep Ones that are spoken about in the *Ponape Scriptures*, or with a particular kind of amphibian creature that are known to reside in certain black lagoons of the Amazon. Tonight, in the basement of your bar, you yourself came face to face with one of them."

Corky swallowed, recalling with a hot feverish wave of adrenaline the monster that nearly killed him.

"Whoever they are" Moira continued, "the Abyss Dwellers stormed the city of the mer-people en masse. They were jealous of the peaceful ones and most jealous of the powerful and pure magic their gemstone possessed. The Abyss Dwellers stole it from their temple, and cold and darkness descended upon the city of the mer-folk."

"The Star of the Sea..." Corky's mouth was hanging open, dumbstruck.

"Exactly. The legends say the Abyss Dwellers took the Star far away from the mer-people's city and onto land so that the rightful owners could never find it. They chose a small island, the place Jimmy Dolan and Alton Treadaway visited yesterday morning, as the Star of the Sea's new home."

Corky's head was swimming: mermaids, magic jewels, creatures from the bottom of the sea... it was all too much to handle, and he unconsciously found himself gripping the rail next to him for support. Was *any* of this stuff real?

"The Abyss Dwellers had magic of their own, and on the island they deposited the Star their sorcerers constructed a twisted shrine to harness its power. The shrine was made from living coral, and they bound the Star of the Sea to the shrine using dark magic that twisted it and made it their own.

"The Abyss Dwellers, they're drawn to the Star's power now. When Alton Treadaway stole the Star, he became tainted with that dark magic: it connected itself to him when he touched the Star itself. When Jimmy found and touched the Star, he became touched by the Abyss Dwellers' magic too, as did you when you touched it."

Corky found it hard to keep his eyes from wanting to stray to the canvas bag on the floor of the boat. *Dark magic, evil sorcery...?*

Moira smiled and touched Corky's arm reassuringly. "Don't worry: it's not dangerous just sitting there by itself. The only harm it can do by itself is what it's already done: as long as the Abyss Dwellers' shrine is standing, anyone who touches the Star of the Sea is marked and those wretched creatures can find them simply by following that magical mark. It's how they found and killed Alton Treadaway; it's how they almost killed your friend Jimmy, and it's how they found you and the Star itself tonight at the bar. They're drawn to the Star and its mark, and under the cover of night they come onto land and come for it and those that bear its mark. They're probably tracking or following this very boat right now."

"But how do you fit into all this, and this Clay fella?" Corky felt confused, even though he was learning the facts. The closer he felt to the situation, the further away he felt.

"Nobody is really sure how, but a long time ago a group of treasure hunters heard of this legend and came looking for the Star of the Sea. Somewhere along the way, a band of pirates visited the island and found the Star. The Abyss Dwellers stopped them and slaughtered nearly all of them. Only a small handful of the pirates were left and one of them drew a map to the island and of the island itself, showing where the Star of the Sea and its altar were located. The surviving pirates never went back to the island themselves."

"I can see why," Corky shook his head.

"The pirate's map changed hands throughout the years, a curiosity and part of a half-forgotten legend. It turned up in finally in New York City, just a few weeks ago, and was auctioned off during the sale of rare occult-related artifacts.

"I own a shop in England that specializes in the esoteric and the occult, and since I've always been a lover of the Star of the Sea's legend, I made it my goal to win that map at any cost. The bidding was furious, and at the end it was a bidding war between me and Lucius Clay.

"I became aware of Clay through the community that deals in esoteric items, and I learned quickly that he's *not* the sort of person who needs to be dabbling with magical artifacts such as the Star of the Sea. The man is *obsessed* with finding it, and even named his yacht after it. Clay thinks that he could somehow harness the Star's power for himself. He wants to be a god on Earth."

Corky was confused. "But we have the Star here, with us. What can Clay do without it?"

"It's true that we have the Star and, unless Jimmy has told him, Clay is unaware that it's not there," Moira replied. "But Clay also plans to use his magic to gain control of the Abyss Dwellers' altar in order to command the Dwellers themselves. He wants them as his own personal army. He's been working on this a long time, and there's been talk that he's done some dark ritual dealings with evil forces in an attempt to help gain some tenuous power over them. He's evil, pure and simple."

"And now he's got Jimmy," Corky said quietly.

Moira nodded soberly, inwardly admiring how much Corky worried for his friend's safety. "I won the map to the Star out from under Lucius Clay during the auction in New York, and I had it in my possession for less than a day before he sent one of his men, Alton Treadaway, to steal it

"…how do you fit into all this…?"

from me. I was keeping it at my shop while preparing to leave for Motugra. Treadaway stole it after shooting one of my associates who was working at the shop that night. Before he died, my friend positively described Alton Treadaway to me but by then he was already on his way to Motugra to use the map to find the Star. I knew that Clay would be on his way himself, too: he'd never trust Treadaway or anyone else with the Star for long. So I radioed ahead to have the authorities stop him. I never suspected he'd actually found the Star already.

"Unfortunately," Moira continued, "Lucius Clay now has the map and is headed toward that island and the altar, and we've got to stop him before he can cause any further damage. I wish that I could have stopped Treadaway before you and your friends became involved with the affair: I have to let you know that Lucius Clay may very well be planning to sacrifice Jimmy to the Abyss Dwellers as part of his bargaining with them. I'm sorry it all had to happen like this, Corky."

"In a way I'm glad it happened this way, Miss LeCain. Otherwise, I wouldn't have met you." Corky smiled at her, hoping that the words he said had come across as sincere as he felt them to be.

"Please, Corky: call me Moira." The dark beauty smiled at Corky, and he felt that thrill again at his scalp.

The two of them fell into a comfortable silence under the stars and the drone of the engine as they moved inexorably toward their confrontation with Lucius Clay.

•••

Clay was furious. The altar of the Abyss Dwellers was empty, and the Star of the Sea was gone.

"I said 'where the hell is it?'" he raged at Jimmy Dolan. The pilot's face was swollen with bruises, his left eyelid puffed up hugely.

"I told you I don't know what you're talking about," Jimmy replied. "Maybe your friend Treadaway took it to Hell with him, why don't you go there and look for it yourself?"

Clay shook with rage, and he kicked Jimmy in the ribs.

"It doesn't matter right now," he spat. "I'll gain control of the altar first, then I'll get them to look for the Star for me. It won't escape me forever!" Clay drew a ceremonial dagger from an ornate wooden box he'd brought with him from the yacht and turned toward the obscene and empty coral shrine. "Drag him to the altar," he commanded his men in a low voice.

Clay's henchmen nervously shifted their feet but they did as they were told. They watched the corners and tunnels warily: in the shadows of the cave, dark shapes were gathering to watch them.

•••

They had arrived. In the darkness the island loomed closer to them as they drifted toward it. Anchored not far from the island lay Lucius Clay's yacht, the *Sea Star*: it lay white and sharp beneath the moonlight like a hound's tooth.

As soon as they had been able to see the lit torches along the beach in the distance, Nick Fortune had cut the *Fortune's Folly*'s engine and the rum-runner coasted along under its dying velocity. Near the torches on the beach a pair of gun-toting members of Clay's yacht crew could be seen standing guard, watching the water for intruders.

"So what do we do now?" Nick said as he eyeballed the guards. The launch from the *Sea Star* was beached on the sand near the men, and there were no other people visible from the water. "Looks like they've already gone ashore."

"Paddle us closer," Khuna said quietly. "Miko and I will take the guards on the beach." The little Chinese woman nodded silently in agreement, and Corky grinned. It was at times like this that he was glad to have these two on his side.

Nick and Corky took to the pair of oars and they silently paddled the boat closer to the island and kept well out of the torchlight. When they were close enough to swim to shore, Khuna and Miko slid from the boat and into the water. Several minutes crept by while Corky, Moira, and Nick waited and watched.

Suddenly a pair of shadows detached themselves from the foliage behind the pair of guards and swiftly dispatched them with a pair of matching broken necks. The trio in the boat watched speechlessly as Clay's guards dropped lifelessly to the sand. Miko disappeared into the shadows again as Khuna stripped the weapons from the guards. She reappeared after a few moments and signaled to the tribesman, who in turn waved the *Fortune's Folly* in. The coast was clear.

Corky and Nick rowed the boat to the shallows of the beach and dropped anchor, and they piled out with Moira and sloshed through the knee-high waves to the island. Corky kept his eyes on Moira, somehow expecting her to avert her eyes from the dead men on the sand. She did not, however.

Moira LeCain was an educated and intelligent woman, but she was also a warrior, he reminded himself. She hadn't batted a lash at slaying an Abyss Dweller sea monster in the Hanging Monkey's basement, and she damn sure didn't seem to be bothered by the slain yacht crewmembers here.

"Well Moira, what now?" he asked her. "You had the map and you know the island better than any of us. Where to?"

Moira was thoughtful, studying the landscape and turning the map's image over in her mind. "Generally we need to be heading in a north-easterly direction. Some stone tribal markers should help show the way, about two hundred yards from here I believe. Let's go." She drew her weird golden sword and stepped toward the jungle. The others followed.

•••

Moira's recall of the map's detail was incredibly accurate, and the group wasted no time in finding the mouth of the cave containing the shrine. There were no guards posted outside the cave, only a single lonely torch staked into the ground. It burned feebly against the dark night.

Before they entered, Corky gave his friends a rundown of the creatures they might face inside, and Nick scoffed until Khuna corroborated the story with his encounter with the Abyss Dweller alongside Jimmy Dolan.

"Sea monsters... okay, sure," the smuggler laughed, but he cocked his pistol nervously just the same.

The five entered the cave and followed Moira LeCain into its blackness, trailing along behind her through every twist and turn. Corky was right behind her, and he carried the bag containing the Star of the Sea slung over his shoulder. In one hand he held his Colt, in the other a flashlight. Moira didn't seem to need it, and he noticed her plunging ahead into the darkness even before the light's beam could illuminate the tunnel ahead. *She's so strange*, he thought with a grin to himself. *And so help me God, I love it.*

An echoing voice, from deep down the cave tunnel they were following, stopped them dead in their tracks.

"...and from the sunless deep and eternally blue grottos, you who follow the call of the Elder voices shall come to heed mine as thine own. Through the blood of this innocent—"

"'Innocent, *ha!*' a second voice interrupted. "Mister, you've must've mistaken me for an altar boy."

"Shut up!" a third voice rang out sharply, and the next sound was of wood smacking flesh and bone. The second voice grunted in pain.

"Through the blood of this innocent one, I shall place a crimson shroud upon this shrine," the first voice began again, its Southern drawl picking up where it had left off. "I will now spill the tribute which I bring to you, the debt that will chain you and all of your kind and kin into my service."

"Clay!" Moira hissed, peering into the darkness.

"An' he's got Jimmy," Corky muttered. "You ready?" he asked Moira.

"I am if everyone else is." The other three nodded.

"Then let's end this," she said, and she bolted down the corridor, Corky and his friends at her heels.

The group burst into the domed chamber of the Abyss Dwellers' shrine and for a moment time stood still. The scene presented to them was frozen: Jimmy Dolan was shackled to the bizarre coral shrine, his head with its beaten and bruised face held in place across the altar's top by one of Lucius Clay's henchmen. Jimmy's neck was exposed, and Clay himself stood over the pilot's awkwardly kneeling form. Clad in a green and scarlet robe, Clay held a weirdly ornamental knife over his head with one hand, a strange brittle old book in his other. Stationed around the perimeter of the room were nervous-looking members of Clay's squad and beyond them horrible shadows crouched in the other tunnels that led to the chamber. Black eyes glinted from the darkness there, illuminated as darkly twinkling spots by the flickering light of half a dozen torch flames. The Abyss Dwellers had gathered around their shrine, drawn by the spells that Lucius Clay was attempting to cast, spells that would bind them under his command forever.

"Stop!" Moira shouted, and the guns of Clay's men snapped up at the sound of her voice to cover the new arrivals.

"The words have all been said, my dear," Clay called out triumphantly. "All that's left now is the blood!" His hand began a downward arc toward Jimmy's throat.

Corky's .45 blasted a shot that caught Clay in the shoulder and the mystic dropped his knife, clutching at his wound. At the same time, Moira leaped forward, her leg outstretched in a flying kick. She seemed to fly through the air and her booted foot collided with the perverse coral shrine of the Abyss Dwellers. It shattered as her kick connected, crumbling into dust as her foot plowed through it.

An inhuman roar went up from the throats of the Abyss Dwellers in attendance, and Corky felt a weird throb pass through him at his hip, emanating from the Star of the Sea in its bag. The Abyss Dwellers' spell was broken. The pulse of magic as the ties were severed was so strong it caused Corky's legs to buckle. The thing in the bag almost felt alive now. He frantically shrugged the canvas bag from his shoulder and it hit the floor of the cave.

Clay's men began to fire on Corky and his friends, gunshots thundering in the domed chamber. Nick, Corky, Khuna, and Miko took cover around the corner of their tunnel and fired back. The man that had been holding Jimmy's head down had let the pilot go and lashed a booted foot out toward Moira where she lay. The girl wasn't there anymore: she was suddenly up on her own feet and slashing out with her sword at her attacker.

The Abyss Dwellers had now begun their attack, striking out at anything human. Clay or his enemies, it didn't matter now. The coral shrine had been destroyed, severing their last ties to the Star of the Sea. In their rage the Abyss Dwellers cared for nothing now save for the taste of human blood.

"They were mine, mine to control!" Lucius Clay screamed into the chaos as he stood amid the sounds of gunfire and shouts of men and monsters. "I nearly had them, even without the Star! You've destroyed it, destroyed it all!"

"Shaddup, dammit!" Jimmy Dolan struck Clay across his face with his shackled hands. The mystic went down beneath the blow. Jimmy raised his hands to strike Clay again, but was tackled by one of the *Sea Star*'s crew.

Mayhem reigned within the chamber now. A pair of Abyss Dwellers was charging the rescuers; Khuna met them with his shark-toothed club swinging wide deadly arcs before him. Moira was a whirling dervish of punches and kicks, punctuated by deadly stabs and slashes of her sword. At her attacks men and monster alike fell around her. Corky and Miko had charged into the chamber all the way and were doing their best to provide covering fire at Clay's men while Nick Fortune had run out to the middle of the chamber. Jimmy was there near the remains of the altar in a mad scrabbling fight with his tackler. Nick threw out a kick, his foot colliding with the man's ribs with a loud crack. The thug rolled off of Jimmy and found himself pounced upon by an Abyss Dweller. He screamed shrilly.

Nick snatched Jimmy to his feet. "C'mon, we gotta get out of here!" They started running back to the entrance tunnel.

"Why Nick, I didn't know you cared," Jimmy mocked the smuggler with a laugh.

"Keep it up, kid, and you'll be fish food, savvy?" As they ducked a thrown crewmember, Nick grinned.

It wasn't taking long for the tide of the fight to turn against Clay's men: they were being slaughtered by the Abyss Dwellers who sought their terrible vengeance from them. Some of the men had been killed outright by the creatures, their blood running red along the chamber floor and staining the stagnant pools of water with crimson. Others still had been dragged from sight, screaming into the tunnels that led away from the chamber and into darkness beyond. A few of the men had run blindly from the carnage and into side alcoves and corridors. None of these tunnels led from the cave system itself, and from the mouths of these passages screams rang and echoed as the men found their doom within.

Corky grinned at Jimmy and Nick. "Lad, yer sure beat to hell and even uglier than usual but it's good to see you again!" he cackled at the pilot. "Let's get out of here before those things get tired of snacking on Clay's men and decide to have us for dessert." They turned toward the entrance tunnel to leave, where Khuna and Miko were gathering now for a retreat.

"Speaking of that southern-fried sonofabitch, where is he?" Jimmy asked, looking around. "I'd like to thank him for the hell he's put me through."

Corky stopped, throwing his gaze around the chamber. Jimmy was right: where *was* Lucius Clay? His eyes stopped on the floor of the passage they'd come in from and he froze in place. The bag, the Star of the Sea, was gone. He looked around the chamber again hurriedly.

"Where's Moira?" he asked. No one had seen her or Lucius Clay leave the cave.

The group hurried out of the chamber, following the snaking tunnel back the way they had come. Corky felt waves of prickly fear creep up and down his neck, an intense worry for the black-haired Irish woman. He scolded himself: *You've only known her for a few hours, you sap! You're acting like you're in love with her. Are you?*

Was he? He shook his head, trying to clear his mind of these thoughts. *Worry about that stuff later, sort it out once you find her,* he told himself.

When they hit the shore the sun was starting to creep up over the horizon, lighting the day up in a brilliant golden glow. The launch from the *Sea Star* was gone, but that wasn't all that was missing from the beach.

"Aw, hell!" Nick shouted. The *Fortune's Folly* was gone too.

"There!" Jimmy pointed out to the water and the others followed the gesture with their eyes.

The *Sea Star* was moving out to sea, her engines pushing her at a good clip. The yacht wasn't alone: behind the *Sea Star* the *Fortune's Folly* sent up a fantail of water as it chased Clay's ship. The rum-runner was gaining on the yacht. In moments it had pulled even with the white ship, was pacing her.

Something dark, barely glimpsed by the group on the beach, leaped from the *Fortune's Folly*. It bounded the high and wide jump as easily as it had been a housecat hopping up onto a windowsill. The *Fortune's Folly*'s throttle must have been cut at the last second because the now-pilotless little craft fell behind the *Sea Star*'s wake. It would take a bit of swimming to reach the drifting craft, but it could be recovered for the ride home.

It wasn't this minor miracle that enthralled Corky and his friends, it was the dark shape that had jumped between the boats. The shape had been barely discernible but it was still clear who it had been.

"Moira..." Corky whispered, eyes widening. "What the hell *are* you?"

•••

On board the *Sea Star*, the disheveled face of Lucius Clay glared triumphantly at the expanse of open water ahead. He himself was at the wheel of his ship, having lost most of his crew to the sea-beasts in the cave. The engine room was giving all they had to give, and the *Sea Star* was running full-speed ahead. He pointed the yacht's bow into the brightening blue sea beyond the jagged teeth of rocks jutting from the far shore of the island. He was glad to be running, grateful to be putting distance between himself and the fiasco in the cave.

That woman, that stupid, stupid woman... she and her friends had robbed him of his chance to command the Abyss Dwellers, to rule them as his own and lead him as their king. He knew he should have had Alton Treadaway or one of his other henchmen hunt her down and kill her when they robbed her of the map in England. If he had done that, maybe he wouldn't have failed to enlist the creatures into his service.

Not all was lost, though: he had lost the command of the Abyss Dwellers, but he had gained something much more valuable in the end. He turned his head to the map table and to the heavy bag that sat upon it. He had stolen a peek at it as he'd run from the cave and snatched it up. The Star of the Sea, that legendary jewel of magic and power that once ruled a city of mer-folk, was now his, all his. It would make him powerful, more powerful than he would have been at the command of his army of Abyss Dwellers...

There was a noise, almost inaudible but enough to make him turn his head.

Moira LeCain stood there in the doorway to the yacht's wheelhouse. Her jet black hair clung wetly to her forehead and cheeks, her leather coat flapping in the breeze. Her weird luminous eyes burrowed a fiery judgment into Clay's, and he caught his breath at the vengeful sight.

"You can't... you can't have it," he stammered to her. "It's mine." As quickly but inconspicuously as he could, he reached under his ceremonial robe and drew a pistol.

"No, it's mine," Moira replied. "It's always been mine. Rightfully mine." She drew her golden short sword and it gleamed in the rising sun through the portholes.

Clay's eyes widened. "The Sword of Atargatis!" he shrieked. "Th-then you – you're...!"

Her movement was an inhuman blur: she was suddenly upon him, across the wheelhouse and against him before he could use his pistol. The sword stabbed up through his abdomen, slicing through bone, muscle, tissue and organs, seeking and piercing his heart. His mouth opened soundlessly, her face only inches from his and her glowing eyes looking into his soul.

"Yes, I am," she said. A dying breath rattled from Clay's mouth and his body dropped, sliding from the sword's blade.

The yacht's wheel spun behind Clay, suddenly without guidance: he had thrown it hard to starboard as he had died.

Moira's head snapped up. Through the windscreen she could see the black, sharp rocks rushing to meet them. There was no time to turn the yacht.

•••

A billowing fireball erupted from Clay's yacht as it careened out of control and struck the rocks. Thick oily smoke boiled into the air around it as smaller explosions rippled out from the dead craft.

"*Moira!*" Corky screamed, running out into the water. Khuna and Nick grabbed him, physically restraining him. He struggled against them, his eyes glued with shock at the burning wreckage on the rocks in the distance. He screamed and shouted again in grief, struggling again to break away from his friends, to swim to the wreckage. His heart hammered as his mind thrashed around in his head, trying to make sense of what had happened. Somewhere inside of him, a calm voice told him it was useless: she could not have survived that explosion.

•••

She had grabbed the bag and had thrown herself from the doomed yacht just as it exploded.

Moira hit the water on her back and sank down into the blue. She clutched the Star of the Sea to her chest as she watched the water's surface rising above her. Looking up as she fell she could clearly see the blooming orange explosions rising into the sky, the black smoke billowing, a fresh cloud of debris peppering the surface; her eyes saw all details beneath the water with crystal clarity. The salt water didn't burn her eyes, and there was no cloudiness in her vision. Her black hair fanned out around her face, framing it elegantly in slow and dreamy waves. She was back in her element.

She smiled in triumph, but it was a sad smile: a lifetime, *her* lifetime, much longer than many, had been spent on her mission, her search for this object, this artifact... so many had come into and out of her life through all those years, so many had loved her. This was the way it worked; it was a part of her being, of what she was. Part of the folklore, the legend. Part of the truth. So many had loved her and she'd never loved any of them back... but Corky O'Brian, she could have loved him. She thought she may have begun to. She hated to leave him behind like this. She knew he would grieve for her. All humans that she had touched grieved when she left. The love was always unrequited and sorrowful. Once again, it was part of what she was and the way those on land reacted to it.

Moira kicked her legs free from her black boots, twisting out of her jacket and her blouse and skirt as the change began, her legs beginning to fuse together, the skin growing between them. Apart from the strange leather belt and scabbard that held her sword, her body was nude now. Moira's alabaster skin was completely free from the clothes she'd been wearing. She pulled her black leather gloves off with her teeth, revealing her slim white hands, lovely skin with small webbing between her fingers.

Her feet were completely fused now, the toes elongating into long spines that fanned out into a wide fin. A peppering of scales rippled along what had been her thighs and calves on land. Iridescent green, the scales shimmered as her muscles moved, testing her transforming musculature.

She cast another look at the world above: she would miss it. Where she came from there were wonders uncounted, but none as simple as a common bird, a tree, the amazing things that humans built, their children... it was a wondrous place, and though it had been her home for uncounted years, she had never lost the awe she felt for it and its people.

She thought of Corky again. Maybe she would see him again one day. She would have to ponder that long and hard. There were rules, now that her mission was done. She would have to follow them and they were strict. But maybe, one day, perhaps she could make her way back there to her second home and apologize to him. She hoped Corky would forgive her then.

It was time now to return to her first home, though. The end of her mission was nearly over. All that was left was the journey back. She ached with sadness and was overjoyed at the same time. It was an odd feeling for her. It was so very… human.

She rolled in the water, her change complete. With a snap of her tail she sped away into the deep blue water and was gone, the prize of her people clutched to her chest.

The End

THE MONKEY, THE ELEPHANT, AND THE STAR

Almost immediately after agreeing to do a story for the second volume of TALES OF THE HANGING MONKEY, I started to get the sweats.

After all, I was (and am) still kinda new at this writing thing. The prospect of writing a short story using primary characters and settings created by others was daunting to me and had me a little worried. Would I be able to play in someone else's sandbox and not make an absolute mess of things? I didn't know, and I wasn't sure what I would do or how I would do it. Nonetheless, I placed confidence upon myself that I would come up with something sooner or later and would be able to step up to the plate when the time came.

And so began the great cycle of procrastination (where I would put the story out of my head as "something I'll get around to") and aimless brainstorming. During the periods where I tried to come up with a tale suitable for Corky O'Brian and company, I would toss around various ideas, most often inspired by an article I'd seen online or read about in the news. Every idea I had I ended up shooting down sooner or later: they were all fun, pulpy seeds that never grew into anything that I wanted to use for the Hanging Monkey and its patrons, and they all ended up sitting forlorn and unused on a notepad file in my computer. Once again I would revert to my "I'll come up with something eventually" mode and would put it out of my mind for a while. I ended up getting pretty good at ignoring the elephant in the room.

I ignored that elephant, off and on, between June 2011 and August 2013. I've said before elsewhere that I'm a very slow writer, but apparently I'm a slow creator as well.

The words "ancient artifact" were somewhere among those rambling ideas on that sad notepad file, and that's where THE STAR OF THE SEA began to take shape. After all, ancient artifacts are one of the great staple MacGuffins of pulp literature, and it's always fun to have a cursed or magical trinket around to keep people running and bullets flying.

Gradually another element began to seep into my long-gestating

Monkey-tale: mermaids. I grew up in Florida, where ads for Weeki Wachee Springs and their famous mermaids are plentiful, where a shipwreck-themed drinkery called "The Wreck Bar" boasts a bevy of lovely fish-tailed swimmers that pass by and wave at the patrons through portal windows. Those sirens of the deep have long held a bit of fascination for me, and I thought throwing them into a south-seas adventure tale would be just perfect.

So with both elements in place I started building things around them: at first I had an idea about a gangster pulling off heists at sea involving his group of nightclub "mermaids" who somehow stumble across an artifact that attracts a very real (and very monstrous) one. This creature of the deep would be hideous and a strong contrast to the comely fake mermaids, and I felt the tale would be a fun caper to write.

Ultimately I started to feel a bit "blah" about this idea but I still wanted to keep some of the elements intact. I still wanted the artifact, and still I wanted sea monsters to be attracted to it. I wanted the Hanging Monkey cast (especially Corky, who didn't seem to get a lot of exposure in volume one) to get sucked into it all, but wanted it all to come to them. That's when I created the Aussie treasure hunter Alton Treadaway, the slick (and slickly evil) southern gentleman/cultist Lucius Clay (named after a ghost in a Charlie Daniels' Band song), and the mysterious Moira LeCain.

Originally planed as a less dynamic figure operating in the shadows, Moira took shape as an adventurous relic-seeker with her own cache of secrets. Ostensibly she's from Ireland and because of this, her presence inspires in Corky a little homesickness along with a surprising tenderness deep inside his rough exterior. Not only did I want Corky to take a more central role in the story, I also wanted him to be seen as something more than everyone's favorite ex-boxer turned drink-slinger. Moira's name also conceals a very obscure "Easter Egg" that ties in with her secrets (thanks, Wikipedia!). I got some pretty good feedback about her, and wouldn't mind this character showing up again down the line. Maybe she'll cross Challenger Storm's path sometime before she heads down to Motugra in pursuit of the Star of the Sea…

Once I had a full outline of the story (and that's the first time I'd ever outlined *everything* in a story before writing it) I finally wrestled that elephant to the ground and went to work. Weirdly, this turned out to be a Jimmy Dolan tale as much as a Corky O'Brien story, as half of the tale is Jimmy's involvement in the adventure. Surprisingly I churned it all out in a pretty short time span… well, short for *me*, anyway: some of the writers

I know could have knocked this thing out in an afternoon. I wrote the entire story over several trips to a bingo hall with my wife and my mom, discovering that the sound of the ball-machine and the callers' monotone voices provided a great "white noise" background.

After all the sweating, worrying, and delaying, the experience of writing the story turned out to be easier, faster, and better than I thought it would be in the end. I ended up having a ball with every single character I wrote in the tale, and I wouldn't mind going back to Motugra to have another drink or two at that famous tropical joint in the future.

•••

DON GATES – was born and raised in Florida; at the time of this writing he is still a relatively recent transplant to the Great White North of Canada, where he and his beloved and feisty wife Annie are having a hell of a time adjusting to a place that actually has more seasons than just a year-round summer. He's held a variety of jobs that include working in a toy store and a bakery, working with developmentally disabled individuals, and doing telephone technical support over the phone. A relative newcomer, his first pulp novel (2011's CHALLENGER STORM: THE ISLE OF BLOOD, also from Airship 27) fulfilled two life-long dreams: to see his writing published and to work with illustrator Michael Wm. Kaluta. The second Challenger Storm novel (THE CURSE OF POSEIDON) came out in 2014 and is another collaboration with Kaluta and he is currently working on the third installment in the Challenger Storm series. THE STAR OF THE SEA is Gates' first short story, and he has since gone on to work on other writing projects (pulp and otherwise) that he hopes will see the light of day.

THE MERCILESS MERMAID

By Lee Houston Jr. & Nancy A. Hansen

It was already a sticky and airless day, and the sun wasn't even high overhead. Today was going to be another scorcher.

Haukea, a young Motugra girl, listlessly swept the floor. Corky O'Brian sat at the edge of the bar, finishing his second Irish coffee of the morning while processing the previous day's receipts. Business was great at his establishment. The bar was a popular watering hole. In fact, there was already someone banging on the front door of The Hanging Monkey. He initially decided to ignore it, since anybody who knew him, knew he was closed in the mornings.

"Come back later," he called out in a voice harsh from too many nights filled by making small talk with the patrons and breathing in their smoke. "We're not open yet."

The knocking grew louder and more insistent, accompanied by coughing and sputtering. Someone out there had obviously drunk his fill for the day somewhere else but still wanted more. Corky grimaced unhappily as he scooped everything up to put back in the strongbox he kept hidden beneath a loose floorboard, before scuffling around some of the fresh sawdust Haukea was spreading over it.

It was still a couple of hours before the bar would be even unofficially open for business, and by then Haukea and any other minors would not be allowed inside. The girl's labor was cheap and her family really needed what little Corky paid her. He should send whoever was beating down the door on his way before he passed out or got sick and made a mess.

As Corky limped around the counter to see what needed to be resupplied for the long afternoon and night ahead, the knocking became more sporadic, but the coughing and hacking continued. The local girl paused with the bucket of sawdust to look at O'Brian, but he just shook his head 'no' and motioned for her to go back to work. He was not expecting any deliveries today, so whoever wanted to get in must be really determined to tie one on.

A hinge pin popped off and shot across the room as someone put their weight into the door. As it bowed inward, Corky grabbed the handgun he kept under the counter in case of emergencies, motioned for Haukea to get behind him, and stalked up to the front cautiously. Standing off to the side where the edge of the door wouldn't hit him, he reached out with his free hand to unlock it.

The moment the lock was open the door swung inward, and a half-prone figure came tumbling in. Haukea shrieked as the stranger landed face first on the barroom floor. The man was weak and exhausted, but had enough wits left to reach out and try breaking his fall. He looked sober enough, but pale and half drowned; barely hanging on to consciousness.

O'Brian took a quick look outside. No one was in sight. He relocked the front door and, after tucking the pistol into his waistband, knelt to examine his unexpected guest.

"You've got a lungful of brine mate, so I'd say you had a bit of a rough start to the day!"

The man was wearing native attire, at least from the waist down. Tropical short pants and one lone, homemade sandal on the left foot were his only clothing. With a touch of gray around the temples of his black hair, he was also soaking wet and gagging up seawater, so O'Brian motioned for Haukea to go fetch a mop. He turned the mystery man's head to the side, making sure he was breathing and his airways were open. The Hanging Monkey wasn't that far from the island docks and the open sea. Did this poor soul escape getting shanghaied? Maybe he'd been out fishing and had fallen overboard?

Corky did not recognize the stranger, but noted that he had also suffered some cuts and bruises upon his hands, face, arms, legs, and chest. They didn't look like wounds someone would get during a fight.

The man had stopped hacking, but his eyes were barely open as Corky tried to ease him into a sitting position.

"Why'n all the places on heaven and earth, did ya decide to come a'knocking at my door?"

The unexpected guest had trouble focusing as he stared at his host. Whether or not the stranger knew where he was, let alone who was with him, the man choked out a string of unintelligible local dialect. The only word the bar owner and the girl understood was, "K-kh-Khuna…"

Then he passed out.

•••

As the blinding tropical sun reached its zenith in the midday sky, Nick Fortune basked in the noon warmth. He had completed another successful operation overnight, and was headed home. That 'delicate task' had required a moonless sky. Far wealthier than he had been before setting out, Nick and the *Fortune's Folly* made their way back to Motugra at a steady yet leisurely pace.

Alone aboard, Nick steered his vessel with expert precision while suppressing a yawn. His only thoughts at the moment concerned a hearty meal, a good stiff drink, and perhaps some female companionship before turning in for a well-deserved rest.

Once in what he considered safe waters, Nick relaxed and cut back the throttle. He was a bit low on fuel, and felt no need to push his craft. He yawned cavernously and stretched, flexing sore muscles. His latest enterprise had been quite ambitious, yet could also have been dangerous; though what was life without some risk? Now that it was completed, he was elated, though dog tired. He was eager to get home, but was running light and easy.

Unfortunately, fatigue made him a bit more careless than normal. He didn't immediately notice the vessel coming up fast on his port side because that was his blind spot, where the patch covered his missing left eye. When he did see it, Nick nonchalantly altered his course to get out of its path.

It came as a total shock when the other ship suddenly opened fire on him, without any cause or provocation. Nick swore at his own stupidity and quickly increased his rum-runner's speed in hopes of losing the larger vessel as its deck-mounted machine guns continued firing.

The initial salvo of bullets thankfully hit just short, peppering the water that churned in the wake of *Fortune's Folly*. He knew it wouldn't take long for his new-found enemies to get the range and increase their accuracy. Nick steered in a zig-zagging pattern across the open sea in hopes of avoiding a fatal hit. Alone, he could do no more than try and outrun them.

Who's after me this time?

A quick glance over his right shoulder could not answer that question. The steel hulled fan-tail was unmarked, which only meant it was no one in a legal-authoritative position, for there were far too many enemies and business rivals to account for.

Fortune knew he was both out manned and outgunned, for he only had his trusty Browning Hi-Power 9mm in its holster on board. There was no chance of trying the old smoke screen trick in hopes of losing his enemy either.

Nick vowed he would not be captured or killed as a shot whizzed past him.

•••

"Aye, I can see this is going to be a rare day," Corky said unhappily as he stared down at the unconscious man. He motioned a big-eyed Haukea over. "I can't leave him alone in here. Run over to the infirmary lass, and ask the doc to step over."

She shook her head negatively. "I go home now, watch the babies for Mama. Golanda is closer, she will come quick."

"No, I don't want Golanda," Corky said with a scowl. He didn't trust the local witch lady; with her beads, rattles, and potions. "Fetch me Doc Bryce."

Haukea crossed her arms and scowled right back at Corky. "Many steps too far. I go home late. Mama will scold. To make Mama happy, I should get two nickels today."

He groaned and riffled a big, scarred-knuckle hand through his thick red hair. "Fine, fine. Just go get the bloody doc already!"

Her palm came up immediately, so Corky had to open the register and give her two nickels before she'd leave. "It's robbing me you are!" he called after her as she flounced out the door. Another quick look outside again revealed no one present who might be interested in his guest, but he still locked up behind her.

It seemed like forever, but more along the line of twenty minutes, when someone else knocked quietly. As he reopened the front door, Corky noted Haukea was tugging on the free arm of the man he had been waiting for, trying to hurry him inside. The doc seemed less rumpled than usual and at least had his bag with him this time. The young girl was either anxious to get home, or wanted to be out of his presence as soon as possible. Maybe both. Although the reasons varied, many on the island did not have a high opinion of Doctor Neville Bryce, and the natives preferred their own healer.

"Thanks for coming so quickly Doctor Bryce. Seems we've a bit of a mystery on our hands," said Corky, welcoming the new arrival.

"I didn't seem to have much of a choice," replied Bryce in his clipped British accent. Haukea had already run off, her job done, and happy to be away. Bryce looked a bit shaky and bleary-eyed, but otherwise sober. "You haven't moved him, have you?" he asked, noticing where the stranger lay.

"Other than flipping him over onto his back because he landed face down when he stumbled in, no," replied Corky, before briefly explaining what happened in greater detail than what Haukea might have told him. "He did cough up part of the bay though."

"Good. Better out than in," replied Bryce, as he set his hat upon the closest table. He knelt next to the man and put his satchel down.

"Is this going to take long? I gotta open up soon," Corky said with a frown, standing nearby. Half-dead men on your floor weren't good advertising.

The doctor shook his head. "He's not a young man, but seems relatively fit for his age. He's more exhausted than anything else. In time…"

Before Bryce could say anything else, Corky held up a hand to silence him. There was a noise coming from the rear of The Hanging Monkey.

The bar owner was about to pull his gun and confront the possible intruder when Miko appeared from the back storeroom. The bar tending serving girl had arrived for duty and simply let herself in the back door with the key Corky gave her. She looked at her employer and the doctor blankly, and then stared at the man on the floor.

"Sorry Miko, it's been an interesting morning," said Corky, shoving the pistol back into his waistband. "We're not ready to open quite yet." He pulled her aside and they had a few quiet words while Bryce examined his latest patient. Instead of having Miko finish setting up for the day, Corky handed her the key to the front door and asked her to find Khuna for him. She rolled her eyes in the direction of Bryce and shook her head before leaving.

Corky ignored her. Neville Bryce had his faults, but was still a fairly competent doctor; at least when sober. Unfortunately the older man loved his liquor, perhaps a little too much.

Corky turned his attention back to the matter at hand. Bryce had removed his outer jacket. It was now folded and resting underneath his patient's head like a pillow. As he approached, the doctor asked Corky, "Any idea who he is?"

"Nope. Never seen him before today. Came banging on the door looking for Khuna and collapsed when I let him in."

"I see. What little he's wearing marks him as probably being from one of the outer islets. I've been out there a few times when Sister Ahern needed help, but I don't recognize him either."

The doctor looked up through his round-framed eyeglasses as he removed a weathered and well-used stethoscope from the stranger's bare chest. "His lungs and heart seem all right under the circumstances, but he's still so weak he can't retain consciousness. We need him conscious or he'll never drain those lungs, and will wind up with pneumonia." He ran a bottle of smelling salts under the native man's nose and his eyes fluttered.

"I'd like some Scotch please," requested Bryce.

"No can do, doc," Corky said flatly. He'd been wondering how long it would take Bryce to ask for a drink. "You treat him first, and then I'll serve you *one*." He had no intention of letting the hard drinking man get soused in his place; on or off duty. Too many people depended on a doctor being sober when they needed him.

"You don't understand," began Bryce, "the drink isn't for me. This man needs it for medicinal purposes. Whoever this poor fellow is, he's showing all the classic signs of extreme exhaustion. He's in shock and on the verge of a complete collapse. While the smelling salts are reestablishing consciousness, the Scotch is the quickest way available to safely bring his body temperature back up and restore his wits."

"Okay, but this is my joint, so I'm administering the treatment," Corky insisted. He went to the bar and returned momentarily with a small glass of the cheap stuff. With the man's neck in the crook of one arm, Corky sat him upright and touched the glass rim to the stranger's lips.

"Let him take it at his own pace, but don't let him gulp it either. Short sips are best," advised Bryce.

Corky shook his head in acknowledgment before proceeding. As a few drops of Scotch passed into the stranger's mouth, he noted that the doctor was watching the proceedings with slightly more than a professional interest. The man consumed a little more liquor, and then began to cough again. More fluid came up, some Scotch and seawater mixed with mucus. It dribbled down his chin onto his chest, with more than a few droplets spraying onto Corky's clean jersey shirt. The big man swore under his breath and smeared at it with a forearm.

"Get him at least into a sitting position and keep his head high," ordered Bryce, as he approached with his stethoscope again. The doctor listened to his patient's lungs, and then nodded. "Much better," he said with a slight smile, before removing an equally weathered sphygmomanometer from his satchel. The doctor wrapped the loose cuff around the stranger's lower arm, stuck the end of the stethoscope between bare skin and the bottom of the cuff to listen to his internal pulse, and then proceeded to take the patient's blood pressure.

After pumping the cuff full of air via a little squeeze bulb at the end of a piece of rubber tubing, Bryce slowly released the pressure until he got a reading. He pursed his lips. "A little off, but understandable for someone his age who has probably gone through a recent traumatic experience. He should be up and around by dusk, but for now, he could use some rest," continued Bryce, as he packed to leave. "It will certainly be interesting to hear what happened to that poor fellow. I'll be back later to check on him."

When the bar's open and there's a better chance of getting someone to buy you a drink, Corky surmised, but never said aloud. "Can I move him? I'll be opening soon and there's a cot in the storeroom."

"I didn't see any indications of internal injuries, but the poor fellow does have a nasty bump forming on the back of his head, so I can't rule out the possibility of a concussion yet. Just be gentle with him when you do. Make sure he only rests in a reclining position, with his head staying above his chest to help clear the lungs."

"I will do this," replied Khuna, walking through the front door of The Hanging Monkey with Miko following behind him. The new arrival was frowning. "Doctor should go now."

Corky shot his friend a black look.

"I was on my way out anyway," Bryce said quietly, brushing the sawdust off his jacket and bag while keeping a wary eye on the island native.

As he left, Khuna glared after him and muttered something under his breath before coming over to help Corky get the man on his feet. Although barely five and a half feet tall, what Khuna might have lacked in height he more than made up for in sheer muscle. Even though Corky was taller, the former prize fighter knew how to judge men. He appreciated how intimidating Khuna could look, especially when he was in a foul mood, like right now.

"Why did you chase Doc Bryce off?" asked Corky. "He probably saved this man's life."

"The Englishman has a demon that makes him drink too much. Evil draws more evil. My friend is weak right now, and cannot fight off demons."

"Oh...*kay*," said Corky, stretching the two syllables of the word out to show his contempt for the idea of demons, but otherwise never commented upon Khuna's superstitious beliefs. "So who is he?"

"Aalona is a friend of my father's from Kaia Akamu. He has a family who needs him, and must be protected from such cursed people. Why is he here? What happened to him?" asked Khuna, with a mixture of concern and rising anger in his voice.

Corky was quick to explain what had transpired.

In the end, Khuna simply nodded. "I do not understand this. Kaia Akamu is only a small fishing village on a small island south of Motugra. What could have happened to cause Aalona to come looking for me? Everything was peaceful when I visited last month."

"Wish I knew," admitted Corky, as he opened the door for Khuna. The other storeroom was no more than a large, walk-in closet for the less valuable supplies a bar needed and the things that Corky's small apartment didn't have the space to hold.

Khuna held Aalona by his underarms as Corky grabbed his feet. Together, they laid the man on the cot positioned against the far wall. It was a bed Corky sometimes let people borrow, depending upon who they were and what the need was.

Just as they were making him as comfortable as they could, Aalona regained consciousness. He looked up with blurry, tired eyes at Khuna and began to speak. The conversation was brief, and Corky didn't understand a word of the native tongue.

Aalona fell back to sleep with a smile on his face, but it was the confused look on Khuna's face that worried Corky more. "What did he say?"

"He said his people are in trouble, and asked me to free them from the evil mermaid. What did he mean by that?" asked Khuna.

"You can ask him when he wakes up," Corky reassured him. "In the meantime, we've *got* to open for business."

•••

The old tar peered around at the Motugra docks with a scowl on his weathered face as he secured the nondescript dinghy he had rowed in. A sailor since he was old enough to walk a ship's deck as a young cabin boy, he was indistinguishable from any other swab working the docks in his short-sleeve shirt, work pants, and red bandana around his neck. Not that he had any difficulties navigating on land, but the older man always fretted at being ashore too long and looked forward to be back on the open sea. However, the Captain's orders had to be obeyed and there was a task that only he could do.

Unless Davy Jones had claimed his soul before he could reach land, the escapee was somewhere nearby. He had to bring the man back before he could talk and ruin everything. Failure was not an option, but if need be, dead men told no tales.

•••

Business was good that late afternoon, although Corky O'Brian was not in a celebratory mood. Despite Khuna being on duty near the front door as his bouncer, the bar owner kept a wary eye out for suspicious looking strangers. Whoever had tried to harm his unexpected guest might return to finish the job.

Miko split her time between tending the bar and taking drinks to the outer tables. Corky could tell she was even more alert than usual, for her eyes focused on the door at every departure and arrival. Someday he hoped the mysterious Oriental girl would learn to relax and let him worry about the shady behavior of some of the regular patrons. Khuna would have no problem bodily tossing out anyone who started a row. Miko always seemed to be examining and categorizing the clientele as potential threats, a nervous habit that Corky found disturbing at times. Her guarded expression and silent disapproval certainly wasn't gaining her any additional tips or the bar many repeat customers the next time their ships docked.

Today however, Corky couldn't blame Miko for her edginess. This islander who had nearly dropped dead on his doorstep made him uneasy as well.

Eventually he found himself lost in the work of keeping The Hanging Monkey running smoothly and his customers happy. He had put thoughts of the mystery man aside, until a familiar face walked in.

"Nick!" shouted Corky from behind the bar.

The man at the front door nodded in response to the greeting and made his way to an empty stool near Corky, taking off his Captain's hat along the way.

"Give me a double. No... make it a triple shot of whiskey," Fortune quipped as he sat down and laid his hat on the counter next to him.

"That's a mite strong, even for you hotshot. Everything going well?" Corky inquired with an edge to his voice as he slid the drink over.

Before Nick could answer, Khuna approached. "I must see how Aalona is doing," he insisted.

"Sure. Doc Bryce should be around soon to check on him," said Corky, to which silence was Khuna's only reply as he stalked towards the storeroom.

"Sounds like you have troubles of your own," observed Nick, as he quickly downed his drink.

"It has been an interesting day so far," agreed Corky.

"Whatever your story is, bet I can top that," bragged Nick. "I was coming back to Motugra when a ship attacked me."

"What ship?" asked the bar owner.

"Never saw it before. Steel fan-tail about one hundred feet long, give or take. No quarter deck. Machine guns mounted port and starboard, fore and aft, all manned; but otherwise no markings. Good set of twin diesel engines on her though. Gave chase and started shooting the moment they spotted *Fortune's Folly*. Normally, since my ship's lighter and faster, I would have outrun them easily. But I was getting low on fuel, so they might have actually caught me if they hadn't given up when they did."

"Ye don't say!" Corky exclaimed in disbelief.

"It was the oddest thing. Once I was well past Kaia Akamu, it was as if they no longer had any interest in me."

"Kaia... Akamu..." Corky repeated slowly. He had a bad feeling about hearing that name twice in one day.

"Yeah. From there, I just barely made it back to port before the engine stalled, that's how empty my tanks were. But the *Folly* is refueled, and after a good meal and this," he raised the oversized shot glass, "so am I." Nick chased the whiskey with a beer Corky shoved his way. "So, how was your day, or should I even ask? Can't be as exciting as mine."

"It's a shame we didn't bet on it, because my story is something you'll definitely be interested in," said Corky, before recounting the arrival of his backroom guest.

•••

With medical bag in hand, Doctor Bryce closed his office and started walking toward The Hanging Monkey. There was a steady, yet hurried pace in his steps, but the man told himself that was just because there was a patient to check on. There was no other need to be there—or was there? He subconsciously licked his lips, but in anticipation of what?

As Bryce entered the bar, wrestling with his inner conflict, he never noticed the old sailor who was quietly following a short distance behind him.

The weathered seaman paused a moment before going in, so it wouldn't appear as if he was actually trailing the doctor. He had been discreetly waiting and watching the sawbones' place under the belief that, wherever he was hiding, the escapee would need medical attention sooner or later.

Thinking enough time had passed, he ambled inside, but was puzzled about his surroundings. Why would a hunted man run to a bar? Well, even if this turned out to be a false lead, he could do with a pint. Sometimes,

...he never noticed the old sailor...following...

carrying out the Captain's orders was right thirsty work.

Taking an out-of-the-way corner seat where he could watch the room and not be too obvious about it, he noticed the doctor talking to a red-haired man behind the bar before being escorted into a backroom. Could the runaway he sought be in there, he wondered, as the big and burly barkeep came back out alone. Whatever the case, that doctor was his best chance of getting near him. The escapee could always be dealt with somewhere else. If necessary, the sawbones might simply have an unfortunate accident too.

He asked the pretty Chinese lady passing by his table for a beer, and bided his time.

•••

Bryce paused to let his eyes adjust to the darkened room as Corky lit an oil lamp hanging from a ceiling rafter. Until then, the only light was a burning candle sitting by the sleeping figure so he wouldn't suddenly awaken in the dark. Although the doctor couldn't recall giving such instructions, this was a good thing. If the man did have a bad concussion, his eyes might be light sensitive for a while. No doubt O'Brian, with his pugilist past, knew a thing or three about concussions.

The storeroom was small; an afterthought when the bar was built, with no windows and only the lone door. Mostly filled by boxes and crates, the clearest area was a straight line between the door and the adult sized cot that looked out of place there. Even Khuna seemed hulking in this tight space. Having never been in this part of the bar before, Bryce wondered idly what else the room might be used for. He set his hat and bag aside, and bent over to examine his patient, ever aware of Khuna constantly glaring at him.

O'Brian watched the two men warily. Neither spoke, but were studying each other covertly whenever possible. Khuna's body language clearly indicated he did not want the doctor there, while Bryce was already edgy, doing his best not to upset the native. They looked like tomcats circling each other; one ready to spit and tangle with the second looking for the nearest exit. He spoke up to break the spell.

"Okay; you two play nice, and holler if ye need anything," said Corky as he went back to the bar.

"How has he been doing since I left?" Bryce asked Khuna quietly.

"Aalona opened his eyes when I came in. He was frightened, but smiled when seeing me, and closed his eyes to sleep again," replied the muscular native in a low-voiced rumble. With that, Khuna moved to stand in the far corner of the room where he could still keep an eye on everything, but not be any physically closer to the doctor than absolutely necessary.

"So he has displayed cognitive functions? Good. Did he say anything?" Bryce asked curiously, as he pulled out his stethoscope.

"He moans. I have not been in here as often as I would like," was the flat voiced answer, not mentioning the weird comment about an 'evil mermaid'.

"Well, there's no signs of any additional discharge around his mouth, so hopefully his lungs are completely clear now," said Bryce, as he knelt to move his stethoscope into position to confirm this.

Khuna watched intently as the doctor set the instrument at various places on his friend's chest. Although he did not think that any demon could pass through the device, he didn't trust the foreign doctor.

"Everything sounds fine. No more sea water in his chest," announced Bryce, repositioning himself to examine Aalona's head. "Now let's check that bump."

He had his back to the door, examining the patient, when a man walked in. Bryce turned and saw the new arrival holding a knife, with every intention of using it.

•••

The sailor nursed his beer, watching for his chance to slip away. The other customers were all minding their own business, lost in their drinks. It was only the serving girl, the red-haired man behind the counter, and the guy the barkeep was talking to who might present problems. They seemed the most alert and agitated, watching the door with each new arrival or departure. It wouldn't be wise to rush things.

An old timer like himself was always cautious, part of the reason he was still amongst the living when others far younger than him had already met their maker. He understood perfectly the Captain's dilemma in not wishing to draw unwanted attention to their presence. You couldn't suffer a man, not even one of these backward and superstitious islanders, to tell the local authorities about things he shouldn't have seen. Someone might actually believe him. So it was important to either capture or silence the heroic fool before he could talk.

Towards the end of his mug of draft, the sailor saw his chance. For some reason, the two at the bar went through another doorway behind it, and then moments later the Chinese girl joined them.

Getting up, he left a coin on the table for a tip as if leaving, but instead scuttled quickly to the other backroom area he saw the doctor disappear into. Not knowing how much time he might have before those three came back; he pressed an ear to the wooden barrier. If caught right now, he could always claim to be looking for a toilet.

He heard the doctor make his prognosis about a chest clear of sea water. The escapee had to be inside! He pulled a knife from one boot and opened the door quietly, quickly stepping in.

Closing it softly behind him, the sailor looked into the small, cramped room and allowed himself a slight smile. The sawbones and the escapee were alone. There were plenty of boxes and barrels to muffle any noise they made.

With no qualms about killing an innocent bystander if necessary, he brandished the knife with the intention of first taking care of the doc, and then his barely conscious patient.

•••

With sick fascination, Neville Bryce stared at the knife as it approached. While every instinct screamed otherwise, he was too shocked to dodge as the stranger moved forward and quickly reached out to grab his hair. With a sudden yank his head was thrown back and the neck exposed, as the well-honed blade came around to make that all important slash...

Although shocked by the abrupt attack, Bryce looked the old sailor directly in the face, staring deep into the other man's hard eyes. "If you are going to slice open my throat efficiently, your weapon needs to be a bit off to the side, where the main blood vessels are," he said coolly. "Otherwise you'll hit more gristle than vein."

That had the desired effect of making the man pause long enough so that no one's throat was getting cut today. With barely a sound, a solid body was wedged between Bryce and his attacker. Something akin to an iron vice had gripped the would-be-assassin's wrist, and the hand with the weapon went instantly numb. The knife clattered to the floor and the man turned at bay, just in time to meet a big fist rapidly coming towards him. He barely managed to duck fast enough to avoid the worst of the blow, but was still stunned as it connected with his jaw.

Another man in native attire, the bar's bouncer, the sailor realized too late, hovered over him. He was far stronger than the wild-eyed one who was scrambling upright on the bed while jabbering something in his native tongue. This new opponent must have been in there the entire time, hidden amongst the clutter. His attacker followed through and body slammed him to the floor.

Sailors learn to fight dirty or they don't live long. When the bouncer moved to grab him again, the man rolled to his feet and made as if to punch his assailant, but used the maneuver as a feint in order to kick his enemy in a vulnerable spot. That trick almost always caught an opponent by surprise and allowed him to gain the upper hand, but the enraged native didn't fall for it.

Khuna let go of him and drew back as a reflexive, defensive action. Even though the hastily out-flung foot still somewhat connected with his unprotected groin, he didn't fall to his knees in pain as weaker men would have. Still, it took the wind from him just long enough for the sailor to regain his knife.

The furious native was at least unarmed, so his opponent lunged quickly with the blade to deliver a devastating stab wound.

Unfortunately for him, the old sailor had forgotten about the doctor, who had the presence of mind to arm himself with the only weapon he had available: his rubber ended plexor, an instrument usually used to tap joints and check reflexes. Without hesitation, Bryce rapped the would-be assassin sharply on each temple, and stood back as the man crumpled like a rag doll.

"I would have torn him apart!" Khuna said angrily.

"I have no doubt you could have Khuna. Yet he's more use to us alive, so that we may question him," Bryce answered quietly. His hands were shaking as he packed his bag. "I doubt he came here on his own accord. Something very complex is involved, and perhaps your friend here," he indicated the wobbly man sitting up on Corky's bunk, "can help us figure out just what that is."

•••

"So that's why I wanted to talk to you back here in private," Corky said to Nick in The Hanging Monkey's other storeroom, since O'Brian never counted the trapdoor hidden behind the bar and what was down there as an *official* part of his establishment's inventory. "With that mess brewing in Europe, I'm starting to have problems getting some of the fancier, high end stuff that my more... *elite* customers prefer. Ya think ye can help me out, Nick me boy?"

"Well...," replied the smuggler, stroking his stubbled chin while thinking things over, "as long as you're not looking for anything rare or expect delivery by a certain time, it should be doable."

"Good. Now about costs..." began Corky, but never got to finish his sentence as the storeroom door opened.

"Sorry to interrupt," said Miko, as she entered. "Corky, do we have any more gin? The bottle behind the counter is getting low."

"Aye. We didn't get a chance to finish setting up for the day. Let me look," replied O'Brian, as he turned to peruse a rack of bottles behind him.

A minute later he handed her one, saying, "Next to last one. Have to order more, so go easy with it."

"I will," replied Miko. "What about those little green balls that sometimes go inside drinks?"

"Right. The olives are on the shelf to your left," said Corky, waiting for her to leave before resuming his chat with Nick. "Take both those loose jars out front. I moved the cases behind them because we're overstocked. They're heavy and I didn't want them falling on someone."

Miko tried an olive once, but didn't like it. Obviously other people did, so she grabbed the jars and was about to leave when the three of them heard a loud crashing noise.

The trio raced out of the storeroom to discover the patrons heading for the exit while a strange man was lying on the floor, on top of the other storeroom door's remains. Khuna was standing over him, fists clenched and ready to continue fighting. A shaky Neville Bryce stood behind him, his bag in one hand and a rather nasty looking knife held gingerly in the other.

Corky and Nick pulled their guns as the man on the floor started to stir.

"Why is this lout lying here, besides owing me a new door!" Corky snapped.

"He came to kill Aalona, and if he does not tell why, I will pull the words from his mouth, one at a time," answered Khuna, grinding his fists together to emphasize the threat.

"I'll not betray my Captain to ye," swore the old sailor, looking at the guns pointed at him.

"It's not us you have to worry about mate," said Corky, as Khuna picked the man up and held him by his feet.

"I already showed you the door. Now talk, or I will show you the floor!"

shouted the enraged native, as he banged the sailor's face against the sawdust covered wooden planks before pulling him back up.

"I'll not betray my Captain," the prisoner repeated stubbornly around swollen lips and possibly broken teeth.

"You must admire the man's loyalty," Miko pointed out. "Some men will die for their masters."

"He will die slowly and painfully then," Khuna said in a low voice full of malice.

"Not that he doesn't deserve it, but that won't do us much good," Corky cautioned.

"Perhaps we should turn him over to the local constabulary for questioning?" suggested Doctor Bryce in a tentative tone, while handing him the knife.

"I'm not sure that's such a great idea. They won't tell us a blasted thing even if they do learn anything, and anyway, you never know who's in whose pockets nowadays," the big man warned him. "It'd probably be for the best if we just tie him up."

"If necessary, I know a few places where we can hide him for a while. Places that no one will ever discover," Nick added.

"The storeroom will do for now," said Corky, before going back there to grab some rope.

Soon enough, the sailor found his hands and feet tied behind his back and bound to a chair, with his own filthy handkerchief stuffed in his mouth and secured by the bandana that was around his neck.

"Don't go drinking all me stock while you're in here, for I doubt your precious Captain will cover your bar tab," joked Corky. He locked the main storeroom behind him before stashing the prisoner's knife behind the bar; then rejoined the others in the adjacent storage area. Everyone was there but Miko, who had elected to keep working outside, in case anyone came back after the ruckus.

"You're just in time Corky," announced Nick. "With Khuna's help, Aalona here was telling us a fascinating story."

"I'll bet he is," said the frustrated bar owner, moving up as close as possible in the crowded storeroom.

"One day, about week ago, Amaya, his granddaughter, was waiting for her father and the other men to come back from fishing," recapped Khuna, while Aalona nodded in agreement. "That was when she saw a mermaid."

"A mermaid?" repeated O'Brian in disbelief. "This girl is how old?"

Aalona held up his right hand to indicate five as Khuna said, "Only

Amaya saw it. When she told them upon their return, the men were concerned."

"Bad omen!" said Aalona, in his best attempt at English.

"Stories of mermaids and sirens causing shipwrecks and death have been handed down by sailors since long before the Motugra region was discovered and explored," added Bryce. "The natives, not knowing otherwise, must have taken the tales as fact."

"Bunch of hogwash," was Corky's only comment.

"Next sun come high, all boats sink," revealed Aalona. "No can fish."

"All of them! How did that happen?" asked O'Brian.

"This is where you came in Corky," Nick said.

"All the boats had holes," explained Khuna. "Not safe on the water. The men spent all day patching, but next morning, all were sunken again!"

"Scuttled," said Nick.

"No," Aalona insisted, "Sea God angry!"

"Did anyone see that um... *mermaid* again?" Corky asked pointedly.

Aalona shook his head negatively, but then, remembering something important, reached inside his shorts' pocket to pull out a water-logged piece of paper that he handed over to Khuna.

As the bouncer began to carefully attempt unfolding it, his friend continued talking. Khuna translated for the others. "Aalona says that is when the bad men with big guns came. His people were told they were..." Then, not knowing what to say next, the two natives conversed for a moment before Khuna turned to look at the others. "He does not know your word. It means, people who must work for no money, and are not free to leave."

"Slaves," suggested Bryce, fearing the answer, but Aalona shook his head negatively.

"Prisoners?" asked Nick, to which Aalona nodded. Then the outer islander continued speaking as Khuna translated.

"Those who would fight were shot. Some of the younger men were taken away at gun point. Families were told their men are needed to help. Everyone else must stay on the island and not make trouble. Bad men would be leaving in several days if everyone works hard."

"What are they doing?" asked Nick, but Aalona shook his head negatively again. He made some kind of protective gesture and looked genuinely frightened.

"Something that brings evil to his village," Khuna said darkly.

"How did your friend get here?" Corky prodded.

"Me build waka," answered Aalona in his broken English. "Bad men not find."

"A waka is a dugout canoe. Quite a clever craft, if you've ever seen one," Bryce told them, interrupting. Khuna stared at him a moment.

"Aalona waited until after sunset and took his chances," Khuna continued, relating the rest of his friend's story. "He got away from Kaia Akamu safely and was headed here to find me."

"But there are closer islets," pointed out Corky.

"Aalona fears others either could not help or were prisoners too. He wanted to tell someone he trusts," said Khuna, a statement to which Aalona added a smile. Through friendship with Khuna's father, Aalona had known the younger man since his childhood. Proud of the man he had become, Khuna was the first person he thought of when the trouble arose. "When the big boat chased him, he thought he would die," added the bouncer.

"What big boat was that?" asked Nick in a suspicious tone.

Aalona held out his hands as far as his arms could stretch, then patted the steel frame of the cot he was lying on.

"Big metal boat," explained Khuna.

"I got that. Can he describe…" began Nick, when Aalona started pointing his fingers and making gun noises.

"There were guns all along the boat that started shooting at him," said Khuna.

"Sound familiar?" Nick asked Corky with a raised eyebrow, to which the Irishman nodded his head and swore.

"Aalona dove into the water and just kept swimming. The boat almost hit him once, but thankfully the guns missed," added Khuna. "He is a good swimmer."

"You mean… he swam the rest of the way from Kaia Akamu to here?" realized Corky. "I'm impressed. No wonder he was exhausted by the time he reached my doorstep."

"Are those bad men still on the island?" Nick wanted to know, balling a fist and striking his palm.

Aalona moved his hand around for a moment and shook his head negatively before Khuna explained. "They circle his island on their boat when not anchored offshore. Keep everyone on land except for those forced to help them."

"Obviously there's something valuable out there they really want, because they chased me away when I accidentally stumbled across them," Nick realized.

"What about Sister Ahren? She's on the outer islands doing more missionary work," said Bryce, who had been thoughtfully silent for a while.

Khuna asked, but thankfully the nun and her party had not made it to Kaia Akamu on their rounds yet, since it was the outermost island of the Motugra chain. At that point, he had finished carefully unfolding the wet paper on top of a crate so everyone could look at it.

"What is it supposed to be?" asked Nick, staring at a crude pencil sketch that survived the journey with Aalona.

"Amaya drew the mermaid," Khuna told them proudly, while Aalona beamed.

"That's no mermaid," scoffed Corky.

"To the eyes of a little girl, it could be," said Bryce. "It definitely has a feminine silhouette," he added, tracing the outline of some rather obvious contours. "After all, have you ever seen a mermaid for yourself?" he asked.

"No, but that ain't one," Corky insisted.

"Corky's right. I think we're looking at something more real life than mythical," said Nick. "See these long humps on her back and that line around her neck with the big circle on it?"

"Deep sea diving gear!" exclaimed Khuna. "Those are air tanks on her back and the mouth piece around her neck. I have seen pictures in one of Corky's magazines."

Nick chuckled. Corky's magazine collection was legendary. His little apartment was wallpapered in pinups from his most cherished periodicals.

"That would be my *National Geographics*," said O'Brian sharply, before anyone asked.

"Someone from enemy boat could swim deep underwater for a long time. A diver with a good knife could be keeping the men from going fishing," Khuna suggested.

"Probably so no one on the island can interfere with whatever nasty little business they're up to," Bryce interjected thoughtfully.

"Doctor is right," Khuna said, reluctantly agreeing with the man he mistrusted. "What do we do now?"

"We stop them, somehow," said Corky, stating the obvious.

"If we're going to attempt a rescue operation, tonight's our best chance. We may not have the element of surprise, but the new moon will just be a sliver at most, giving us the best cover we can hope for," explained Nick. "A small raiding party would be preferable. While we don't know how many we're up against, if we can sneak up to the enemy boat and rescue the prisoners that will give us more manpower against them."

"Count me in," said Khuna. Aalona nodded and pointed to himself. "Aalona will come too."

"I can't advise that," warned Bryce, addressing the island natives. "Your friend is not young, and he needs time to rest and recover."

"Time we don't have," Khuna pointed out. "It is Aalona's right. They have his son, Amaya's father."

"Well then Doc, why don't you come with us?" asked Nick.

"*Me?*"Bryce said in a state of shock and surprise. "I'm a doctor, not…"

"You can stay on the *Fortune's Folly* with me," said Nick. "Besides the fact I can use a second pair of eyes on the water, you can keep tabs on your patient and be there if any of the other islanders need medical attention."

The doctor remained silent for a moment, and then nodded his head in agreement. *Well, I wasn't looking for an adventure, but it's either myself or Golanda. Then again, she might be more useful in a fight,* mused Bryce.

"So, since that's all settled," began Corky, "Miko and I will stay here with the prisoner. If we don't at least get word from you before I open in the morning, I'll hand him over to the law and explain what's going on."

"Agreed," was all Nick could say, not being able to imagine the authorities on his side for a change. In low voices, they discussed their plans further.

Afterward, Nick looked at his wristwatch and said, "We'd best be going. The sun will be setting soon, which means the enemy will hopefully cease all activity for the night, except for maybe their patrol schedule. Either way, we can observe them for a while and proceed accordingly."

I wonder if there's a chance of getting a last meal, or at least a good stiff drink, thought Bryce as he started following the others out of The Hanging Monkey, gripping his medical bag harder than necessary.

•••

With a spectacular tropical sunset on the watery horizon obscured by only a few stray clouds; Nick navigated his rum-runner for Kalia, Kaia Akamu's closest neighbor, at a leisurely pace, as if on legitimate business. Just when the islet started to appear upon the horizon, he changed course for Aalona's home and turned off his lights to travel undetected.

There was no immediate sign of their target as *Fortune's Folly* began traversing in a wide, clockwise circle. Everyone on board was alert and watching the surrounding sea, for there was always the risk that the enemy vessel could have altered course and was now patrolling counterclockwise. Nick maintained a low speed, so no engine noise would herald

"I can use a second pair of eyes on the water."

their arrival, but was prepared to elude them if a chase occurred.

With just the four of them on this mission, the possibility of stopping long enough to acquire more men on Kaia Akamu was raised again enroute, but dismissed. There was no guarantee that whoever was behind the islet's troubles hadn't decided to leave guards on shore after Aalona's escape, and the last thing Nick wanted to do was walk into either a possible ambush or potential gunfight. Better to go in light, stick to the plan, and hope for the best.

As their ship began to clear the southernmost tip of Kaia Akamu, Neville Bryce called out quietly from his position at the bow that their target laid ahead.

Despite running dark, Nick repositioned the *Fortune's Folly* so the islet would obscure anyone possibly sighting his boat before bringing the engines to a full stop. Khuna dropped the anchor as Nick joined the doctor at the bow. Taking the binoculars from Bryce and looking for himself, Fortune saw the steel fan-tail anchored southwest of the islet. While the machine guns were unmanned at the moment, the deck was still quite lit and active, with sailors going about their nightly chores.

"I see seven men above. How many do you think below?" asked Khuna.

"Not sure. A vessel that size could have up to a fifty member crew," Nick ventured, wondering just how badly the odds were against them.

"I seriously doubt there are that many," commented Bryce.

Nick turned to face the doctor and asked why.

"Simple mathematics. The more people that are involved, the more risk of discovery and the smaller their shares will be," reasoned Bryce. "Whatever nefarious undertaking these people are executing, their merciless and hostile behavior indicates they're also quite greedy and don't want to be discovered. Such avaricious people tend to be secretive and antisocial creatures."

"Very astute Doctor Bryce," admitted Nick, trying hard not to relate that to some of the operations he had been a part of.

"No see my people. Must be inside boat," commented Aalona, staring ahead at the other ship.

"What gets me is that I don't see any women," said Nick.

"Why is that important?" asked Khuna.

"Our mermaid had to be a woman," replied Nick. "Even if the deep sea diving outfit fooled little Amaya into thinking she saw a mermaid, the child's old enough to tell the difference between men and women. So where is she?" he asked, before peering through the binoculars again.

"Does it matter? Enough talk. When do we free Aalona's people?" Khuna demanded, grinding his fists together in anxious anticipation of what lay ahead.

Nick looked at his wristwatch and replied, "It's only a little after nine now. Let's get some rest and we'll attack after midnight, when hopefully most of them will be asleep. Who wants to take first watch?"

"I will," volunteered Bryce. "I'm too nervous to sleep anyway."

"Okay. We should be relatively safe this far out, off in the dark, but keep your eyes and ears open," Nick warned him, glancing up at the starry, but moonless sky. "Wake me up in two hours, unless either that boat moves or someone else arrives."

"You gentlemen should rest too," Bryce told the Motugra natives. "Especially Aalona. You have a long and difficult night ahead."

•••

Corky would never admit it publicly, because it would tarnish his reputation, but he was worried about his friends; especially the doctor. There was a part of him that believed he should have spoken up and argued against Neville Bryce accompanying the others, yet there was no legitimate reason other than concern for his safety, an excuse that was actually applicable to all of them. The only thing O'Brian knew for sure was that it was doubtful he would get much sleep tonight.

It was nearing closing time after a long and eventful day. The last customer was staggering out of The Hanging Monkey when she entered the bar. A walking dream with bright red hair, she was packed into a tight black dress that greatly accented every curve. Oh she was a looker all right, and one he would never have missed, had she been on Motugra before. He wondered idly how she had arrived. Maybe Jimmy Dolan was back?

Without any hesitation, she walked right up to the bar and asked for a brandy, while occupying a stool directly in front of Corky, giving him a healthy view of her well-appointed personal assets.

"What do I owe you?" she asked in a voice both exotic and seductive, while reaching into the handbag she had placed on the countertop between them.

He stopped her with a gentle pat. "It's on the house lass, 'cause it's rare to see such a charmer like yourself in my place," Corky insisted. He placed the bottle nearby, just in case.

"So... I take it you own this joint?" she asked with genuine curiosity and a slightly wicked smile. Her lips left faint carmine prints on the glass.

"Yes ma'am. Corky O'Brian, at your service," he replied with a lopsided grin, offering his hand. She took his fingers, and shook them gently, letting her own slide down suggestively between them.

"Sirene," she replied, eying him with more than a hint of what might be possible in the future.

"Enchanting name if I've ever heard one," Corky said with great interest. He was leaning against the bar on his elbows, a bit lost for words as he stared longingly into her deep blue eyes.

"I'm... looking for someone," she added, taking in the broken storeroom door, as she started reaching into her handbag again. "The authorities couldn't help me and this is the only place still open this late."

"Motugra's a big island, but I get to meet a lot of the new folks," Corky admitted, hoping to become far better acquainted with Sirene. "Do ye have a photograph?"

"Oh, I've got something even better," she replied smoothly as she pulled out a small pistol with her right hand and pointed it right between Corky's eyes.

Although startled to be taken by surprise in such a manner, Corky still considered himself a man of action.

He stared deeper into what he now perceived to be her ice cold eyes, hoping to distract the lady, and asked, "Is this necessary?"

"I need information. Consider this my version of a thorough interrogation. I'm looking for a man."

"Not me, I take it," Corky said sarcastically, with just a hint of genuine disappointment.

"Sorry handsome," replied Sirene with a smirk. "I…"

It was at that moment that Corky reached up and grabbed her gun hand by the wrist, and yanked her half over the counter.

Sirene swore like a dockworker as they struggled for control of the pistol. She clawed and slapped at Corky, trying to gouge his eyes, as he tried hard to subdue her without having to resort to punching her. Sirene picked up on his reluctance right away, thinking it was simply misplaced chivalry. Having no such sense of fair play herself, she grabbed the brandy bottle with her free hand, and hit him over the head with it as hard and as fast as she could.

Corky fought to stay conscious and lost. He was swearing off redheads for good even as he sagged to the floor, covered with expensive liquor and the shards of broken glass.

•••

By 1 a.m. the rescue operation was underway. The steel fan-tail had dimmed most of her lights over an hour ago, and there was now only one sentry present at each end of the vessel. But each man had a rifle, which might present a problem when Aalona and Khuna tried to board the boat.

The Motugrans swam just below the surface of the water, coming up occasionally, but only long enough for more air as they made their way to the other vessel. Both men had bundled fish nets tied to their backs. Once they reached their destination, they would use the nets to foul the ship's props; preventing it from giving chase or getting away if everything didn't go according to plan.

Yet, as they were helping each other untie the nets from their bodies, Khuna realized he had no idea how they were going to actually climb on board.

•••

Sirene peeked through the remains of the smaller storeroom door only long enough to confirm it was empty, then hurried around to the other side of the bar without a second thought to the prone body lying on the floor.

As she had told Corky, coming here was her last shot. The rendezvous had been missed, so it fell to her to discreetly discover what happened.

Pausing only long enough to make sure the bar owner would not be regaining consciousness and interfering any time soon, Sirene spotted the missing man's knife sitting on the under counter shelf next to a stack of clean glasses. Doubting anyone else would have the same initials carved into the handle, she grabbed it and briefly considered slitting Corky's throat, but decided against it. Too messy, and murdering a white man would bring the authorities down on their necks quicker than harming any native would. Besides, under different circumstances...

She smirked and shoved the blade in her purse, preferring the revolver in case anyone else was still in the bar.

Cautiously, Sirene opened the other storeroom door.

As the back area came into view, she saw no one else inside except the man she had been looking for, tied to a chair in the far corner. He spotted her and struggled against his bonds, trying to talk; which was useless, being gagged.

In her haste to free the sailor, Sirene didn't check the room thoroughly. A hand came roughly down on her wrist in a chopping motion, knocking the gun out of her grasp.

Sirene turned at bay and just barely caught sight of Miko, already lashing out with a sweeping kick of her left leg as she pivoted on her right.

The wily redhead was no stranger to this kind of fighting. She threw her purse out to deflect the kick even as she shifted to avoid the blow that would follow.

The Oriental woman kicked the gun across the floor, out of play, but her opponent was already out of range of the punch she tried to deliver afterward.

Taking a defensive position, Sirene was ready and able to combat this new threat, as her blue eyes glanced around quickly, looking for something else to fight with.

•••

After fouling the prop blades with the fishing nets, Aalona and Khuna silently swam around the steel fan-tail, looking for a way on board. The ramp for transferring between vessels was too far above the waterline to reach, and the diving ladder had been pulled up too, leaving their only point of possible access the anchor chains.

Khuna pantomimed what was necessary to accomplish their objective and then, swimming to the starboard side of the bow where the guard had last been seen, began climbing upward, holding onto the chain with his feet against the boat hull.

Waiting until Khuna was about halfway up, Aalona began to climb the port side anchor chain. He was more tired than he was willing to admit, and didn't move as quickly as the younger man. Still, he was determined not to let his friend's son, his family, or his fellow islanders down.

•••

Miko had been on edge all day. Her instincts told her that the islander who had shown up at the front door of The Hanging Monkey, along with the old sailor who attacked the trio in the other storeroom, were part of some far larger and very hostile menace. Consequently she was slow to depart that night, not wanting to leave Corky and the man they had tied up alone.

She was gathering needed supplies in the storeroom when she heard the bottle shatter and the sound of a body hitting the floor. She was extremely concerned for Corky, but knew better than to rush out into a possible trap.

Instead she hid behind the sweep of the door, figuring that this was too much coincidence in one day to be simply a desperate thief who would settle for whatever was in the cash register before fleeing. The intruder was gingerly picking his way around something, and would soon come to her.

As the door opened, she was surprised to see a woman enter; but the handgun marked her as an enemy, and neutralizing that weapon was Miko's first objective.

Combat would be difficult within the close quarters of the storeroom, but Miko assumed she had the advantage of familiar ground and launched a blinding speed offensive against her foe. She was met with a fury of battering hands and feet. The red-haired woman countered Miko's every move with an instinctual skill that only years of training could achieve.

As they backed off to take stock of each other, each looking for an opening to attack anew, Miko paused only long enough to bow slightly, acknowledging the expertise of her opponent.

Sirene nodded in response before lashing out with a flying kick, her hands poised to strike.

Miko easily blocked the move as the women continued fighting.

•••

They climbed until the end of the anchor chain disappeared into the chute and hawse pipe that ran into the hull, well below the ship's deck railing. Finding a decent foothold on the anchor chain, Khuna reached up as high as possible and cautiously grabbed the gunwale, before slowly pulling himself up to peer through a scupper.

The sentry had his back to Khuna, just mere feet away. The man was half crouched between the windlass and the side rail, next to the unmanned machine gun, trying to protect his match against the land breeze coming off the island as he attempted to light a cigarette. His rifle hung against his back by its sling.

There would never be a better time, but he had to be closer to take the man out without too much noise. Khuna pulled himself erect on the gunwale, and edged silently like a cat along the outside of the rail. In one fluid motion he pushed the machine gun muzzle toward the sailor, knocking him off balance.

Although it wasn't strong enough to deck him, the man's first thought was that the wind had caused it to pivot. As he scrambled awkwardly to secure the gun, Khuna lunged over the rail and grabbed the sentry, pinning the rifle to his back. One hand went over the man's mouth and nose while the other arm encircled his neck in a choke hold.

The sentry struggled fiercely; clawing at his unseen attacker, throwing his weight around to try and break free. Small as he was, Khuna was powerfully built. He wrapped his arms ever tighter, muscles straining and bulging to maintain his stranglehold.

For the hapless guard, it was a losing battle. He crumpled to the deck unconscious.

Khuna ripped the sling off the rifle and dropped the weapon overboard, then trussed up the man with the strapping, shoving his own crumpled pack of cigarettes into the guard's mouth. After helping him on board, Khuna motioned to Aalona that they had to take out the sentry at the far end just as quietly and efficiently.

They split up, each silently creeping down the catwalk on either side of the bridge structure. A quick peek through the glass windows showed Khuna no one was currently occupying the command center, but how many more were still below deck remained a mystery.

Aalona walked cautiously toward the rear, having never been on such a big boat before. He had not been as quiet as Khuna, or as brutally effective, and felt diminished by that. Unfortunately it was that inexperience that would prove to be his undoing, as the older man suddenly felt a cold, metallic object pressing against his bare back.

•••

Neither woman knew who her opponent was, but both respected the skills displayed, and realized that victory would be hard fought for.

Miko studied the red-haired stranger. With the side slits, the tight dress didn't restrict leg movement as much as she figured it would. While it had been ages since she last fought a worthy opponent, Miko knew she would have to end this battle quickly, before someone else came looking for them and discovered the Chinese waitress was more capable than she appeared to be.

Sirene took stock of her situation too, because it was taking too long, and they were making too much noise. The man she came to rescue was still tied to a chair, while an Oriental hellion in shorts and a loose shirt was endangering her mission. Blue eyes narrowed upon her opponent. They were about the same height, but Sirene weighed a bit more; otherwise they were evenly matched. This woman was too well versed in unarmed combat to be a simple barmaid.

The revolver was on the floor back by the door, while her handbag with the knife inside was behind the black haired tigress, who looked like she wanted to tear Sirene apart with her bare hands. To win, she would have to do something unexpected.

Or someone else would.

While the two women fought, the old sailor renewed his attempt at escape. Although an expert at knots, his fingers could never gain enough purchase upon the ropes binding him to do any good.

His only other option was to start rocking back and forth in the chair, hoping to tip it over and find freedom in the aftermath.

•••

"Don't move," warned a gruff voice. "I have no idea how you got out of the hold, but I'm gonna put ye back with yer mates. I hope you're the only one, because it's me hide if'n the Captain finds out! Now turn around," added the man, as he pressed the muzzle of his gun harder into Aalona's back. In the semi-darkness, he couldn't tell that this was an older man and not one of their prisoners.

The islander acted as if to comply, but as he turned to face the man, Aalona moved quickly. He grabbed the hand holding the gun in both of his, and then slammed it hard against the metal wall.

Unfortunately the sailor was stronger. He held tightly to his gun, thinking the escapee was trying to wrestle it from him. He punched Aalona repeatedly, in the face and stomach, until the wheezing old man managed to bring a crushing knee up into his groin. The gun went off with a deafening sound, though fortunately the bullet hit the deck instead of Aalona, splintering the wooden planking; yet the damage was done. Within moments the alarm would be raised that there were intruders on board that must be dealt with.

•••

Sitting silently in the night, they had been watching the steel fan-tail for some time when a lone gunshot shattered the otherwise still air of the pre-dawn hours.

"What the blazes…" began Neville Bryce, as Nick Fortune started his rum-runner's engines.

"Trouble Doc, with a capital T. Help me haul anchor," Nick ordered as he burst from the wheelhouse. Both men raced to the windlass. While not as big as that of the enemy vessel, it still took the two of them many straining moments of effort to crank and haul it back aboard.

Nick raced back to the controls and within seconds, *Fortune's Folly* began to move out.

"What's the plan now?" Bryce called loudly over the roaring sound of the engine.

"Hope for the best but prepare for the worst," answered Nick, as he reached for something below deck. "Here, take this," he added, handing Bryce a rifle he had loaded aboard before departing Motugra.

"What am I to do with a firearm?" asked the confused man as he glanced down at the long barreled weapon in his hands. "I'm a doctor, not..."

"What do you think?" said Nick in return, as the boat approached the fan-tail. "Point it at anybody you don't know and act like you mean to use it."

•••

As Miko launched her new attack, both women heard the sound of a body dropping and splintering wood. In his latest escape attempt, the sailor had overturned his chair.

Miko glanced just long enough to make sure the prisoner was still secured and not about to enter the fray.

It was too long.

The well-timed distraction worked in Sirene's favor. She charged forward, not as concerned about blocking her opponent's blows this time as slamming into her as hard and as fast as possible, using her slightly higher weight as an advantage.

Caught off guard, Miko felt the bodily impact even as her fists started making solid contact.

Momentum carried them along, Miko receiving the worst of it as they crashed into the shelving unit next to the stockroom door.

The edge of the shelving caught Miko squarely in the back. The boards buckled and were forced upward as she was shoved further into the fixture. Miko felt wood scraping the skin under her shirt as her head hit the back wall beneath a bowed shelf, scattering supplies all around her.

Sirene staggered back a step, trying to regain her footing so she could assume a defensive position.

Although dazed, Miko was fast to bring her guard up and ward the other woman off. As she grabbed the shelving unit's support rails to pull herself out of her predicament, a jingling box of glass jars overhead slid off the displaced shelf.

As the box struck the back of her head, Miko's last thoughts before losing consciousness concerned a growing hatred toward olives.

•••

The two men continued to wrestle for control of the gun even as Aalona heard the noises heralding the impending arrival of more men. He spotted an open metal door, which must have been where this man came from. It was closed when he passed it and, in the dim deck light, had originally appeared to be just part of the wall, which was how the sailor was able to surprise him.

Fortunately, many of the man's companions aboard had been asleep when the gunshot went off. There was general confusion as they all scrambled and tried to get up through the hatch at the same time.

Just as the first sailor was about to emerge, Aalona shoved his opponent head first into the metal door, forcing him and it backwards.

A smile of satisfaction briefly appeared on Aalona's face as he heard a couple of solid thuds, along with curses and yelps of pain. Whoever was behind that door had fallen. He yanked the gun out of the dazed sailor's hand and, not knowing how or wanting to use it to shoot the man, hit him over the head with it. It went off harmlessly, the round impacting the cabin wall.

Aalona tossed the gun overboard as the unconscious man collapsed at his feet. He quickly arranged him so that his body would block the door when he heard a third gunshot.

•••

Corky stirred and groaned. Pleasant dreams of a beautiful redhead turned into nightmares of a she-devil in a black dress as he awoke.

He waited until the room stopped spinning before he managed to rise to his knees.

The ex-fighter told himself he was down, but not out, as he fought to regain his footing.

Noises from the main storeroom explained where that treacherous little hellion went, and what she was more than likely after. His head

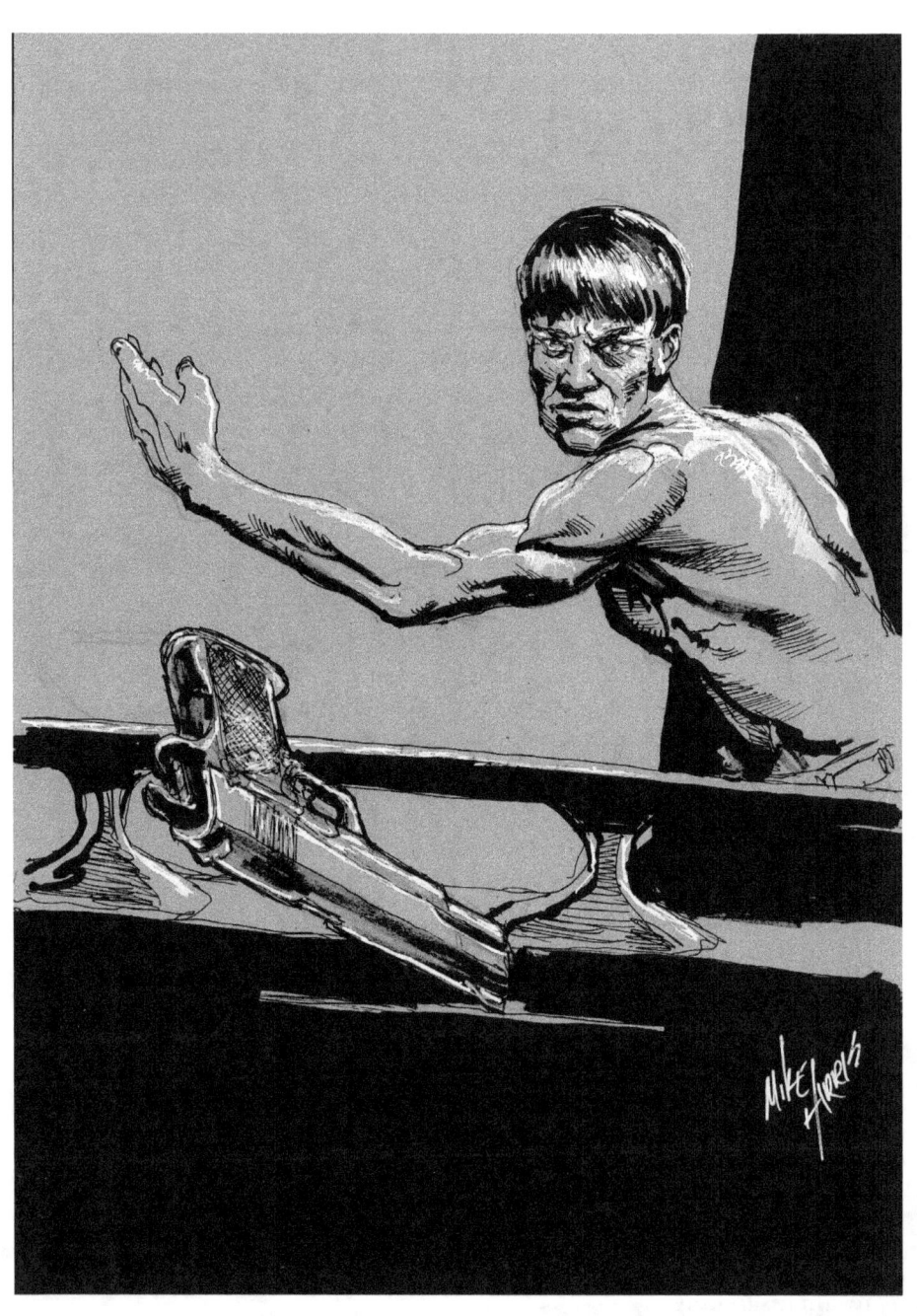

Aalona tossed the gun overboard…

cleared the bar counter, as Corky reached out to grab the opposite edge for additional support, attempting to pull himself upright.

While not totally erect, Corky was at least off the floor as he reached around with his free hand to feel his gun still tucked into the waistband of his pants, hidden by his shirttail.

One way or another, this was going to end now.

•••

Khuna reached the stern and spotted the other sentry ahead of him. While he had his back to the Motugran, this man was more alert. He was constantly walking back and forth along the aft railing, keeping an eye upon the horizon, but missed seeing the *Fortune's Folly* since it approached from the port side.

Sticking close to the exterior wall, Khuna slowly began to creep up on the sentry. He hoped to be able to pounce quickly enough to subdue him before he could raise an alarm.

Unfortunately, the opportunity never arose as both men heard a gunshot.

The sentry stopped in mid-step and wheeled in the direction of the noise, just as Khuna came charging at him.

Far too dependent on firepower, the sentry pivoted and tried to aim, but there was no time. Khuna's left hand yanked the barrel upward just before his right fist slammed directly in the sailor's gut.

As the other man expelled all his breath and doubled over in pain, Khuna landed a solid uppercut directly against the man's glass jaw. The sailor reeled backward from the force of the blow, releasing his hold on the rifle. It fired as the weapon hit the ground stock first, the bullet whining off into the night.

While dazed enough to think he was now fighting three men, the sailor had enough wits still about him to attempt reaching for the knife at his side. But before it could be drawn, he went flying through the air, landing in the water behind the stationary ship.

•••

They heard a second, and then a third shot echo in the night. Nick cut the rum-runner's engines as soon as his boat came alongside the enemy's. *Fortune's Folly* throbbed to a stop underneath the boarding ramp as Bryce dropped anchor. Now only the gentle bobbing of the waves gave his vessel any motion as Nick reached up and managed to grab the underside of the ramp and yank it down. They were expecting somebody to come back, otherwise it never would have been accessible.

Starting to climb up, Nick warned Bryce quietly to be alert, and not let anyone on board. "Shoot them if you have to, just don't hit the fuel tanks or you'll blow us to Kingdom Come."

"Lovely," was Bryce's only comment and he appeared a bit green.

Once he had purchase, Nick scrambled aboard in a low crouch, his trusty Browning already in hand.

•••

As Corky approached the storeroom door, he spotted Miko lying on the floor near the damaged shelving. Juice from a carton of olives was leaking out and wetting her hair, indicating most, if not all of the jars in that box were broken.

His gun was drawn, but he hesitated pulling the trigger as Sirene appeared in the doorway.

"You wouldn't shoot an unarmed lady, would you?" she asked, dangling her purse and looking helpless.

"No," admitted Corky. "But you ain't no lady," he added, as he swung a meaty fist. It connected, but so did her purse, the strap tangling around his gun arm.

As Sirene reeled back from the force of the blow, Corky's gun was yanked sideways. That's when the old sailor leapt at him. Corky realized too late that the man was free and had been laying in wait. He had a chair leg in each hand and was using them as clubs.

Corky tried to bring his gun back into play as the first chair leg hit his wrist, sending the firearm to the floor, while the other was rammed into his gut.

An experienced fighter, O'Brian tried to backpedal and cover to avoid the full force of the next blow. He was not completely successful, as the sailor brought both chair legs to bear on his skull.

Corky lost his already tedious hold on consciousness and joined Miko on the floor.

The old sailor grabbed his knife from his boot, returned after Sirene used it to cut him free. But before he could do any damage, Sirene grabbed his wrist. "No!" she insisted. "Let's just cut our losses and get out of here before things heat up more than we can handle."

The man grunted unhappily, but resheathed his knife while she grabbed both guns.

•••

As Nick boarded the enemy vessel he spotted Aalona, doing his best to keep the sailors trapped behind their side of the metal hatch. He had put his whole weight against the door, but was fighting a losing battle.

With gun drawn, Nick nodded to Aalona, who stepped back away from the door in anticipation of the fight that lay ahead.

The first man came out in a rush. The metal door swung open and banged against the hull as the sailor tripped over the unconscious body of his fallen comrade. As he fell, Aalona grabbed him by the back of his shirt near both his neck and waist. Instinctively using the man's momentum to help carry him forward, Aalona wedged the sailor between the metallic bars of the ship's railing, before seizing the gun out of the dazed man's hand and hurling it over the side.

The next sailor, seeing Aalona's actions, was about to shoot the native in the back when Nick stepped between them, his Browning 9mm pointed right at the man's chest as Fortune ordered the sailors to drop their weapons and surrender.

"Why should we?" someone shouted.

"Because I'll be perfectly happy to shoot you all, like fish in a barrel," Nick quipped.

Packed in the hatchway, the men realized their predicament rather quickly. Some had managed to turn around unobserved and were opening the port side hatch.

As the metal door swung open, another obstacle presented itself.

Khuna's muscular frame blocked their other exit. He punched the lead sailor in the jaw without a second thought.

That man reeled back into his companions as the enraged fighter worked his way into the group of enemies before him.

•••

Doctor Neville Bryce was concerned about his friends and allies, but couldn't see much from his position on board *Fortune's Folly*.

Wondering what was happening overhead, Bryce heard a splash toward the rear of the boat.

Heading astern, the doctor would never discover that it was the gun Aalona tossed over the side that gained his attention, for he spotted a dripping wet sailor about to attempt boarding the *Folly* with evil intent, for he had a knife in his right hand.

"I'm a doctor, so don't make me put a bullet hole in you that I will have to fix later," said Bryce, pointing the gun at him. "Now, raise your hands where I can see them, then let that knife fall into the ocean."

The sailor stared coldly at the man on board, but reluctantly complied with his orders.

"Good," said Bryce, not being able to hide the relief in his voice. "Now keep treading water until I tell you otherwise."

•••

Miko awoke with a start as a strange smell assailed her nostrils. As her consciousness returned, she remembered the fight and...

She sat upright, fighting dizziness as she felt the dampness of her hair and upper shirt. It wasn't blood. Another sniff of the vinegary stench solidified what would be Miko's lifelong hatred of the pickled Mediterranean fruit.

She heard a man moan.

Miko turned her head slowly to avoid another bout of vertigo and saw Corky lying on the floor nearby.

Not trusting her balance yet, she crawled over to him. Miko had heard the Irishman brag about some of his past fights, but he had taken the worst of this one. Corky's breathing was steady, but he was barely conscious, his face swollen and bruised.

Slowly, she managed to rise. The open, empty cash register told the rest of the story. The woman and the old sailor were gone, not even bothering to close the front door in their hasty departure.

Miko staggered forward to correct that situation, pausing only long enough to make sure no one was still lurking about. With the door locked, The Hanging Monkey was officially closed for the night.

Still a bit unsteady on her feet, she made her way back to the bar to start a pot of fresh, strong coffee. They would both need some once Corky awakened.

•••

The fight was more of a formality than an actual battle.

Not feeling very charitable towards his fellow human beings, Khuna tore into the sailors before him with no remorse. While the confining space of the small corridor made throwing a punch difficult at times, every blow was delivered with the full physical force he was capable of. Most of these men were not well armed or knew how to fight. Only those who tried to escape out the starboard hatch avoided spending any time in an infirmary.

Yet those sailors were unable to escape justice, for Aalona and Nick Fortune were dealing with them.

Khuna's friend, while not as young or as strong as the bouncer, held his own against the sailors he faced. The first man, thinking he could easily defeat the older native, swung and missed as a grinning Aalona delivered a punch to the sailor's jaw that knocked a tooth loose. "That for my people," he said.

The man reeled as the sailor behind him tried to step forward, but Aalona was waiting for him. "This one for me," he added, punching him in the gut.

•••

At first, Nick thought all he had to do was just enjoy watching the Motugrans deal with the situation and be prepared in case one did manage to get past Aalona.

Then he heard a noise behind him.

Nick turned and saw an ambitious sailor trying to open one of the bridge windows, desperate to escape the fury that was Khuna.

Before the sailor could react, Fortune ran up and bodily yanked him out of the portal, making sure he landed head first on the hard wooden deck.

With his opponent out of the fight, Nick turned to check on Aalona, but he was nowhere in sight.

•••

Swept up in the moment, Aalona fought his way inside.

There were more aboard than they first thought. The finally tally would be fifteen crewmen, counting the one Doctor Bryce was keeping a wary eye on, but that didn't matter at the moment. All the Kaia Akamu denizen wanted to do was free his son and the others.

With that thought in mind, Aalona was about to tackle what he thought was his next opponent when Khuna blocked the punch with his big, open hand.

"It's over," he told his friend with a smile.

Aalona looked to see all their enemies lying helpless at their feet. That the sailors were still alive might have been a bit of a disappointment, but the older man never commented on that as he returned Khuna's smile.

"Look's like everything went well," said Nick, trying to make his way through the mess to rejoin the others.

"Where you hiding?" asked Aalona in his broken English.

"I dealt with a few stragglers and took care of some other things," Fortune bragged, examining his bruised knuckles like they were prized jewels, "like finding a way into the radio room to contact the authorities. They'll be here soon."

"Good. Let's finish this rescue," said Khuna, as he started down the stairs to the lowest deck of the ship.

•••

"I'll be the first to admit that I've had better days, lass," said Corky, nursing his second cup of strong coffee while sitting next to Miko at the bar. "But what's that smell?" he asked, while sniffing the air.

"Olives," replied the barmaid in disgust, as she tried working her fingers through her matted hair.

"Don't worry. A good shower will get rid of it."

"I hope so," said Miko, then stopped to stare at Corky.

"What's the matter?" he asked, but her only reply was to point at his forehead.

Corky looked up, and between the bottles along the back wall, spied his image in the big mirror. He brushed his red hair aside and saw Sirene's calling card.

The Hanging Monkey's owner muttered something obscene as he sipped his coffee, his face almost as scarlet as the perfect lipstick print on his forehead.

•••

They stood watch over the sailors until the authorities arrived. Nick was a bit anxious to be out of there. It seemed odd to be on the legal side of this.

As Bryce's captive was hauled out of the water and the other sailors were taken into custody, Aalona finally got his wish.

A crowbar broke the lock and chain, releasing the men locked in the storage hold. They led the rescuers to what their captors were after in a nearby cabin.

Treasure!

There were crates of Spanish minted gold coins, goblets, plates, jewelry, and all sorts of artifacts.

In time, with translations by Khuna, the story was pieced together. The crew of the steel fan-tail was exploring and hauling up anything of value from the wreck of the *Isabella Hermosa*, an ancient pirate vessel reported lost at sea in this area long ago.

The prisoners had been forced to dive for days, always led by a mermaid who became human once on board. Yet no females had been arrested.

How their captors knew of the wreck's location was a mystery. While common knowledge amongst themselves, the islanders never said a word to anyone, especially not to any outsiders. They had always respected the sea god's dominion over the spirits of the dead and stayed clear of the area, no matter how good the fishing might be around it.

Later questioning indicated the captain was a much older man; and was also not amongst the imprisoned sailors the authorities were preparing to haul away.

"'I will not betray me Captain,'" repeated Nick, recalling the old sailor's words back at The Hanging Monkey, "and we fell for it!"

"The woman obviously decided to escape while she could," guessed Bryce. "Which reminds me, don't we need to tell them about the attempted murder of Aalona, and our uninvited guest back on Motugra?"

"Corky and Miko can handle that," Nick said confidently. "Right now, I'm wondering what happens to all of this?" he asked, staring longingly at the treasure, now under guard.

"Aalona's people won't touch it. Tribal superstitions," explained Bryce. "The government will probably claim it, though hopefully some of the proceeds will eventually benefit Kaia Akamu. Personally, I would love to see it go into a museum, and a clinic built out here on this side of the island chain to help Sister Ahren's work."

"Afraid my first thoughts on the subject weren't that charitable," admitted Nick, "but I wouldn't of minded a souvenir."

•••

"Well Captain, we certainly pulled off another successful operation," said the old sailor, as he steered their launch across the open sea.

"That we have," agreed Sirene. "But how many times do I have to remind you that when we're alone, you don't have to be so formal, Daddy."

"Old habits, me girl. I learned to respect my superiors a long time ago."

"I understand," she said, putting an arm around the older man. "We're still on schedule for the rendezvous?"

"Should be there in time for the meeting later tonight. Be glad to unload that thing though," he said, indicating the small chest tied down in the back of the boat. "Ya have any idea how your client knew about it, let alone why he's willing to pay so much for a small statue of a black enameled bird?"

"No, but the finders' fee and our share of the gold coins from that wreck will keep us solvent for quite a while," bragged Sirene.

"Well, 'borrowing' that boat, let alone skipping out on paying the crew, will certainly cut down on our expenses," agreed her father. "Though you should've let me silence those two at the bar. That cash register didn't even yield decent pocket money."

"Forget about those island fools," she said dismissively. "They're small change in a big world that's just waiting to be plundered."

"So what's next on our agenda then?"

"Some well deserved R & R. Then, who knows?" said Sirene, leaning back in her seat to enjoy the warm, rising sun.

Maybe I'll come back here someday. That bar owner was a handsome bloke...

The End
For now...

TWO WRITERS ARE BETTER THAN....

Ron Fortier was one story shy of completing the volume you now read, but had two authors working on stories. His solution? Ask if they could combine their talents on a joint production.

Nancy A. Hansen and Lee Houston Jr. had been friends and writing buddies since the old Prodigy Writers' Bulletin Board, back in the days when Internet communities were more than just posting rants and raves.

Thinking it over, they decided to work on Lee's plot for "The Merciless Mermaid," since it was the furthest along of the two, and started trading the manuscript back and forth via e-mail, each adding new material after proofreading the previous addition. Lee took pity on Doctor Bryce, and gave the ol' chap more to do in this story, while Nancy added homages to another famous physician.

"We've beta read and kibitzed on each others material for years, but this is the first time we have ever shared a byline. It was a lot of fun and I hope we get to do it again," said Lee. "The Hanging Monkey and the Motugra island chain are an interesting locale. Besides, there was a cameo with the bar's namesake I was unable to work in, and it will be interesting to see if Miko is ever able to overcome her hatred of olives, though I doubt it."

"The best part was making the final pass over the manuscript," added Nancy. "Not because it was the end, but because until that point, I honestly didn't know about the twist ending Lee snuck in, let alone what the overall objective of Sirene and company was. Reading those last paragraphs and realizing what they had locked up in that chest was a big surprise to me."

While the duo plan to eventually finish Nancy's story for a future *Hanging Monkey* volume, will the mysterious redhead return? Maybe. Sirene certainly has at least one reason to consider another visit to Motugra," added Nancy.

•••

NANCY A. HANSEN – An avid reader and prolific writer of fantasy and adventure fiction for over 25 years, Nancy A. Hansen is the author of the novels FORTUNE'S PAWN and PROPHECY'S GAMBIT, the anthologies TALES OF THE VAGABOND BARDS and THE HUNTRESS OF

GREENWOOD, and the novella COMPANION DRAGON'S TALES: *A FAMILIAR NAME*. Her short stories have been featured in multiple issues of Pro Se Presents, and she has a tale in THE NEW ADVENTURES OF SENORITA SCORPION, while the E-story TO RULE THE SKY is offered as a Pro Se SINGLE SHOT. Nancy has also contributed stories to both Airship 27's SINBAD: THE NEW VOYAGES Volume 1 and Mechanoid Press' debut book, MONSTER EARTH, and the charity anthology THE LOST CHILDREN. Nancy is also the author of Airship 27's JEZEBEL JOHNSTON pirate novels. Nancy currently resides on an old farm in beautiful, rural eastern Connecticut with an eclectic cast of family members, and one very spoiled dog.

LEE HOUSTON, JUNIOR is the writer-creator of *Hugh Monn, Private Detective* and *Alpha* the superhero, published by Pro Se Press.

His other creative credits include serving as the Editor-In-Chief of The Free Choice E-zine (www.thefreechoice.info) and writing numerous short stories.

In what he laughing refers to as his "spare" time, Lee is an avid reader of pulps, science-fiction, detective/mystery stories, fantasy, and comic books.

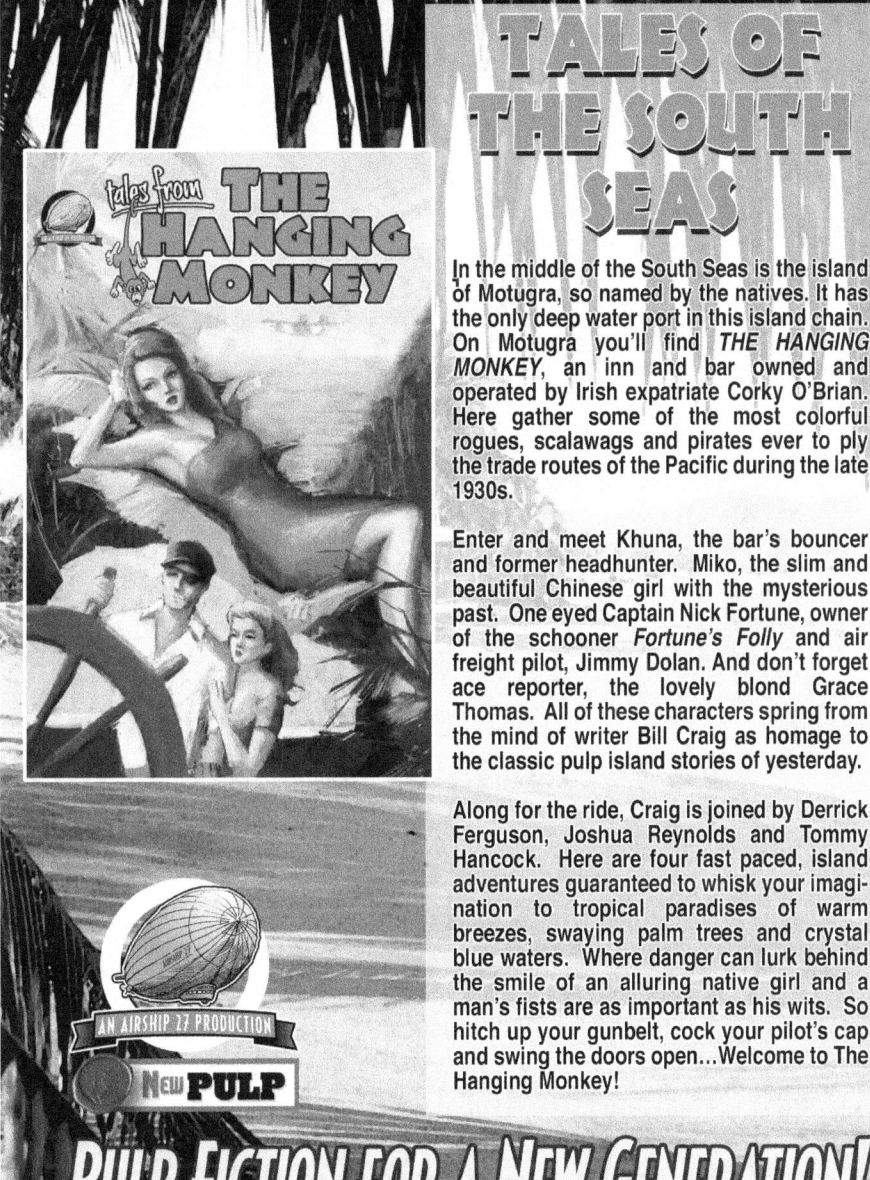

TALES OF THE SOUTH SEAS

In the middle of the South Seas is the island of Motugra, so named by the natives. It has the only deep water port in this island chain. On Motugra you'll find *THE HANGING MONKEY*, an inn and bar owned and operated by Irish expatriate Corky O'Brian. Here gather some of the most colorful rogues, scalawags and pirates ever to ply the trade routes of the Pacific during the late 1930s.

Enter and meet Khuna, the bar's bouncer and former headhunter. Miko, the slim and beautiful Chinese girl with the mysterious past. One eyed Captain Nick Fortune, owner of the schooner *Fortune's Folly* and air freight pilot, Jimmy Dolan. And don't forget ace reporter, the lovely blond Grace Thomas. All of these characters spring from the mind of writer Bill Craig as homage to the classic pulp island stories of yesterday.

Along for the ride, Craig is joined by Derrick Ferguson, Joshua Reynolds and Tommy Hancock. Here are four fast paced, island adventures guaranteed to whisk your imagination to tropical paradises of warm breezes, swaying palm trees and crystal blue waters. Where danger can lurk behind the smile of an alluring native girl and a man's fists are as important as his wits. So hitch up your gunbelt, cock your pilot's cap and swing the doors open...Welcome to The Hanging Monkey!

PULP FICTION FOR A NEW GENERATION!
FOR AVAILABILITY: AIRSHIP27HANGAR.COM

SET SAIL FOR ADVENTURE

The greatest seafaring adventurer of all time returns to the high seas, *Sinbad the Sailor!*

Born of countless legends and myths, this fearless rogue sets sail across the seven seas aboard his ship, the Blue Nymph, accompanied by an international crew of colorful, larger-than-life characters. Chief among these are the irascible Omar, a veteran seamen and trusted first mate, the blond Viking giant, Ralf Gunarson, the sophisticated archer from Gaul, Henri Delacrois and the mysterious, lovely and deadly female samurai, Tishimi Osara. All of them banded together to follow their famous captain on perilous new voyages across the world's oceans.

So pack up your you traveling bags, bid ado to your loved ones and get ready to sail with the tide as Sinbad El Ari takes the tiller and the Blue Nymph sets sails once more; its destination worlds of wonder, mystery and high adventure.

www.ingramcontent.com/pod-product-compliance
Lightning Source LLC
Chambersburg PA
CBHW050657290626
47170CB00015B/1625